THE WEEK
I RUINED
MY LIFE

THE WEEK I RUINED MY LIFE

Caroline Grace-Cassidy

BLACK & WHITE PUBLISHING

First published 2016
by Black & White Publishing Ltd
29 Ocean Drive, Edinburgh EH6 6JL

1 3 5 7 9 10 8 6 4 2   16 17 18 19

ISBN: 978 1 78530 039 4

A CIP catalogue record for this book is available from the British Library.

ALBA | CHRUTHACHAIL

Typeset by Iolaire, Newtonmore
Printed and bound by Nørhaven, Denmark

For my daughters, Grace and Maggie Cassidy
Follow your dreams girls. . . Always.

part
1

1

Sunday morning. 1 December. The week before. At home.

'What the hell is wrong with you?' I exaggerate the words, slowly rounding them out, mouthing them silently into my mirrors. A conclave of lips, teeth and tongue.

'What is happening to us?' I enunciate carefully.

Surveying my reflections carefully in the side-by-side mirrors, I scrutinise the pair of me in our white polka-dot towelling dressing gowns. Both the MDF white, mirrored wardrobe doors are swung slightly open so I can perfectly see me times two. I take another step forward on my spongy beige carpet. I wish at least one of me had the answers. But I don't. I'm trying to look inside my head. Trying to figure out my own thoughts. Trying to analyse what has gone wrong. My heads fall gently to lean on the glass and my eyes begin to water as I fight them on their primal need to blink.

Am I restless and searching for focus in my marriage? Yes.

Am I really unhappy? No.

Well … no, not really. Not altogether.

However, I am completely confused. I squeeze my eyes shut tight now and I feel the damp of the water inching from eye to cheek. My tongue extends, outstretched to its limit, it blindly finds the salty tear. The tear vanishes but its sour taste lingers on my palate. I'm visualising my age in my mind's eye. Drawing the numbers in thick black permanent marker behind my eyelids. I pull my head up straight now and stand back, stationary in front of my mirrors, barefoot in my bedroom and squeeze my deep-red-painted toenails into the thickness of the beige. I squeeze so tight it hurts. Cherry Bomb, I think the colour is called. I should know better. I am a grown up. I should feel settled. I should feel content. I should consider myself lucky. I am none of the aforementioned on this murky Sunday morning. The weather outside reports in as dismal and dreary, as winter delivers on its dark dependable consistency. Three and five. I move my head, making the shapes of the numbers. Around and around and across and down and around. It feels almost meditative. I am thirty-five years old. I have two beautiful children, a fulfilling career and a husband.

You will have noticed I didn't prefix him with a compliment and nor will I recite an appropriate encomium after his name. He's not a bad man at all, please don't get me wrong. He is an excellent, loving, committed father and provider, but something has gone drastically wrong between us. Between husband and wife. 'Till death do us part' feels way, way too long off. Once my perfect soulmate. One time I couldn't keep my hands off him. But not now. On this Sunday in early December, our marriage is in real trouble. I have absolutely no desire for him. We cannot find a civil word. There is no common dominator apart from our amazing children. What is commonly known as

4

'on the rocks', I guess? Sing it to me Neil Diamond – sing it to Mrs Ali Devlin.

Right now there is little of anything congenial between us. I don't know what has happened exactly; I have my suspicions obviously, but not as to how it happened or when exactly it happened. All I do know for sure is that we are drifting like two broken branches, rushing downstream towards a treacherous cataract.

Now might also be the time to mention something else that isn't helping matters. I have recently started to fancy a guy in work. My friend. My colleague. I'm embarrassed to admit this to myself and I would never admit it to another living soul, but I've started to fantasise about him and it's dirty. Pushing him up against a public bathroom wall kinda stuff. George Michael's 'Outside' lyrics spring to mind. Teenage stuff. Exciting stuff. I cannot get him out of my head.

This is a million miles away from how I feel sexually about my husband. So when I say something's not quite right between us, you get it now, right? Me, a married mother of two, how could I say such a thing, right? Awful, I know. I totally agree with you. I am ever so slowly, metaphorically ripping, from the bottom up, my marriage certificate. I know that. I keep moving my head.

'Mom?' Jade, my eleven-year-old daughter, speaks from my half-closed bedroom door and I snap my eyes open.

'Yes, love?' I answer her. Bang back into reality. My Worzel Gummidge Mummy head screws on tight.

'Seriously, Mom? What're y'doing in the mirror? And where're m'grey Hollister leggings with the black stripes down the sides, huh?' Jade drawls.

5

'Er … grey leggings.' I tip my head repeatedly with my index finger. I must know the answer to this one; I've literally finished putting away all the laundry in the house. It comes to me.

'Ahh … they're in the hot press but I have just taken them off my radiator so they may still be damp,' I warn her.

'But Dad said he's taking us zip-lining so I need them.'

I look at her slouching in the frame of the doorway. She never used to slouch. Once the most tactile child, she now talks in an American accent and spends hours huddled over an iPad watching videos of random strangers test out random products.

'Hey guys!' is all I hear coming from the thin rectangular electronic device. Obsessed with watching Seven Super Girls, which don't seem all that super to me, talking about nothing worthwhile. Taking selfie after selfie. Pouting at a camera. Image obsessed. It doesn't seem to bother Colin, that's the way the world is now is all he says. I don't get it so I'm finding it hard to get her at the moment. She recoils from my loving advances all the time lately. Oh, I know she still loves me and I worship the very ground she walks upon but her attitude of late is challenging. If this is eleven then what are the teenage years going to be like? Where is my little girl who couldn't keep her hands off me? The little girl who wanted to marry me. Me and only me. I can, almost, still smell her little girl, pink satin-soft skin.

'Marry me, Mummy? Pinky promise, so, so, so promise, so promise?' four-year-old, bouncing pig-tailed Jade would beg of me, extending her tiny pinkie finger for me to link.

'I will boo boo, I pinky promise, I so, so, so, promise, I so promise.' I'd join our pinkies before falling to my knees and we would lock lips and I was in a little piece of mummy heaven. My nostrils vacuuming up her wonderful body scent. She would stand on my knees, her tiny pink feet gripping into my flesh and I'd take her two hands as she rocked forwards and backwards. Totally safe in her mummy's hands.

'I love you, Mummy, so, so, so, so much.' She'd kiss me again, so hard, on the lips and for as long as she possibly could hold it.

Seems like a lifetime ago that oath … that bond … as I study her bored expression still slouched in the doorframe. Jade is beautiful if slightly on the too thin side – nothing to do with her diet, she eats really well – genetics.

'Genetically blessed,' Corina, my best friend, tells me.

I'm not so sure, I'd rather she was a bit stronger.

'Let me throw them in the dryer for ten minutes. Did you clean the muck off your trainers from running through all that mud after gymnastics?'

It takes her so long to answer questions nowadays. She thinks before she speaks apparently, so as I stand and await her response I look at her. Her long white-blonde hair is piled on top of her head in a messy bun. She looks more like her dad's side of the family; she has pale skin, a narrow face, a small nose and bright full rosebud lips. Dressed in her freshly ironed pink flannel cream love-heart pyjamas now she looks so young but as soon as she is ready to go out she will look five years older. She is exceptionally pretty. Her baby-blue eyes narrow at me, the sign her answer is ready.

'Dawwhh, serioooously, Moooom? Obviiiiiously.'

It's like a song: every vowel is dragged out. She slouches away.

'I love you, boo …' I stop myself as I call after her. She has asked me not to call her boo boo any more and I get it: she is eleven; I just forget sometimes. I shut the wardrobe doors gently and turn to the bed. I pull the goose-feathered duvet up and smooth it out with my right hand. Plump up the pillows. It's a dark purple leaf print duvet set from House of Fraser. Corina had been given a voucher as a thank you from one of her work clients and she'd insisted I use it. I slept alone under it last night; he must have slept on the couch. Again. I have already made the kids beds, their clothes have been put away and the two upstairs bathrooms thoroughly cleaned. Upstairs is done.

You are probably still wondering what am I doing daydreaming about a thirty-six-year-old guy I work with? About Owen O'Neill. Like I said, he is my friend, my work colleague, and this is all sorts of wrong. Fifty shades of wrong. I'm too young for a mid-life crisis. I'd never actually do anything about it, don't worry. *Cop yourself on, Ali Devlin,* I tell myself.

I hang up my polka-dot dressing gown and pull on my cream skinny jeans that are draped across our wicker bedroom chair and slide my size five feet into a pair of black slip-on flats that are underneath. I drag a cosy Kilkenny Shop black wool knitted sweater from my chest of drawers, and pull it over my head. I leave my bedroom. It's becoming a room I'm no longer comfortable in. A room I try to avoid at all costs when the dark drops down. In this room we cannot pretend.

8

Across the landing I take the leggings out of the hot press. I pick up a wet towel Jade has just draped across the banisters as I feel the leggings. I press them to my cheek. Not really that damp but my beloved late granny, Margaret, still has me so paranoid about damp clothes and them causing chest infections. I fold the towel and return it to the towel rail in the bathroom. I go downstairs and pass into the kitchen, collecting two glasses that have been deserted on the glass hall table as I go. Milk-stained rim.

Colin, my husband of twelve years, is at the table on his MacBook watching some football match at full volume. The kids' breakfast bowls and his empty coffee cup and cafetiere sit on the countertop awaiting my attention. I can hear the commentators raging about the billions some player cost. They are very cross and agitated. The afore-mentioned player has obviously let them all down. Poor unfortunate youthful billionaire. Colin doesn't look up.

'Damp leggings,' I say by way of explanation as I put them into the dryer. I don't think we spoke one word to one another yesterday. Please let today be better. Yesterday I annoyed Colin because I invited Mark's friend in to play when Manchester United were on the TV in some cup. The boys were running in and out of the room as the whistle blew and the Red Army lost; Colin was in a foul mood.

'I get one afternoon to myself all week. One lousy free afternoon! Is it too much to ask I get to watch the match in peace?' he'd sulked.

'Well, you don't like Mark out on the road, so I'd no alternative,' I'd said and he'd gone up to our room with his MacBook to watch the highlights of other rolling balls.

Now he says, 'You're putting *one* thing into the dryer, Ali?' He looks up at me, stabbing at the volume button on the laptop with his thumb to lower it. The silence is a welcome relief. The beginning of a new argument is not. We cannot seem to converse on anything without arguing any more.

'They're still damp, Colin,' I inform him as I slam the white circular door shut, twist the appropriate dial and press the 'on' button. It only takes seconds for it to whirr to life. The grey leggings are thrown around.

'That's a ridiculous waste of energy, Ali. Tell her to wear something else.' Colin Devlin stands. All six foot two of him. Tall, very broad and dressed this morning in a grey Nike tracksuit with black stripes down each arm and leg, and white runners. He has the hoody pulled up. Colin isn't one for central heating; he thinks a few extra layers are all we need. He has the exact same baby-blue eyes as Jade, floppy light brown hair and a huge dimple in the centre of his chin. A strong jawline. Athletic. I don't fancy him any more and I just do not know why. There's obviously something wrong with me because I can see he is clearly gorgeous.

'Sexy Col.' Corina calls him that all the time. Corina Martin is thirty-eight years old, three years older than me, and she isn't married and she doesn't have any kids and she tells me she is sometimes lonely but her Facebook page would tell me differently. She's out five nights a week. It's her occupation, events manager and sometimes PR person, so she always has various events to organise and attend. I think she isn't lonely at all, I think she's having the time of her life. She's taking about

10

getting a shih tzu but that's just to make me feel better.

'It's work, Ali,' she tells me every Sunday afternoon at our sacred lunches.

'Facebook isn't real, you must believe that, everything you see on Facebook – like, I mean, eeevveerryytthiinngg – is planned and approved and pre-mediated and Photoshopped and filtered out of its little social media mind. It's up there because people *want* you to see it … always remember that, although it may make you feel like you are prying, being voyeuristic, you're not – it's the complete opposite.'

Over our weekly sneaky glass of wine with lunch, she will reiterate over and over again: 'You have a real family, a real home. I envy you. I want all that too.'

'Is Mark nearly ready?' Colin breaks my thoughts of Corina as he moves beside me. I lean against the swishing machine.

The tension between us is almost comedic. I feel itchy and ill at ease with him so close. It's like we haven't seen each other for years. Like old lovers reunited, we are emotionally awkward around one another. I have the urge to laugh. Nervous energy. I look down to the dark slate kitchen floor and slip my foot in and out of my shoe. Cherry Bomb is playing peek-a-boo. I don't ask him why he never came up to bed last night.

'I don't know where Mark is, Colin,' I say slowly. 'I've been upstairs making all the beds.' I choose my words very carefully so as not to entice an argument.

'*Alllllll* the beds, it's not a hospital ward up there!' He drags out the word and half laughs. 'Sounds tough though, three whole beds … *aaaaannnnd* two of them are singles!'

11

He makes this noise through his nose as his snorts air out fast, as a racehorse might do after running in the Grand National. He squeezes my arm. It's a joke, I know that, but he also knows that by saying what he's saying and the way he's saying it, he's winding me up. We cannot seem to avoid annoying each other. He removes his hand from my arm, he must feel my tension.

I pick up the bowls and scrape the hardening mass of old Weetabix into the open bin. I move back to the sink, his eyes never leaving me, and I twist on the hot tap to wash the dishes. I stuff in the dark stopper with no chain attached, set the bowls, cup and glasses down gently and add some washing up liquid. I swirl to bubble. The noise of the glasses rattling takes the edge off. I stuff the yellow kitchen brush in and out of them.

'Really? The breakfast bowls in with the cup and glasses?' He is staring into the sink.

I say nothing but I remove the offending bowls and I lay them on the draining board to be washed separately. Colin is very fussy about how we wash the dishes.

'What? Don't make me feel like some kind of dish-washing freak again ... the bits of Weetabix will be floating in the water, Ali.'

'Yup, fine, that's why I have removed the offenders and I will wash them separately.' I wish he would just go away. I do not want Jade to hear us arguing again. I'm surprised I have a tongue left in my head, I've been biting it so much these last few weeks. How can you fancy someone who irritates the absolute shit out of you?

'At least you are speaking, I thought you'd had a mini-stroke yesterday.' He laughs.

'That's not funny, Colin,' I say.

He shrugs his shoulders, his hood coming loose on his head as he does so. He pulls it down tighter with both hands.

'So you don't know where our five-year-old son is then?' he says now. Then he tut-tuts several times, shakes his head at me and smiles. I'm riled. I don't want to be. I can't help it. Why is he doing this?

'No, I don't actually – but aren't you supposed to be minding them today? Wasn't that the deal – taking them zip-lining? You know I'm going for my Sunday afternoon lunch with Corina later.'

He pulls an apple from the brown bamboo wooden salad bowl on the chrome countertop and examines it. Turning it over and over in his hand. As the world turns. It disappoints him, I see, as he makes a face and replaces it.

'What's wrong with the apple, Colin?' I demand.

'It's gone off, Ali ... It's soft ... withered.' He stretches his arms high above his head and yawns very loudly, bringing his left hand down slowly to fix his hood.

'So put it in the bin then, why did you put it back in the bowl?' I yank the hot tap off and wipe my hands on the black-and-white chequered tea towel that's on the countertop.

'Why is it out if it's gone off?' he asks me.

'Are you actually serious?' I scratch my head hard – something I do when I'm stressed and he knows this. Once it was endearing. Now it makes him wince.

'Stop scratching ... Jesus, you are only up and already you have a puss on you ... are you due or something? The never-ending period or what? Calm down … I'm going outside to look for our son.'

'He's on the road playing with Daniel, you know that.' My voice is raised and I don't mean it to be.

He holds his right hand up behind his ear and screws up his nose. 'I'm right here, Hilda Ogden … I told you before I don't think he should be out on the road on his own, he's too young.'

He shakes his head at me. Another row is brewing. I'm conscious of Jade's movements upstairs. She's at the banister leaning over to listen, I just know she is. I lower my voice. I can't let her hear another argument. My eyes are holding the anger though, I can feel them bulge. Through gritted teeth I say, 'OK … OK, Colin, so every day after school Daniel calls in for Mark, they play football in our driveway. I can see them out the window. Just why do you want me to keep him in? It's a cul-de-sac. I'm even slightly embarrassed now when Maeve, that's Daniel's mother by the way, comes to collect him that I won't take her up on her offer of them playing in Daniel's driveway occasionally because I know you'll blow a fuse therefore making me look like a psycho, over-protective mother!'

Colin is just staring at my mouth. His eyes never make contact with any other part of my face. I go on.

'I,' I bang my chest hard, 'I, me, Ali – I am the one who has to rush home from work to pick them up at five every day from Laura's, and then get a dinner ready by six o'clock for four people. Sometimes you join us, sometimes you don't. You never bother to confirm that any more. I need the hour to do that without him under my

14

feet pleading with me to go out and play … pulling out of me every second.'

'Life is really tough for you, isn't it, poor old Ali?' Colin puts his bottom lip over his top.

I want to tell him to *Fffffuck off!* But I don't. Inside my head I am screaming. I can't let Jade hear me raise my voice.

Yes! Sometimes it is tough. But I know it's not *that* tough. I'm not unfortunate or hapless by any means. Yet he makes me feel like I shouldn't ever have a little moan or complain about anything. I cannot vent. Cannot get stuff off my chest. Built-up frustration, however trivial, still needs an outlet. An ear. I don't even think I do moan or complain, to be honest. I just get on with it but then sometimes, like just right now when he picks on how I am managing and points out the faults within my system, I can't handle it. He just doesn't refer to the fact I juggle it all. He never sees fit to thank me in any small, minute, miniscule, teeny-weeny way for keeping it all together. It's like he just expects me to do it. Lunches, uniforms, homework, school pick-ups, parent-teacher meetings, extracurricular activities, play dates, my full-time job, the household – and it gets under my skin. I'm not looking for a marching band or a diamond ring, but now and then maybe a bunch of garage flowers would be nice.

'Thanks for all you do, Ali.'
'No problem, Colin.'

He's the major breadwinner. He has his own company, Devlin's Designs, a green company who design greeting cards and sell on their own website and on the internet. It's a growing company and doing quite well. Lately they have been getting their cards in independent newsagents all across the country. He employs four people and one manager, Maia Crowley, who is also a very green girl. Maia drives an electric car and has a compost heap in her front garden. She grows her own vegetables. She is also vegan. Maia looks vegan, I think. Colin used to work for Hallmark Cards but went out to set up on his own. Like I said, his cards are green. His cards care about the environment. His cards are made from waste material. The *e*'s in D*e*vlin's D*e*signs logo are green and shaped like the globe with two hands wrapped around them. Caring. Me? I work as a coordinator for an arts' centre in the inner city, very low wages, but I love my job and they are very flexible with my hours. If I need to be somewhere for the children, if the school rings in the middle of an important work meeting and they are running a high temperature, I'm OK to leave, to go do what I have to do as a mother. My boss is a woman with two grown-up kids, but she gets it. She understands the working mummy. Thank God.

'It's on your head then. Look … I'm messing with you. I dunno what's melted your sense of humour recently, but I'll take them off your hands till teatime, like I do every single Sunday afternoon, feed them like I do every single Sunday afternoon.' He moves away to the kitchen door, his large hand resting on the slim gold handle, and then he turns back. I'm not sure he gets just how bad things really are between us.

'You know that I have had absolutely no problem with you having these Sunday gossips with crazy winky Corina Martin but I think Mark is at an age now where

16

we should all be sitting down together for a family dinner on a Sunday.' He takes a deep breath in through his nose and releases it slowly. 'Jade had it for years, until you ... well ... so, why shouldn't he?' His dimple is pulsating, his floppy hair dropping down over his left eye.

'I cook six days a week, Colin, I don't want to cook on a Sunday.' I pick up the chequered tea towel again and walk over to him, wiping my bone-dry hands. I wring it hard between my fists. I detest it when he calls Corina crazy and winky. Again, he knows this, just like I know the 'until you' was about to proceed into the whole 'until you started working full-time' tirade.

'Well, I'll cook then.' He pushes his hair back and stares down at me. I'm around five foot five in my flats.

Is he trying to put a stop to my Sunday lunches with Corina? Or am I so selfish that I don't want to do a Sunday roast dinner for my family? True, I used to do a roast every Sunday before Mark was born. I'd start the prep at midday, peeling carrots, parsnips and potatoes to roast, stuffing a chicken or whatever we had and I'd sit down after cleaning up at five o'clock. I became weary of roast chicken, roast beef, roast lamb, roast potatoes, roast parsnips and carrots. The whole roast shebang. Most times Colin would rush it at the kitchen table to get back to see the match. Other Sundays he'd actually be in Manchester at the match. Or in Liverpool, or Southampton, or Birmingham, or Newcastle, or Blackburn. Wherever his Red Army were playing. Most of the dinner time I'd spend coercing Jade into eating the meat and the vegetables. Jade prefers lasagne, or spaghetti bolognese; she isn't into roast dinners. Colin doesn't allow food anywhere else in the house except at the dining table in the kitchen. I sigh internally. Maybe we should all be sitting down together. Maybe I'm not a good mother?

'Fine,' I give in. I want to be a good mother. I want to be a good mother more than I want to be anything else in the entire world. That is my one true desire. Always has been and always will be. I can't state that enough. Moving back to the sink, I fold the tea towel neatly into fours once more and place it on the side of the draining board again. He releases the handle of the door with a rattle and follows me.

'Ahh, look, we'll see … It's just … I always had a family dinner as a lad on a Sunday when me da' was still relatively well … It was important. I loved it when we did it here, Ali. We talked …' He picks the apple up again and from where he is standing, pulls down his hood, closes one eye and stands on the tippy-toes of his white runners then he fires it into the open bin.

He misses.

'He shoots! He misses! See ya later, OK? Have a nice gossip.' He claps his four fingers and thumb together, opens and closes them repeatedly and he leaves the kitchen this time. He also leaves the apple on the floor for me to pick up. I could call him back and argue but everything is an argument these days and I'm tired of it. I'm drained.

'OK,' I manage. I have a lump in my throat. He moves away down the hall to the front door and I watch him go out to get Mark. Colin Devlin. My soulmate. My boyfriend at seventeen and then my husband at twenty-three. The true love of my life. Right now I just don't want to be in the same room as him. What is happening to us?

18

2

**Sunday afternoon. Malan's Restaurant.
Dawson Street, Dublin 1.**

'Are you maybe just over-thinking it all?' Corina says as she twirls her large wine glass by the slim stem in front of her face and dips her nose in. She inhales the bouquet deeply.

'Come to mamma, big boy,' she echoes into the glass, fogging up the sides. I've just filled her in on this morning's new set of arguments and how I'm feeling.

'How am I over-thinking it? I'm not having sex with my husband; we can't talk without it escalating into a fully blown row. I'm really worried, Corina. We really are in a bad place.' I hiss across the table at her and stab my heavy-duty stainless steel fork into my chicken Caesar salad with extra dressing. I manage to collect a crunchy crouton, chicken and romaine lettuce all on the fork. Score. I push it all into my mouth and chew, releasing the flavours of the combination of Parmesan cheese, lemon juice, olive oil, egg, garlic, Worcestershire sauce and black pepper. Malan's do a seriously tasty Caesar salad and this afternoon the restaurant is energetic. Both young and old enjoying a lazy work-free afternoon.

A baby cries loudly and hysterically in the corner. As

I crunch on my bite I glance over at the frazzled parents and make sure I catch the mother's eye. She is standing, bouncing baby in one arm balanced on her hip with her fork full of twisted spaghetti in the other. Trying to wrap her mouth around it, she only serves to drop it all down the front of her dress. I smile widely but softly at her to show I understand and hope I give her some reassurance with my smile. I have been that spaghetti-covered frustrated soldier. But I think all children have a place in public restaurants until late evening. It's great for the parents to get out together. If you want a silent meal, stay at home or wait until after nine o'clock.

We are sitting in a booth at the window seat and I gaze across at Dublin's Mansion House, where the Lord Mayor lives, as I wash my food down with the sharp-tasting grape. It is bad that I have no idea who the current Lord Mayor is. The building is monumental and always extra impressive at Christmas. I remember it well from my history books in school – the black-and-white pictures of an Irish crowd gathered outside on 8 July 1921 ahead of the War of Independence truce. Funny how some images from history books stay with you for ever. I love Dublin. I love being Irish. I'm very patriotic. I love feeling European too. I especially love being in the city centre on a Sunday afternoon, the feeling of being free, a day for me, all alone – not that I don't cherish being a mother. Like I said, I do, I really do. I just like to have some me time on a Sunday. Is that selfish? Sometimes I feel so guilty about it. I work hard the other six days a week. The earlier threatening rain now sleets diagonally across the busy road. I live in a world of perpetual guilt.

20

'Hello?' Corina is waving her stainless-steel fork in front of my face.

'Sorry, what?' I answer, still chewing. That's another thing I simply adore about Corina: we don't need to talk all the time.

'I was going to say I'm no expert, right, but you have two kids with an awkward age gap. Like, Jade was five and you were almost heading in a new direction when you fell pregnant with Mark. You had to start all over again. Nappies, bottles, sterilisers, teething, temperatures, sleepless nights … and you guys have lots of financial stress with your big mortgage, so many bills coming in, routines to stick to, school runs, and pick-ups, drop-offs, full time jobs, you never ever have a night out together …'

'Because …' I interrupt and spit a square of Parmesan cheese out as she raises her hand.

'I know, I know because you can't afford a babysitter, seriously that landed in my wine? I'm still going to drink it obviously but ew, Ali,' she fishes the intruder out with her unused fork.

Corina smiles at me. I don't really feel comfortable lambasting Colin to Corina, as I am doing it so often lately, so I try not to. I tell her things are tough, and I have only recently admitted that things in the bedroom are bad too but I haven't told her the whole story. I haven't told her how he makes me feel physically. I'm not sure I understand it enough myself to explain it to another person, to be honest. More often than not I wonder if there is something wrong with me. It's unfair of me to ask her to give me marriage advice. Also Corina is clever enough to know you never disrespect or slag off someone's husband or wife too much because odds are they will reunite and you'll be the one left with egg on your face.

Corina and I have been friends for three years now. A new friend who breezed into my life and with her brought a Jo Malone, nectarine-blossom-and-honey-scented blast of glorious, fresh, jocular, buoyant, independent air. She was employed to help me plan the opening of the City Arts Centre's new government-funded, sixty-eight-seat theatre, The Inner. I had more or less lost touch with any school friends as I married so young and had the babies. I have friends, don't get me wrong, fantastic neighbours, some great mummies from the school. I'm really close to my older sister Victoria but she lives in Los Angeles so I don't see her very often, maybe once every five years. Victoria works for Paramount Pictures and lives in a very different world to me. I love her, she's my sister, but I didn't have a Corina. Corina and I hit it off the instant our paths crossed. If we were lines on the palm of a hand, our perpendicular lines crossed right through one another.

'Sorry, I am reeking of garlic and eminently hung-over,' she informed me immediately and oh so matter-of-factly the first time I greeted her at the door of the City Arts Centre.

'Corina Martin.' She extended her hand. I took it. Firm handshake. Warm. If it were a teenage movie, a bolt of electricity would have been visible when we touched. Connected.

'Ali Devlin, and don't worry I can't smell anything, probably because I'm reeking of garlic too: I made a very strong chilli last night. This way.'

She followed me into our small staff kitchen behind the centre's cafe, Beans and Other Stuff.

'Coffee?' I offered.

'I'd ride Shane MacGowan in a mankini with his old teeth for a strong coffee right now: black, two sugars. Don't supposed you've a choccy biccy going?' She had pulled herself up onto the countertop, legs swinging. Then she went on.

'So, Ali ... Alison?' She raised her gorgeous well-shaped eyebrows at me.

'Ali,' I confirmed.

She goes on. 'So, Ali, get this: I have been seeing this guy the last three weeks, right, nice enough, had a job, his own hair, still hadn't sent me a dick pic ... all good signs ... but last night he just stood me up. I sat in the Trocodero restaurant and waited. Then I texted him, three times – it was on Whatsapp so I could see he was reading them. It had the two blue tick marks. No reply. Then I called and his phone was turned off. I even tweeted him. Jesus, why did I tweet him? Anyway, then I simply took off my long wraparound, stomach-hiding cardigan, slipped off the bastard high heels, loosened my elasticised belt and ordered for one. Garlic prawns in filo for starters, garlic chicken with asparagus and honey mash for mains, extra gravy, a bottle of Merlot and a messy nest of fresh cream strawberry meringue. I rolled out of the place, Ali.'

We never looked back.

I relish having her around me; she makes me feel so at ease and God she makes me laugh so much. Corina loves life and is the type of person everyone wants to be around.

Corina, simply put, is loyal, funny and great craic. Three ingredients I adore.

'So are you going to Amsterdam or not?' She cuts into her medium-rare steak with ease and pops it into her mouth. Corina loves her grub.

But I still can't tell her how much I fancy Owen. Owen O'Neill. I know she'd be horrified, rightly so, and immediately put me in my place on that one. I get that I just have to cop myself on. Corina just wouldn't understand it. I don't understand it myself. I still can't believe I actually fancy another man. I mean I haven't properly fancied anyone since I clapped eyes on Colin Devlin in sixth year. He'd strutted into our classroom, 6A2, white shirt hanging out, the top button open and the blue-and-white stripy school tie loose and messy. Something happened to me. I kind of saw him in slow-motion. I was lolling at my desk by the window – Mr Woodcock had just opened it a little, as it was an unusually warm, bright April morning – and I heard the hum of a faraway lawnmower but could still smell the freshly cut grass. Mr Woodcock held Colin at the top of the classroom, clasping his shoulder tightly and introduced him. I was transfixed. Him. That guy. Holy cowabunga. Yer man standing up beside the confusing pie-charted blackboard with a graffiti-covered khaki canvas bag slung over his shoulder. Not a word of what Mr Woodcock was saying went into my head. A massive Manchester United Football Club crest was sewn onto the bag. *Long Live the Red Army* written underneath it. *Busby Babes* inked down the side. The names *Whiteside* and *Giles* written in white Tippex. Funny how I've come to despise that Red Army over the last number of years. If only I'd known the number of overnight trips to Manchester, the Champions League games weekends in Barcelona, Turin, Berlin, the lost Sunday afternoons, and the mood he falls into when they lose. I just find it, nowadays, all so idiotic and childish. Anyway back then Colin Devlin had just moved from Belfast to Rathfarnham in south county Dublin. Today his Belfast accent is less accentuated but still very much there. Owen O'Neill. If I don't say it out loud, this crush, because I know that's what it must be, a pathetic adult crush that might just go away. It's certainly not helping my marriage crisis. It's not the reason for my marriage crisis; at least I don't think it is.

'I think so. We leave this Friday coming so I have to tell them for definite tomorrow morning. There is just so much for me to organise to be gone two whole days and two whole nights?' She's allowed me to daydream again with my delayed answer as I pick up my glass and gently swirl my beloved vino. I'd dance the tango with it if I could.

'Like what? I think the little break would do you and Colin good to be honest. Absence makes the heart grow fonder and all that. Pick up some outrageous dirty lingerie in the red-light district. Some filthy shit. Go see a peep show yourself. Look how passionately Madonna recommended it. Kinky old cow. Marriage isn't easy, my mother still tells me this, and her and dad are fifty years this summer. Sex is very important. You can't let that slide. The kids are in school Friday right and Laura will collect them?'

I nod and stab some more chicken pieces onto my fork. *Prong. Prong. Prong.*

'So, Colin can just leave work early and get them from Laura's by five. Can't he take them out over the weekend? Daddy-time. Dublin is a hub of children's activities at the weekend. I have event-organised so many, if he wants to call me I can give him a foolscap page of things that are happening. The Ark theatre has weekend shows for kids that are always worth seeing. You're back Sunday, right? You aren't going to Mumbai via the kibbutz in Brother Sebastian sandals, a tie-dye bandana and a sarong to find your inner self, for crying out loud.' Corina shakes her head.

I swallow. 'Yeah, I know, I know … but Jade has a gymnastics competition on Friday after school at two-thirty which I'll be missing. One of the mothers said she can collect her after and bring her home with her and Colin can collect her from them at seven, she will give her dinner … I just feel crappy I'm missing it, why do these work things always overlap with kids' events?' I sigh.

'Is it an important thing?' Corina asks.

'No … well, yes for her, but she's only doing it for fun really. It's not serious. They are, like, little competition exhibitions, you know? Because it's "Active Week" in the school they are allowed to rehearse in the school hall from eleven o'clock. I mean, she's never going to be yer McKayla Maroney, gold-medallist at it,' I pause. 'I, I just get the feeling Colin thinks me going to Amsterdam … He thinks it's all a big huge pain in the arse, he's just so unsupportive about my job lately.' I shrug.

'He's not exactly unsupportive, Ali, come on. Wasn't he the one who urged you to go for the job in the first place when you showed him that flyer?'

I wouldn't exactly use the word *urged* but I keep my mouth shut as she continues, 'Look … and I know he's not my number one fan, for whatever his reasons – no doubt it's because he finds my subscription to spinster-hood threatening – but he is under pressure to pay for pretty much everything, right? He's carrying a lot on his shoulders. You earn such a low salary and you're left with feck all to play with after you pay Laura but maybe just sit him down and actually tell him how much you love your job … how much it means to you? Tell him what it is exactly that you do, the importance of your work and thank him for all his support. Then give him the ride, that's what's really wrong.'

'Maybe,' I say as I take a long slow drink of my chilled glass of Pinot Grigio. Swishing the liquid around my mouth, tasting its flavours before swallowing the relaxation down. True, he was enthusiastic initially as a little part-time thing until he saw I was actually serious. I drink another precious sip. Corina got hundreds of those 'over the limit' tests from an event she did promoting a safe-driving event in Croke Park, her boot is still full of them, and we always do them before we leave after our one glass of wine. It has never once read over the limit. We drink a jug of water also. After our glass of wine, we have dessert and coffee.

Corina excuses herself to answer an email on her beeping Blackberry and I catch my reflection in the mirror behind. I can't stop looking at myself lately for some reason. I don't look thirty-five, I don't think. I have short blonde hair, with a sweeping side fringe, green eyes, a slightly prominent nose but a good chin. An oval face. I sit up straighter. I never slouch, I hold myself up tall always. I have pretty good posture so I can't be to blame for Jade's slouching. That is not a case of monkey see, monkey do. I have a reasonably good figure. It could be better around my tummy area, I guess, but both my babies were over nine pounds. I ain't ever wearing midriff tops again – not that I ever did. Even when I had a flat tummy, I never had much of an opinion about myself physically.

This afternoon I am wearing a TK Maxx V-neck red long-sleeved T-shirt that says *Boutique Chic* (don't ask me why) and black skinny jeans with high, black, strappy wedges. My make-up is minimal. Well, face make-up: my foundation is minimal. I like to concentrate on my eyes. I like a good cat eye effect and I'm pretty good at it now. I can do my eyes in six minutes flat. I take my liquid gel eyeliner and make a small line from the edge of my eye, flicking up. Then I take the gel liner down and into the corner of my eye and then literally colour it in. A tip I got from Corina. A tip she got at the Irish Film & Television Awards from the incredible Irish actress Victoria Smurfit. Saves me ages on mixing and blending eye shadows. So, I do just a small bit of BB cream foundation and I'm all about the black mascara and gel eyeliner. Rose Vaseline for the lips.

I wonder what Colin sees when he looks at me now. I know he still fancies me. He used to tell me I looked like the actress Naomi Watts. Every time she came on a movie on the TV or we saw her in a magazine, he'd say, 'There ya are, Ali Devlin, you're doing well for yourself!'

I'd say, 'Go away, I'm nothing like her!' But secretly I'd be ridiculously chuffed.

Naomi and I are about the same height, I surmise now into my mirror as Corina types at breakneck speed. At one stage she did have a haircut like mine. Me and Naomi. Aliomi. Ha!

I wonder what Owen sees when he looks at me. I know just how bad I fancy him right now. I fancy him something rotten. Grotesquely. I can't tell if he fancies me back. I know he really likes me but he also knows I'm married with kids. Out of bounds. I've never had a male friend who I just relate to so exactly. We like all the same things. We find the same things hilariously funny. We finish each other's sentences. I can't watch *Frozen* with Mark any more without comparing me and Owen to Anna and Hans when they sing 'Love Is An Open Door'. Ridiculous. But we just get one another. It's like we have known each other all our lives, not just for the last six months. The instant thought of him puts me off my food. I can't eat another bite. Belly like jelly. This is bordering on the insane. I have to stop this. It's why I have been unsure about going to Amsterdam: he's going too.

Owen O'Neill only joined the Arts Centre at the end of June, coincidentally not all that long after things started going really pear-shaped between me and Colin. Just at the time when I was becoming really busy in work and we couldn't say 'good morning' to one another without fighting. True, I had been getting more and more involved in my work. I had a new programme on the go with the elderly of the community in the St Andrew's Resource Centre on Pearse Street that I was very dedicated to making happen and Colin was a bit miffed. Neglecting him, he told me one night when he came home a bit drunk after a Manchester United Cup Final game and I was still working on the family shared computer in the kitchen. He was trying to tell me about Wayne Rooney's missed penalty and because I didn't look up immediately and give him my full attention he went off on one. I remember that night now.

* * *

'What is it you are actually doing there at ten o'clock at night?' He nods to my spreadsheet for the St Andrew's Resource Centre.

'Work.' He's had a few and I'm not in the mood for defending my job again.

'There's real work!' He flings his right hand out wide to land pointing at the massive pile of ironing piled up on the kitchen table.

'Sorry?' I ask the word as a question and I hit Save and minimise my spreadsheet.

'Why is there a massive pile of ironing, and you are pissing around with the arty oldies? This is your job, Ali, you are supposed to be a wife and mother. The place is a tip!' He spits the word 'mother'. Then he moves to the sink and takes the pint glass off the draining board and fills it up with tap water. I could leave it and go up to bed but I'm starting to unravel when it comes to not standing up for myself.

'Why should I be doing the ironing, Colin?' I keep my voice conversational. It's an enormous effort in self-control but I do it.

He huffs a sarcastic laugh at me.

'No, you are right, Ali, quite right, why should you do your kids' ironing? I don't ask you to do mine, ever. I do my own. So don't give me that poor housewife-has-to-do-it-all bullshit.' He necks half the pint glass of water gasping loudly at the end.

I rise from the family computer and walk to him. This mood when Manchester United loses is not washing with me any more.

'You do it,' I say.

'I'm not doing it!' He recoils from me. I put on my baby voice.

'Oooooh, did Rooney Pooney miss his penno wenno? Oh no, Colin, oh no … How will he cope tonight in his million pound house with his million pound salary?' I squash up both my fists and twist them in front of my eyes. Like I am boo-hooing.

'That's just so pathetic … is that supposed to annoy me?' He refills the glass to the top and takes another drink as he walks to the pile on the kitchen table. That, by the way, I was about to tackle after I finished my spreadsheet. I'm not touching it now.

He picks up Jade's cream cardigan.

'Jade's.' Moves through the pile, dropping them onto the dark slate floor. 'Mark's, Jade's, Mark's, Jade's, Mark's, Mark's, Mark's …'

Neglecting the family, he had gone on to tell me that night. Kids are suffering. I had stupidly apologised over and over and tried to convince him that wasn't my intention. I never once brought up the fact when his beloved Man United were playing he may as well not exist to the family.

31

Corina is still tapping away.

I think about Amsterdam as I prod my chicken salad around the plate.

There are four of us invited to see the Very Messy Theatre Company at the opening of the Danker Arts Centre in Amsterdam. We would like to programme them next year with their new work, *The Treasury of Fairytales*, for our Christmas show for inner-city kids in the centre's theatre. I saw a promoted tweet about the show that directed me to their website and I contacted them immediately after I watched the first five minutes of the show. They have kindly invited to put us up. We also intend on implementing a scheme I suggested where we swap students on work experience from different arts centres around Europe. The team travelling over is my boss, Colette Flood, the director of programming Michael McKenna, myself the coordinator and Owen O'Neill the artist-in-residence. I'm back to the mirror. I'm not sure about this thirty-five malarkey.

'Corina, have you had any cosmetic work done?' I stare at my nose. I reach up and tug it gently from side to side.

'No.' She's still typing.

'Never?'

'No.' She's leaning back and half looking up, the universal sign of 'I've almost finished this'.

'Oh,' I say.

'I would though,' she says, tucking the Blackberry into the side pocket of her bag.

'Like what?' I ask.

'Oh, the bloody works.' She stands up in the booth, knees slightly buckled, running her hands all over her upper and lower body.

'I'd do here, here, here, here, here and here. Lipo it all off!' I laugh and she sits down again.

'I'd have it all sucked out, full face lift, double-chin removal, smaller face if they can do that, can they make your fat face smaller? I have fat eyes.' She winks at me. She is always winking, Corina. Colin thinks it's weird. I think it's fabulous.

I'm still laughing hard as I sit back and rest my straightened back against the soft red leather-backed frame of the booth. Then I remember why I haven't laughed all day until now.

'Ali, what is wrong? You do seem really disjointed.' Corina fills our water glasses and kindly allows the generous lemon segment to fall into my glass.

'It's Colin!' I throw my hand in the air. I'm incredulous. 'Haven't I just told you all this?' I shake my head from side to side, mouth open.

'It's a blip, right? A rough patch, isn't that all? Don't let it escalate. Don't focus too much on it. He's a good man, Colin. A good provider. He loves you, right?' She looks steadily into my eyes. Questioningly.

'You're right … Sorry, I am due. I'm finding my PMT is lasting at least two weeks before they even arrive. Colin threw that one at me this morning too. He loves to throw the menstruating monster at me. Christ, Corina, listen to me: I'm all me, me, me! Enough about me, tell me how was your week? I wasn't on Facebook, I wanted to keep it a surprise.' I tease her.

She throws her head back and guffaws. Nothing affects Corina. She is small in height, curvy in frame and huge in personality. She is attractive with a splattering of tiny freckles and wild red curly hair that she always wears in a loose bun at the back of her head with curly side bits tumbling around her face. Corina wears lashings of black mascara but no other make-up. She's fiery. Always in flowing knee-length skirts that meet her knee-high black leather boots and colourful wrap tops.

'Ahhh, ya know, nothing much, Ali, just work all week. We launched the new SlipperOH range last night in Dundrum town centre, yeah … Big launch, lots of media coverage, huge campaign – just big slippers really. One of the big Irish models launched them and I thought I'd puke trying so hard not to laugh. Her frame was so emaciated in a skin-tight yellow-and-red-striped dress and then the huge red slippers on her feet, she looked like Ronald McDonald! Nearly pissed myself … Eh, not much else new to tell.' She rolls her eyes from side to side in deep concentration.

'Oh! I did join that life-drawing class for beginners in the City Arts Centre on Thursday evenings … remember I was telling you I might join, well that new artist-in-residence, Owen O'Neill, isn't it? He takes it. Man, I wish he was the model. *Ba-ba-boom!*' She links her hands together and pushes them backwards and forwards over her heart. Every part of my body tenses up. She doesn't miss a beat, clueless, as she goes on.

'Ali, the first class was so hilarious.' She cuts another piece from her steak and dips it generously into her garlic butter on the side. She holds it aloft before adding, 'An elderly lady, the model, was in great nick, I have to admit – but her stomach rumbled like Posh Spice's in a French patisserie for the entire hour. The noise! She looked like a basketball hoop when I was done drawing her on my page. I nearly wet myself again! Lucky I can amuse myself so much, eh? Van Gough, I am not; Picasso, well, maybe. I enjoyed it though. I'm going to keep it up mainly for the exceptionally hot art teacher and the fact it kept me away from the fridge! Both good for my figure and my liver.'

She pops the steak into her mouth and raises her glass to me now, still chewing, tilting it from side to side across the table in front of my face. The exceptionally hot art teacher, never a truer word was spoken. I'm avoiding that conversation like the plague, even though her words stab at my mind. Corina chews. Elton John quietly sings out about the blues from the small black speaker above our booth. I stare at the gorgeous splattering of freckles on the bridge of her nose. It would be so easy to live life with Corina.

'I'd murder another one of these, would you? Inhale it actually!' She holds her wine glass out at arm's length.

'Oh, man, I so would,' I sigh.

'Let's then?' Corina makes a cheeky face.

'I have the car!' I groan.

'So leave it – it's free parking today, just put the lousy coins in for the three hours in the morning. Surely Colin won't mind dropping you here on his way to work after you both drop the kids off. Call him?' she suggests.

I know he won't like this idea but I am actually too embarrassed to say this to Corina. It just sounds like I am bashing him all the time. Maybe I should give him the benefit of the doubt. Maybe he will say, 'You know what, love, you need a break, enjoy and we will see you when we see you.'

'I'll text him.' I pull my cream suede Mango bag from the back of my chair and grope around the mess for my iPhone. I pull it out, blow off the debris, enter my password and I type.

Might have another drink or two and leave the car if that's OK?

Seconds later the phone rings, it's Colin.

'Colin.' I hold the caller ID out for Corina to see.

She gives me the two thumbs up and is already signalling the waitress.

'Hiya,' I keep my voice bright. Breezy wife.

He says nothing for a second.

'What're you doing, Ali?' His voice is terse. I can hear Mark screaming in the background. My heart races. I hate when I hear my kids crying and I'm not there. I get an actual dull ache in the pit of my stomach. My heart races.

'Is Mark OK? What's he screaming for?' I ask.

'His mummy,' Colin spits down the line, and then continues, 'What's this about, this text? I'm driving, I had to pull in to read it, he's screaming because he didn't want me to stop as he's starving! I hate texting, you know that.' He's pissed off.

'OK, OK, sorry … Mark gets fierce food rage, all right … Well, I'm still here, I'm in Malan's having a bite with Corina. We were just enjoying the … having a laugh, ya know. How's all your end? How's Jade?'

'And you want to stay out on the piss all day and night? Seriously what is wrong with you?' Terser still.

I don't want Corina to know how he speaks to me, I'm embarrassed, so I keep my voice at the same breezy level so he will know this. He knows she's sitting opposite me by my tone.

'Yeah … just enjoying the catch up and thought another glass would be nice.'

'So have another glass but make it a spritzer, a few black coffees, then drive home.' He spits the advice at me.

'I'd be over the limit, wouldn't I, though?' I'm making a face of pretend deliberation while licking my index finger and rubbing an imaginary stain off the table.

'Do whatever the hell you want, Ali, but Maia's picking me up at seven in the morning to drive to Carlingford on an overnighter. We have a meeting with the MD of NewsXtreme newsagents, so I don't know how you are going to get the kids to school.' He rings off at that. I do not.

'Ahh, right, sorry, I totally forgot. Yeah that's grand … Yeah, OK, see you later, bye, bye, bye, bye.' I ring off now and drop my phone onto the table. The amount of times I got the call to say he'd missed the flight home from Manchester and would now be on the last one, or the early morning one, I couldn't count on two hands.

Corina is making a sad face.

'No can do?' she asks.

'No can do,' I manage.

'Next time maybe,' she says as she unsignals the approaching waitress. If she knows, she is playing along nicely. I'm guessing she could hear him. Oscar nominee stuff. Meryl Martin.

My heart is racing. Listen, I'm not annoyed he has to leave early to go to work or that it's not practical for me to leave my car overnight. I get it. All I want is his attitude to be nicer. He sounds so hostile towards me all the time. Pissed off. Bitter. Impatient. Angry.

'Actually, will I just order our desserts then?' Corina asks.

'May as well,' I say.

Our friendly waitress returns, Corina apologies for playing 'table tennis' with her and they both laugh. Corina knows I'm upset but she also knows I don't want to talk about it. She orders our favourite desert in this establishment, two banoffee pies with extra Devon clotted cream, a pot of strong tea for me and a large hazelnut latté for herself and we talk about the effect worldwide notoriety is having on young Kylie Jenner.

When we are full up and have split our bill I hug Corina tightly at the door, the rain has stopped but it's deathly dark at five thirty. The smell of Christmas is actually tangible. Almost like mulled wine is making its way through the streets. Like when Scooby-Doo used to follow that long line of visible scent. Dawson Street twinkles. Early shoppers brush past me laden down with bags. People to see, places to go.

Corina pulls on her lime green soft leather gloves and before she walks away she says softly, her nose crinkling up at me, 'Maybe you guys should think about some marriage counselling, Ali? It can't hurt.'

She winks at me with a smile and walks away, head down, tapping on her Blackberry, undoubtedly to meet some friends for drinks somewhere trendy and dimly lit with fairy lights and lounge music as I trudge towards my grey car. Wager she's going somewhere that brews their own craft beer.

I don't want to go home. I would if Colin wasn't there; if it was just my children I'd race home. The constant keeping my mouth shut so as not to upset them with another row is starting to become more and more difficult for me. Draining my soul. I wrap my un-winter-worthy brown leather jacket tighter around my chest and I see the orange neon sign for Nectar Wines just where my car is parked. My beacon of hope. And I head straight for it. It is necessary to press a buzzer to gain access, reads the sign on the door, so I do. I'm authorized and buzzed in. Alcohol approval. I buy myself a bottle of the same Pinot Grigio from Malan's, almost ten euros cheaper, and armed with my brown-paper-bagged bottle I get into my grey Mazda car and I slowly drive myself home.

3

Sunday night. At home.

'Mummy's home! Mummmmyyy'sssss hooommmeee!'
Mark zigzags towards me at the hall door. His little face
overjoyed to see his mummy. He grabs me in a tight
hug around my legs. He is wearing his filthy dirty Olaf
costume and his Fireman Sam wellington boots. Mark is
a real mixture of us both. Sandy blond hair and blue eyes.

'Careful, darling,' I say, as I hold onto the glass hall table
with my brown paper bag in the other hand. I kick the hall
door shut behind me. The house is cold. Colin hasn't got
the heating on. Again. It's December and, although I do
love our planet, I live in Ireland, an island in the North
Atlantic. Gas heating is a necessity. I'm bloody freezing.

'Mummy doesn't want to drop her booze, Markey boy.'
Colin walks out of the living room in his stocking feet,
MacBook surgically attached under his arm, straight past
me and straight up the stairs as he ruffles Mark's floppy
Olaf head.

I plaster a smile on my face for my baby and fix his
hood. His carrot nose bobbing.

Some people are worth melting for.

'Where is Jade? Did you guys have any tea?'

His tiny features warm my heart.

'Just Maccy Donald's earlier.' Mark is still stuck to my legs. He's small in stature for five. The smallest in his class. I've had him with the paediatric doctor and they don't see any immediate growth issues.

'He'll probably never play full back for Ireland, mind you,' the specialist had said as he charged me an arm and a leg, but told me there was no need to reschedule an appointment.

'OK, well, how about some toasted fingers and dippy boiled eggs? I'll give you some grapes while you wait,' I say now as I put the wine down carefully on the hall table, undo my wedges and pick him up. I know I shouldn't, it's another huge bone of contention between Colin and me. Colin literally flips out when I carry Mark. I know he is five but he's still my baby. Junior infants. I have argued the use of the word *infant* with Colin a lot lately and I quote: 'Infant: denoting something in an early stage of its development.'

Colin thinks it's weird that I still want to pick him up and says I'm doing Mark no favours by babying him all the time. But he is my baby. My last baby. I kiss him gently on the lips. I inhale him.

'Yayyyyy, Mummy, do I have big school 'gain t'morrow?'

'You do, sweetie.' I hold him close and carry him into the kitchen. He smells of Monster Munch and markers.

'Not long to go now before you get Christmas holidays and Santa comes!' I whisper in my excited voice and I start to hum 'Rudolf the Red Nose Reindeer'.

I stop in my tracks. The kitchen is a total bomb site. Dirty dishes, arts and crafts all over the table, Lego pieces all over the floor, the dirty washing strewn around by the machine, uniforms and tracksuits to be ironed piled up on the chair. I sigh.

'What am I getting for lunch tomorrow? Alistair gets chocolate spread on crackers and when he squishes them together the chocolate comes out through the holes and it's so funny, can I have that? Can I Mummy? Can I?' Mark asks as I gently release him down to the floor.

'Can I go out to Karen's for, like, an hour?' Jade is lounging against the kitchen door again. Looking sixteen. Light military-style denim shirt, grey legging and Uggs. Her blonde hair falling around her shoulders. A hand-made loom-band chocker around her long neck. Red and black. I did not look like that at her age.

'No, it's too late and too dark now ... do you want a boiled egg, love?' I ask her.

'Can I, Mummy, can I?' Mark pulls hard at my duffel.

'Um ... how come everyone else is allowed to go to Karen's?' Jade darts the words at me.

'Can I, Mummy, can I? Can I? Can I?' Mark tugs and tugs.

'No, Mark, you are having Billy Bear Roll tomorrow OK?' I look down at him, then to Jade. 'Because I said so, now do you want a boiled egg?'

The wait for her answer begins. It's irritating me already because of the Colin-inflicted situation I find myself in, I know, but nonetheless I brush past her out to the hall table, pick up my wine and return to the kitchen, open the fridge and put it in to chill more. I take a wine glass from the top shelf and add that to the freezer too. I love a frosted wine glass.

'Uh no, coz, like, Brooklyn and Bailey are posting a new

video anysecondnow and I have to be in m'room to watch it – and you know Dad won't let me eat in m'room, Mom,' she drawls.

'All right, well, when you have watched it come down and I'll make it for you then, OK, love?' She is only eleven years old, I constantly have to remind myself. Still just a child. Growing up in a grown-up world. Jade slouches away in her fake cream eBay Uggs. I start to pick the clothes up off the floor and put them into the washing machine. I pull on a pair of dirty socks. The grey slate floor is freezing under me, but there's no way I'm going upstairs to get my slippers.

'Mark, why don't you go in and watch CBeebies and I will call you when tea is ready?' I take off my brown leather jacket, hang it on the back of the kitchen chair, walk over and flick on the central heating and suddenly I feel dog-tired. Weary. I prepare Mark a bowl of seedless red grapes and set about getting the kitchen back in order, making the lunches, locating all the bits of each uniform, ironing the uniforms and making the teas. Colin does not come back down. I see from the silver cartons and the leftovers on his unwashed plate he had ordered himself a Chinese takeaway. But not the kids. My kids hate Chinese takeaway. One year they both got a vomiting bug and the last food they had eaten was a Chinese takeaway. They can't look at one since. I should be glad, I suppose, but sometimes it's a bummer. I feed the kids their boiled eggs with toast separately, and get them both up the stairs, washed, teeth cleaned into their pyjamas and ready for bed. A new dawn, another new day, another chance for it to be better. I can hear the commentary from a football match blaring out of our bedroom. I read Mark another chapter from *Rover Saves Christmas*, the latest in our series of library borrowed Roddy Doyle books, for his bedtime story and allow Jade another half an hour in her treasured iPad world.

* * *

Pop! The wonderful sound of medicated relaxation. If only Pilates *popped*! If only fitness *fizzed*! I am bent over with the cold wine bottle between my legs and have successfully uncorked my reward.

Taking my wine glass out of the freezer, I pour myself a large, unmeasured chilled glass.

The unruly kitchen is now spotless, back to the way I left it earlier. I love my kitchen, don't get me wrong. I don't own a NutriBullet and I don't shop organic at my local farmers' market, but I do like to cook. The Greatest Cook in the World Award will never adorn my shelf but I do try and I just like spending time in the kitchen. It's the warmest room in the house. That, and the fact there is a constant supply of strong tea, probably adds to my affection for it. Until I have ingested my first cup of tea of the day I'm still clinically asleep. Then another, then another, then another and I'm just about ready to face the day.

I'm not bad at the few things I make, mind you. I taught myself how to make a great stew and I like homely dinners, like a baked ham and baked potatoes and broccoli. Mine will both eat broccoli, possibly the only veg they actually like. Mark is a bit better than Jade; he'll eat corn and peas. Jade is afraid of any other veg, so broccoli it is.

44

Like everyone, I'm afraid of all processed foods and hidden sugars now, so even the one-of-your-5-a-day smoothies I used to pay ridiculous money for and beg the kids to drink are now removed from my shopping list. I don't have time to make fresh smoothies, sorry, but I just don't. I'm not a juicer. I don't want to become a raw, green, frightened human being. There is always fresh fruit in the house (don't mind Colin and his withered apple comment) and that's the best I can do. I slice banana into their Weetabix in the mornings (also now the only cereal I can apparently buy – given Coco Pops is almost as bad as dipping your licked finger deep down into the sugar bowl, I understand). I give grapes and apples for lunches, and I always try to hand them plates of cut-up fruit when they are watching TV. I remember fruit being considered a treat. When Granny Margaret gave me a ripe pear or a plate of strawberries I was in heaven. Ha!

Anyway, my kitchen is a nice place. It's all open plan with dark slate flooring and a long row of dark oak shelves; the American-style fridge is a vibrant glossy red and the kitchen table is also dark oak but with four red chairs around it. 'Seriously stylish', Corina calls it. There's a sliding patio door that leads out onto our large back garden. The cream walls are covered in framed photos of the kids. Mostly black-and-white. Colin prefers black-and-white; I prefer colour. One wall is painted with metallic blackboard paint but no one ever chalks on it. It is too dark to see anything but out the back there are three wheelie bins – one brown, one black and one green – swings, a wrecked piece of garden furniture, a filthy barbecue and various bikes, flickers and scooters scattered around.

We live in Dublin 6, in Ranelagh, just off Milltown Road, and it's a lovely three-bedroom semi-detached house with real physical character. Castlebrick Road. All the houses on the street are painted a different colour – right now ours is a canary yellow. They must be freshly painted every year, in May, by law of the county council and it costs a bloody fortune!

We live in No. 13.

The superstitious digits put me off the house at first but Colin just told me to cop myself on, 'It's only a number. Would ya hand back thirteen million on the Lotto if ya won it?'

Fair point.

We were aware of it about to come on the market as a friend of Colin's, Ado, the president of the Ranelagh Manchester United Supporters Group, had been renting it but was told he had to vacate as the landlord wanted to sell. That was twelve years ago, just before we were married, and we got it for what was considered, in the ridiculous Irish property boom, to be a good price!

We still have a huge mortgage on it. Huge. Huge pressure to meet it every month.

I take a sip of my fermented grape juice. It tangs on my tongue and rolls sharply down my throat. Nice drop of plonk, if I say so myself.

I put it back on the table as I locate the two school bags and leave them out by the door with the coats on top. I Chubb lock and chain the hall door and finally I can sit down. Jobs all done.

Closing the kitchen door softly, I pick up my wine and wearily plod into the sitting room. I'm so cold-blooded

I still find the room chilly, so I throw the fleece blanket around my shoulders, grab the Sky remote controls – I draw the heavy navy curtains with silver threading, then I settle back into the black leather sofa and sip my wine. I flick. Nothing much catching my attention.

Flick. Flick. Flick.

The amount of Christmas ads for certain insanely expensive toys is so early, it's bordering on propaganda.

Don't get me wrong, I understand the pressure Colin is under to make this house tick along. No, I don't earn much of a salary to contribute, but the plain fact is I'm not qualified for any high-paid work.

Flick.

Grand Designs. Seen it. Still I watch for a while. Kevin McCloud's voice is hypnotic. I can hear the muffled noise from Colin's MacBook up above in our bedroom. I can't go up to bed until he's asleep. I can't face it.

Flick.

I settle on a *Friends* repeat. 'The One Where Rachel Tells Ross She Still Loves Him'. Ross and Rachel. Their wonderful on-screen chemistry and easy banter takes my mind off the day. Escapism. I'm only half watching – I've seen it so many times, I can say the dialogue word for word almost – but I have finished the glass already, so I pop back into the kitchen. When I return I take the bottle with me and put it on the floor, I relax back into my warm seat with the blanket. I'm laughing at something Ross did when the door opens and Colin is standing there in his Manchester United boxer shorts. I jump.

'The fucking heat in this house, Ali, is that heating still

on? Jade's still on that iPad too, do you know that? It's a quarter to ten, Ali!'

He stares at the watch on his wrist as though it had just shouted the time out at him. His back-up. His ally. His second-in-command. The watch I bought him for his thirtieth. A Tag. I saved up half my children's allowance for a year for it. Silver strap with a deep red face. He adores it. He had picked me up and swung me around the bedroom. I'd kicked the wicker chair over and then he'd pretended he'd done his back in. We'd laughed and kissed and I was thrilled he'd liked it so much. Good times. He never took it off.

Colin had never got much by way of presents as a kid. He was an only child and his dad suffered badly with MS from the early age of thirty, so his mother, Janet, had worked full-time in the local bakery and money was scarce. When they moved down to Dublin to live with his wealthy brother in Terenure, she got a job in Londis on the checkout. When his dad finally passed away fourteen years ago, Janet jacked in the job and moved back up to Belfast. Colin goes up now and then and sometimes takes the kids but not very often.

'Ali?' He throws his hands dramatically in the air now. The Tag moves slightly up his arm.

'Oh, sorry, yeah, I forgot. Sorry, I'll go up to her now.' I go to stand up.

'No, stay where you are, I'll do it. And can ya keep the telly turned down and turn off the heating?' He nods at my wine bottle on the floor and smirks out a laugh.

'What's so funny?' I ask.

'No … nothing … oh, by the way, are we going to talk

about you going away for this whole weekend? Because I know you have to tell yer woman Collette tomorrow, don't you, and it doesn't look like you are coming up to bed anytime soon.'

'I'd like to go to bed now, actually.' Dutch courage. I move the blanket off me. *It has to be done. This can't go on. He'll be in a better mood once we do it. Get it out of the way.*

He eyes me suspiciously. His tone softens, though.

'Have you sorted anyone to collect Jade after this gymnastics thing, because honestly I'm up to my tits on Friday with NewsXtreme paperwork, I'll be lucky to make Laura's by six.' His face is less annoyed looking.

'Yeah, I have, you can collect her from Emma's mum's at seven, she's having her tea there. I'll text you the address and Laura's fine with six, and she's taking Mark to McDonald's.'

'Wow … very healthy,' he says.

'You took them there today!' I'm kind of incredulous.

'Ya know it's a joke. Yer mother's rented her house in Rathfarnham and is swanning around India when we are desperate for help with the kids.'

He loves slagging my mum off. Granted she isn't the most hands-on grandparent but she has every right to travel the world; she has no husband or other children. She is free. I never slag his mother. Janet Devlin is a lovely woman. Life has just exhausted her, so I never expect her to travel down from Belfast to mind my kids. Just like my mother has every right to live her life wherever she wants to now. He has some cheek.

The will to try to do *it* has completely vanished.

49

'I might watch the end of this actually.' I turn back to *Friends*, grab the controls from the couch and notch up the volume. I pull the blanket back up to under my chin.

He stands there and says nothing for what feels like an age.

'I suppose I have to give you money as well for this trip?' he asks me, his voice full of anger again. His finger now resting in his dimple.

'No.' Rachel is so tanned. So beach ready. So golden. So independent. Probably I do need to join a gym in the not-too-distant future. Maintenance. Or I'll be Curly Watts not Naomi.

'So what are you going to do for spending money?' He pursues his line of questioning. Detective Inspector Devlin.

'I'll manage, Colin.' I stare at him now.

'I have no problem giving you spending money, Ali.' He can sense my temper rising.

'Well, it seems like you do. I don't want anything from you,' I say through the blanket that's now covering my mouth.

'Oh, Little Miss Career Woman, now are we? Angela Merkel what?' He makes a fist with his left hand and covers his mouth with it stifling a fake laugh.

'Oh, go 'way, Colin, I'm too tired for this.' I boldly pick up my wine glass and even more boldly I bloody drain it.

'You're too tired for everything lately, I see. More wine? Maybe you need to pop into the ole AA?'

'Huh?' I wipe my mouth with the back of my hand.

He nods to my other hand.

'The old desperate housewife crutch. A glass here, a

50

glass there, a bottle a night, two bottles a night. Sure, you didn't want to come home, did you? You wanted to stay boozing with the crazy lonely winky woman.' He flicks the elasticised band on his preposterous Manchester United boxer shorts.

'I wanted to have another glass of wine, yeah, so shoot me. That would have made a whole two glasses in total. That's a lot less booze than you consume on one of your football trips, I imagine.' I pull the blanket away from my face now and glare at him.

'What does crazy lonely winky woman think you are? A single woman who can spend all her Sunday afternoon drinking wine and talking shite?'

'Her name is Corina,' I spit the name at him. I release the three syllables at him like bullets from a gun.

Pppccchhhuuuuuuuuuu!
Pppccchhhuuuuuuuuuu!
Pppccchhhuuuuuuuuuu!

I hear three gun shots in my head.

'Well, I don't think Corina has any respect for me or our family if she persuades you to ring me to ask can you stay out all night drinking with her, just cause she has to go home to her empty shithole on South Circular Road.'

'Oh, go away … please!' I plead.

He steps back now, holding the door slightly open still.

'Actually, on your way to the AA pop into the Well Woman Centre and ask them to give you a once-over too, give you a lady MOT if you will.'

'I don't know what you are talking about.' I stare at Ross and Rachel as they look lovingly into one another's eyes.

'Check if your parts are still working. You're always too

tired for sex, aren't you, Ali?' His voice is raised now and I am alertly conscious that Jade is still awake.

I throw off the blanket, jump off the couch and ask him quietly to step back in and close the door. Please let us not subject her to another argument.

'I'll come up now, Colin …'

He moves away. 'You're grand, I'm not begging—'

'But I want to,' I interrupt. But I don't, but I do.

I turn back to the couch and grab the controls, point them at the TV and press. The room falls dark. I reach for my iPhone in my back pocket and use it to light up the room. I just want this family to be all right again.

'Let's go,' I whisper.

He doesn't refuse me a second time.

I brush my teeth slowly as he takes the iPad off Jade and closes her bedroom door. As I rinse and spit I hear him whisper to her from the landing, 'Love you, Jadey.' It's been quite a while since he whispered anything like that to me and actually meant it. I only ever seem to hear those words when he's trying to get something out of me. To be honest, I can't remember the last time Colin had a kind word to say to me. Trying to calm the anger I feel towards him, I embrace the cold night as I strip naked in my bathroom and then slowly walk into the bedroom closing the door behind me. He is sitting up with his bedside lamp on, the room only illuminated on his side. He's looking down at his MacBook and he doesn't look up. I climb in beside him. I feel like we are worlds apart.

'Ya OK?' he asks me.

'Yeah, fine,' I answer him as I wiggle down beside him. The bed is toasty warm. He is naked.

'Wanna take a look at this?' His breath is heavy as he turns the MacBook to face me.

He is watching porn. All I see is a poor young woman being violated by two men by way of making her living. I try and watch but all I feel is sorrow for this poor young woman. How old could she be? Nineteen, twenty at most? Eight years older than our daughter. Turned on, I am not.

'Ya like that, Ali?' he whispers as he leans over and kisses me. Hard. Forceful. Sloppy. He grabs my breasts and drops his head. I feel like he is having sex with the young woman in the video. I want to roar. My whole body feels like it's being subjugated by him.

'Ohh, Ali,' he moves up now and moans into my ear. I feel like he is invading me. I try to get on with it, hurry it up.

'Woah!' He pulls his head up.

'Whatever happened to foreplay?' he half laughs taking my face in his hands. 'Maybe I was wrong and maybe you have wanted it as much as me these last few weeks … could be months now even … What are we like? You are so sexy … I love you, Ali …'

See? See how he only says these words at times like this, which are very rare these days. He ducks down under the covers. I know where he is heading and right now I simply can't cope with it. I zip my legs up tight. It's involuntary, I can't help it.

'What's wrong now?' He pops his head back up.

'Sorry,' is all I can manage.

'Sorry?' He pauses.

'I can't do this, Colin,' I whimper and then he flips. It's not even the porn. How can I be intimate with someone

53

I am fighting with? I physically can't. I cannot dig that deep.

'Fffffuck this! Fffffuck this shit!' he thunders.

'Shush, please, Colin,' I beg. 'Jade will hear you.'

'I don't give a flying fuck who hears me! It's my house! I can't live like this any more! I have needs. You are a complete, frigid bit—' He stops himself.

I don't answer.

'You are a fucking useless wife, Ali, you know that!'

He flings the goose-feathered duvet back and jumps out of the bed and grabs the MacBook and takes it into the en suite bathroom.

I know he is relieving himself and I am glad.

I turn over and shut my eyes. I know it's all wrong of me. I feel so bad, I really do, but I just can't help it. Why am I feeling like this? What is wrong with me? Why can't I just do it? I know it will all be better if I just do it. How hard can that be? But he makes me unable to physically want him by irritating me so much. I feel physical emotion with my brain not my vagina. Plus, I admit, I just don't think that Colin should want dirty sex from me any more. I'm the mother of his two children. How does he get off on desperate young women? Can't he see the fact that in the other room lays a girl not all that much younger? Would it be better if he had showed me a middle-aged woman? I don't know. I don't know when I started to feel like this, but I wish to God I didn't. How can I fix it? Maybe Corina is right, maybe I should look into counselling. It's only sex, it really shouldn't be this difficult.

Owen.

Owen O'Neill.

Would I feel like this in bed with Owen? No. I wouldn't. I know I wouldn't. And that's all sorts of wrong. Nothing works with Colin and me any more. It's broken. I lie still and wait for him to come out of the bathroom. The toilet flushes. Colin's back. He slips under the covers. I remain motionless.

'I don't know why you don't want to make love to me any more, Ali, but it really hurts.' He curls up into the foetal position.

I cry quietly.

4

The week of. Monday morning.
The City Arts Centre, Moss Street, Dublin 1.
'Morning, gorgeous!' Owen O'Neill pushes open the full-length glass door to my tiny office with his outstretched chin, carrying two coffees, one in each hand.

'Morning.' I jump up to help him. All my thoughts of Colin and last night immediately disappear, as if by magic.

Poof. Gone.

He's nowhere near as classically good-looking as Colin, but he is just incredibly attractive to me. Everything about him interests me. I take the cup he offers me and I return to behind my messy desk.

This morning he is wearing wrecked-looking, ripped blue denim jeans and white Adidas runners, a black round-neck T-shirt under a black leather biker jacket. Upon his head lies a grey beanie hat. He isn't shaven. I've yet to see him clean-shaven. The thick dark stubble catches my eye as he pulls off the beanie hat and runs his hands over his dark, closely shaven head. The deepest darkest brown eyes I have ever seen pour into mine. He doesn't have perfect teeth like Colin's, but they add character to his face, I think. His incisors are pointy and very slightly longer than his front two teeth. Even our teeth are similar and, get this, he is exactly the same height as me when I'm in my high heels.

'What's the craic? You OK?' He flops himself into the seat opposite me and lifts the lid off his black coffee. Steam rises to escape. The silver zips from his leather jacket sleeves rattle and then relax.

'Ahh, yeah, I'm OK, I suppose.' I sigh deeply.

'Sounds like a dark, cold December Monday morning response to "you OK", all right. Nice shirt, by the way. So I didn't hear from you at all over the weekend, are you coming to Amsterdam or not? Did Daddy Pig give you permission?' He is tongue in cheek. Colin and Owen have met each other a few times over the last while at various events in the centre, mainly when Colin has come in to pick me up. Colin isn't one for the arts, or artists, but they always got on fine. The reason he calls him Daddy Pig is that Colin was still wearing his *Happy Birthday, Daddy Pig* badge from Mark's *Peppa Pig* birthday card to him on his jumper. Owen, having never heard of *Peppa Pig*, thought this was some sort of critical analysis of Colin's inner angst with parenting.

'What, this old thaaang?' I respond in a Southern accent and pull at my brand new Zara shirt. 'Why thank you, kind sir.' I pretend to fan myself with the palm of my hand.

He laughs and slaps his bare knee through the rips. I see speckles of dark hair.

Then I say, 'Sorry I didn't text you back with my answer. Still wasn't sure I could go but Daddy Pig did give permission and I am indeed travelling this Friday to the land of tulips, sweet Amsterdam. Yippie. Yappie. And Yahooey.' I remove my plastic lid now and blow into the white hot foamy liquid. He got me a latté. Extra hot, just the way I like it.

'Permission?' He tilts his head slightly and squints his brown eyes at me before saying, 'But deadly!' He seems genuinely delighted and I get a small shiver up my spine.

'Hope our rooms aren't adjoining, mind you? Bit of "tomfoolery in the middle of the night" buddy-style.' He puts down his coffee and runs his hands up and down his knees like Vic Mortimer in *Shooting Stars*. He's messing.

'Stop that!' I giggle though.

Not laugh, giggle. I'm ridiculous.

He's so different to Colin in every way. He's so easy going. *Comme ci comme ça*. I guess it's that he's arty and I am arty. I wasn't always arty though and this, I believe, could be the real root of the problem. My inner artiness has come out. It had always been there, but hidden. Dormant. In school, I always only really liked English, drama and art. I had devoured *Romeo and Juliet* and *Othello* for my Inter and Leaving Certificate exams, whereas all my friends found them torturous, double Dutch. Colin thinks it's all bullshit, I know he does. I'm not overly arty or snobby about art, I just love drama and music and painting and work that isn't confined solely to an office desk, I suppose. Expression.

For a moment I think back to this morning.

Waking up was just horrendous. Colin's alarm went off before six and he jumped up immediately. I was already awake and I think he was too. It was pitch dark and bitterly cold.

'Will you be home early tomorrow?' I asked in a croaked

whisper, pulling the blankets back over me from where he had disturbed them.

'Probably,' Colin muttered, his knees bent as he pulled on his socks.

'Colin …' I put my hand on his bare back. He jerked away, grabbed his clothes off the wicker chair and left the room.

I had waited until I heard his car reverse out of the driveway before I padded down barefoot and turned the heating on. I grabbed a cup of tea and brought it back up to the warmness of my bed. When I'd finished I got up and put the kids' uniforms on the radiators to heat before waking them early and making them grilled rashers on toast.

I know Jade senses the tension, no matter how hard I try to carve that smile into my face. I am a mess. I am a woman who's in danger of losing her husband, but more importantly, of breaking up a family. I can't seem to control it. It's spiralling. Colin works hard for us, I know he does. I feel a lunge in my heart. Is he really to blame or is it all me? I can't expect him to change. He shouldn't have to; he is still the man I married.

Owen puts his poly-coated paper cup down on my desk.

'Hang on, I need to open the skylight window in the studio to dry the kids' paintings fully before they all arrive off the bus.' Owen drags me back but as he takes his leave, I'm back inside my head to scrutinise my husband.

Like I said, Colin doesn't really get 'The Arts'. He thinks this job is all a bit of a laugh really. Nonsensical. A thing to keep me amused. He likes Owen but deep down thinks he's slightly odd. He said so himself.

'All those arty people are a bit odd, are they not?' Colin asked me the first time I took him to see an installation piece in the centre's gallery. You see, I changed and Colin didn't. I evolved a new interest, he didn't. No one's fault.

'I mean, I'd love to stand in a white room and splash blobs of paint on the walls all day and get paid for it, but I can't. I have to go out to work for a living,' Colin informed me on another occasion.

'That is work. That is the artist's work,' I told him.

'Well, I'm in the wrong business, so.' He'd more scoffed than laughed.

He just didn't get it. That's not me being a snob; I understand he doesn't get it.

I don't get lots of things too. I don't get his fascination with Manchester United now that he is a grown man. Or how he can spend hours watching football results pop up on *Sky Sports*. Transfixed by them. Nor do I get why the female presenters on *Sky Sports* are made to dress like they are going to a summer wedding not to work. Nor do I get how he can scream insults and threats at players that couldn't care less about him. I don't get that he can't see it's all a money-making racket, a multi-million-pound business and these supporters are the mugs paying those grotesque, excessive, vulgar wages. I don't get how he can waste so much of our money on it.

Just like he doesn't get blobs of paint on canvas are a work of art.

Just like he doesn't get how Lenny Abrahamson's film *Room* is a masterpiece. Owen and I have spent hours and hours going over every detail of that film. Talking over one another with excitement and admiration.

Colin thought it was shite.

Listen, I don't want to end my marriage over differences of sporting or creative opinions. I don't think I want to end my marriage full stop. I know I don't want to ruin my kids' lives. I realise it doesn't seem like that, but I can't help how I am feeling, can I? It's not a conscious thing. The chemistry is gone. It's dead in the water. How do I get it back? How do I get us back? My mind takes me back further as I await my artist to return.

Hand on heart, we really were love's young dream. After sixth year, we literally collapsed into one another like Noah and Allie in *The Notebook*. We were so instantly and intensely involved with each other and therefore neither of us got amazing results in our Leaving Cert exams. Not surprisingly, I could not get my head into studying when it was crammed full with this incredible new boyfriend. But we decided to go to a vocational college together and we both enrolled in a marketing diploma course in Rathmines Town Hall and we both got in. I never really knew what I wanted to do except marry Colin and have his babies. We were completely smitten with one another. After a year in college I dropped out when I got offered a job in *Buy For Less*, a free ads magazine, taking the calls from people and wording the ads for the items they wanted to sell; it was fine but it was just a job. Colin finished out the two-year diploma and went to work for Hallmark, the big greeting card company, out on the road.

Back then I didn't have work ambition. I just had no clue what really interested me apart from Colin Devlin. I knew I adored going to the movies, reading books and seeing plays whenever I could, but they were just my hobbies, right? They had nothing to do with any job I may ever get. No one paid you for that stuff. I had no head for figures, or anything scientific. To be honest my careers guidance teacher had no clue what area to point me in. On one occasion she basically told me to find myself a rich farmer!

When we got married and I fell pregnant with Jade on our wedding night, I was over the moon. Ecstatic. I had come off the pill a few weeks before and I had been taking folic acid. I was educated. I was prepared. I was ready to procreate. We had just moved into our new house in Ranelagh. I gave up my job in *Buy For Less* at seven months and concentrated on getting the nursery right. Being a wife and mummy-to-be was total contentment for me. I was perfectly serene playing house. Colin had made no apologies that he wanted me to be a stay-at-home mum and I had wholeheartedly agreed.

When Jade was born, the love I felt was so overwhelming it was magical.

Nothing I'd read or seen or done had prepared me for motherhood, I just found my own way with my perfect baby girl. Life ticked along just fine, just as it was supposed to, but it all happened in the blink of an eye. That moment, when I walked away, hysterically sobbing, from Jade's first day in St Theresa's junior school, but she never looked back – that's when I questioned my future life's fulfilment. Other mothers were waving, blowing kisses and rushing off to work.

Women in power suits. Women in gym gear. Women going off to have a full day ahead of them. Women who had other interests.

I didn't even have a hobby! I'd only had one focus after

Jade was born: having another one. We had been trying for another baby for years. Years. Tortuous months of unwelcomed stained pants, and unwanted cramping. I went for every test possible. Colin didn't go for one. He refused point-blank on the very good grounds that we had Jade so there was nothing wrong with his sperm. It was my fault. My body just wasn't doing what it had done so easily the first time round conceiving Jade. And he point-blank refused to talk about IVF. It wasn't that he didn't agree with it, he refused to even consider it.

'It either happens or it doesn't,' he would say.

Or: 'If it's meant to be it will be.'

'But it's not happening and why are we ignoring the fact when we have loads of options?' I'd try and explain them.

'Test-tube babies! No way!' He'd ignorantly argued against all my suggestions.

'Don't be ridiculous, it would still be our baby, just with medical assistance,' I'd pleaded. He wouldn't budge.

I did it all. Everything the fertility books had told me to do. I cut out alcohol, caffeine, sugar, dairy. I'd taken to meditation and visualisation and acupuncture. I was taking traditional Chinese medicine Every time we had sex I would lay, my legs in the air for up to an hour before clutching my knees to my chest still deteremind not to roll over should anything escape. My Google history was like a fertility encyclopaedia. I'd tried it all. Nothing worked. I was dumbstruck that we were having so much sex, at the right times, yet zero was happening. I was single-handedly keeping ovulation sticks in business. I could have built a raft out of all my used ones, and sailed out and collected

Tom Hanks and Wilson. How could it be that over three hundred million sperm were floating around inside me? Sure, less than one hundred thousand of Colin's soldiers were passing into my cervix every month – and, yes, only about two hundred of them would successfully reach my egg – but why wasn't I becoming pregnant?

Anyway, that September morning when Jade started school, I dabbed my sodden tissue at my wet eyes on the slow walk home to my then coral blue-painted empty nest. As I watched the world start its day I decided to look up courses for mature students. A eureka moment, if you will. I was lonely, I admitted to myself for the first time. Defiantly I lifted my chin up high and sniffed up my snot. I was on a mission. As soon as I shut the front door behind me I went straight to the family computer in the kitchen, I didn't even take my coat off or address the household mess. Searching, I came across a course in Griffith College that looked really interesting: Arts and Communications. On a whim I clicked the button and sent off for the application form. I can't quite explain the relief that flooded through me. Colin was supportive, once he understood it didn't interfere with Jade's school drop-off and pick-up or his job. It didn't; it was at night. The administrator called me for interview and a practical examination and when I got the letter to say I had secured a place I was thrilled. A new challenge.

Just before the first evening, as I was packing my college bag, I discovered I was pregnant. I'd had the Clearblue test hiding in the zipper part of my handbag for five days. You see, I wasn't sure I wanted a baby any more. I'd wanted another baby for far too long. It was more than

64

a want: it was a yearning. The yearning had exhausted me. The relentless yearning had become a scary thing. The relentless want and yearning and longing had left me feeling useless and empty. Now I was moving on.

But the test was positive.

The pregnancy meant much more to Colin in those early days and he suggested I defer the course until the baby was old enough; I'd have enough on my plate. Slowly I unpacked my college bag, dropped out of my place and got ready for our new baby. Once Mark was born I fell, instantly, head over heels in love and I completely forgot about any idea of an outside education and possible career.

Mark was an extremely difficult baby. He had colic, milk allergies; he bawled all day every day and all night every night, not a wink of sleep for the first six months. As Colin was up early and out on the road he needed his sleep so I was the one doing the night shifts and the day shifts. I was literally sick with exhaustion. A zombie. Just to see some different faces really, I joined a mother-and-babies Claphandies group once Mark had become a thriving one-year-old. It was there I saw the flyer for a part-time position at the City Arts Centre. The flyer was burnt orange and was sort of hiding behind another flyer for a breastfeeding club. I'd stood on my tippy-toes, prised the gold flat thumbtack out with my thumbnail and folded the flyer carefully into my bag.

Something about the words *Arts Centre* had given me a tingle of excitement.

So I told Colin about it, it was only part-time then, three mornings a week as part of a back-to-work scheme and he told me to go for it if that's what I wanted. I don't think he actually thought I was serious. So I went for it and the rest is history. Now, I eat, sleep and breathe my job. That doesn't mean I don't want to be a completely present mum. I do. I worship my children, they are the greatest gifts ever bestowed on me but after staying at home with Jade until she started school and after being at home with Mark for a year I knew I wanted to work outside the home. I knew I didn't want to walk home to an empty nest the day Mark started school the way I had done after Jade's first day. Seeing that flyer was meant to be. Colin's business was growing every day, he was busier than he had ever been and I wanted some of that working life satisfaction for myself.

Anyhow, that was four years ago. When Colette offered me the job, I found a wonderful, retired woman on our road, Laura Delaney, who was a terrific child minder. I moved quickly from scheme trainee to the full-time paid coordinator all in one year. I adored the place. I adored the people, all the actors, musicians and artists, the creatives. Oh, how I adored the artist who had just returned to my office.

'There are too many steps in this world.' He flops in front of me again and picks up his coffee. 'Just an observation I have wanted to share with you for some time, Alison dearest. Discuss?'

He crosses his legs and stretches them out.

'Well, I dunno, I mean … they all lead somewhere right?' I cross my skinny-jeaned legs and swirl my paper cup anticlockwise to gather the foam.

'Do they, though? When we can see where they lead, are they really going anywhere at all?' He laughs.

I laugh.

We both laugh.

I love how abstract conversations with him are. We always have the 'Is drinking coffee really as arbitrary as eating caramels?' conversations. I love them. If I started a conversation with Colin about where steps lead to, he wouldn't know where to start.

'Good morning, you two.' Colette enters my office, a huge black ring binder tucked under her arm.

'Michael is still in Merrion Square at the Arts Council meeting, so we will just get started. Ali, can you come on this trip or not?' Colette, my boss, is gay; she is smart, kind, tough, an incredible mother to her two adopted sons from Cambodia and dedicated to helping children from the inner city become educated in the arts. Also a qualified social worker, she turned her hand to this job five years ago.

'I'm on board, captain.' I make the sign of a sailor and Owen laughs. He uncrosses his legs now and sits up straight.

'Super, that's great, I really want your opinions on various shows, so I'm booking the flights now. I have a printout of times here. Owen, I need to talk to you before we book your flight about something I'm looking into, can you pop up to me this afternoon?'

'Sure, no probs,' he says.

Colette opens her black ring binder with a click and removes a couple of stapled pages from a clear plastic pocket. She moves her clear-polished nail and dances it down the page.

'A-ha, OK, so, Ali, you will leave Friday morning on

the Aer Lingus to Amsterdam at six thirty; Michael and I will follow on the two o'clock after the opening of the new gallery exhibition. Owen, like I said, I need to see about your flight out, but we will all return Sunday night together on the eight thirty into Dublin.' She licks her thumb as she flicks forward a few pages.

Immediately my stomach tightens. I thought we would be back by early Sunday afternoon. That's a whole other day. Now I have to tell Colin it's three days and two nights. *Please don't let there be a Manchester United game on this Sunday.*

'That all right with you? Jade and Mark sorted and all that?' Colette looks up and studies me closely now.

'Yeah, they are, that's fine with me, Colette.' I dip my finger into the creamy froth and lick it. It's tepid now.

Colette continues, sliding the pages back into the clear plastic pocket.

'We each have our own rooms. The Danker have been really generous with their funding for this trip, they are very well supported. They've got us a nice hotel, central location. Programming-wise we all need to split up Friday night and go see separate shows that we can possibly bring over here next spring. I have a list of what could travel cheaply and are suitable for our stage dimensions. Expect an email before the end of the day – choose your shows when you get a second and let me know. Saturday night we all watch the Very Messy Theatre Company's work and we are invited to dinner with the company after. They are taking us to Ciel Blue, the only two-starred Michelin restaurant in Amsterdam; their beneficiary and board are joining us. I just had a look at it, here.' She pulls her phone out of her shirt pocket, taps something in and hands it to me.

It looks stunning.

'I am super excited to eat here! You know what a foodie I am. Read it out for Owen there,' Colette says, her eyes dancing with the culinary excitement to come.

I adjust my eyes to the small text on Colette's phone. Holding it at arm's length to read.

'Right, OK, the restaurant is located on the twenty-third floor of the delightful Hotel Okura with Chefs Onno Kok … Kok … Kok … KOKmeijer.' I get the pronunciation after three attempts and go on reading. 'And Arjan Speelman. They use fresh, locally produced ingredients to create gastronomic masterpieces.'

Owen makes a guttural sound and then he erupts with laughter.

'What?' I say but the sound of my voice saying the word *cock* over and over is spinning around my brain too. *Keep it together.* I glare at him and bite my lip. I can feel the laughter rolling from my stomach and gathering momentum. I can't speak. My eyes are running.

'What is going on with you two?' Colette is genuinely puzzled as she leans in and takes her phone from me.

'Are you all right, Owen?' She doesn't wait for his answer as he pinches his cheeks and she goes on.

'Too much caffeine, I'm assuming. The days, as far as I'm concerned, are all yours team, just stay away from the hashish, you pair!' Colette raises her eyebrows at Owen as she pushes her pencil into her ponytail. He raises his hand by way of apology.

'What time are the Steffi Street gang arriving?' she asks

him as she gets up with her black folder. Her high street black suit and open-necked pink shirt are professional yet casual.

He's composed now, thank God.

'Ten thirty, I'm making sure their paintings are dry enough to take home today – just popped the windows open.'

'Right, don't give James Rafter his painting to take home; it's the one of the crying ballerina, it's so beautiful and as you know he told me his da' will rip that faggoty shit up – so I'd like to frame it here and put it on Corridor One upstairs.'

'Great, I'll do that this afternoon.' Owen nods his approval at Colette.

When Colette leaves, Owen closes the glass door. He sits on my desk now.

'Sorry, I couldn't cope.'

We both fall around laughing.

'What are we like? A pair of kids!' he gasps.

'Absolute idiots! Morons … I'm mortified by us!' I clutch my stomach tightly. 'Colette must think we are mad.' I let out a slow breath and sit back at my desk. I hit the return button on my laptop and the screen jumps back to life.

'I'm really looking forward to this weekend away though … I do honestly wonder, will we have adjoining rooms? I could nip in and out when I wanted …'

'Stop …' Suddenly I'm not laughing.

'Hey, what's wrong?' He stares into my eyes. 'I'm messing with ya!' He moves over and pokes me gently in the ribs.

'I know you are, but … It's Colin … We are … we're really going through a bad patch. We're killing each other all the time … I think it's run its course.' I can't believe those words have come out of my mouth. Deadly thing to say! Alarm bells ring inside my head.

Bong!

Bong!

Bong!

They echo. I know exactly what I'm doing and I am a witch! I have planted that seed in Owen's head now. I instantly try to take it back.

'Sorry, this isn't anything for you to worry about. I'm sure we can work it out, maybe I just need a break! He is a great dad …' I hate myself.

'It's genuinely not any of my business, your marriage. However, we are friends … but I'm not going to say anything, Ali … well, because …' He looks down at the floor and then raises his eyes and looks up at me coyly with those deep brown eyes. I am floating in them.

'Well, you know why, I guess, by now. And it wouldn't be fair on you or on Colin for me to add to the issues that you are already having. I'll see you in the Beans at lunch, yeah?'

He runs his hands over his shaven head speedily. Then he drains his coffee, takes his paper cup, stands on the bin pedal and drops it in. The bin lid clatters. Just like my bin lid at home. I don't jump from the noise but my heart is pumping. He fancies me too. He basically just said it there. I am euphoric. I am horrified.

My desk phone rings and its Colin's mobile on the caller ID.

'I better get this,' I say.

'I'm gone, girl, gone,' he says and takes his leave.

'Hi.' I hold the receiver tight to my right ear.

'We need to talk. I can't concentrate on anything today … and I have a big day ahead.' He pauses.

'I know.' I lean forward and roll some soft Blu-Tack between my fingers, making a small round ball.

'Is there anything you need to tell me? Is there something going on with you and that artist bloke?' he huffs.

Thank God in heaven he didn't ask me this face to face because I would have gone beetroot red from head to toe. I'm on fire. I don't answer quickly enough. I squeeze the Blu-Tackball out flat between my index finger and thumb. Splat.

'Ali?' he has to prod.

'No … no, Colin, no … don't be ridiculous,' I reaffirm with three no's.

'Because he's a total knob and he wants to ride you.' I can hear an indicator ticking away. It's in time to my heartbeat.

'Is Maia in the car with you there?' I ask horrified.

'No, she's gone into the meeting. I'm parking the car.' There is silence.

'I'm telling you he wants to ride you,' he repeats.

'That's not true …' I swallow hard.

'It is.'

'It is not …'

'I tell you one thing, Ali, if I ever get wind of anything between you two, he's dead and so are you.'

My heart starts to beat heavy in my chest.

'Charming,' is all I can manage.

We both remain silent, only our breaths meeting.

'Look, I didn't ring for another fight,' he says.

'You could have fooled me,' I say.

'I just can't seem to find the girl I married any more, Ali. Where is she?'

'Well, I'm still here, Colin. I'm just not a girl any more.' I twist the cord around my fingers.

A pause.

'You'll always be my girl.' His voice is sad.

A pause.

'We'll try and talk later, yeah?' I say.

'Yeah. I miss you, Ali.'

He hangs up before I have to answer and I'm glad.

My phone rings immediately and I leap on it. It's not him ringing back, it's a call in relation to the exchange programme, so I take a deep breath and I try to busy myself in my work. When I get off the call I have lots to do with my elders in the St Andrew's Resource Centre and that takes my mind off everything for the rest of the morning.

At lunchtime I'm starving. I didn't bother with the rashers on toast this morning; I just drowned myself in strong tea. I make my way down to the ground floor, to the Beans slightly before one o'clock. I say hi to Patricia, the lease owner and head chef. Patricia does great food: wholesome soups and salads, yes, but also egg and chips, home-made shepherd's pie and fried chicken rolls. Comfort food. She has an allotment near the Four Courts. Today her specials are lentil bean soup, tomato soup, tuna burgers with sweet potato chips, and a mixed grill with freshly baked warm white crusty rolls. I get a ten per cent discount. Office workers from all over Dublin 1 will arrive any second now. Sliding my brown tray along the metallic line I order the lentil soup with two small crusty white bread rolls, pour myself a pint of tap water and take my tray to the far end of the cafe. We can use the little kitchen for staff behind the cafe to make lunch but I rarely bother. I have to cook enough when I get home. Owen is outside the Inners, its box office opposite the Beans entrance. He waves. He's on his phone. Pacing up and down. I sit and immediately add salt and grind plenty of black pepper into my soup and I text Corina.

Want to come over later for a glass of vino, Colin's on an overnighter? Xx

'What's the soup?' Owen is standing over me now, picking green paint from his long, lean fingers.

'Lentil,' I tell him, stuffing my phone back in my bag.

He pulls out a chair opposite me and scrapes it noisily off the ceramic tiles. Sitting opposite me, he makes two fists with his hands, brings them up under his chin and bursts into song, 'Papa, can you hear me? Papa, can you see me? Papa, can you find me in the niiigghhtttttt?' He is all closed eyes and deep, intense, booming voice.

'That's *Yentl*, ya loon!' I roar, laughing at him. As we found out early on in our friendship, we are both huge Barbra Streisand fans. We are always looking for a reason to break into a Barbra tune. When I stop, he is staring into my eyes. We stare at each other. Suddenly my mouth is dry. I lick my lips before reaching in my pocket for my rosy Vaseline and slather it all over my lips. Owen watches me intently.

'I'm still laughing at your triple cock outburst. I've

74

just been busting my ass laughing at various moments throughout the morning.' He shakes his head. 'You're mad.'

'I'm gonna get you back for that … I'm gonna ask Chef Kok'whatever to come out and meet us after the meal and I'm going to tell him you can do the Riverdance backwards and—'

'You deserve to be happy, Ali,' he interrupts me, deadly serious face, 'that's all I'm going to say.'

His hands come to rest on top of his head and he leaves them there, linked together.

We continue to look at each other. Really look at each other. I can look into his eyes so easily. We can maintain eye contact for hours. It's so comfortable.

'I know I do …' I can't find any other words. I don't know what to say. I know what I should say: 'I am happy, Owen. It's a blip … a rough patch. All marriages go through one and we will get through this.'

But I don't.

He drops his hands now and picks up one of my bread rolls, tears it in half, leans across and dips it into my soup.

'Mmmm, excellent soup, Patricia.' He chews quietly. 'If I ever get my act together and have an exhibition, Patricia is doing the nibbly bits.'

'Work away, I'm happy to share, I'm not really that hungry.' I push the bowl into the middle of the table. It's true: my appetite has dissipated.

'I can't see how anyone, any person, can tell another person what's worthy to them isn't worthy. I hate that shit … That's what I wanted to say.'

He picks up my spoon and helps himself to soup. When

he replaces the spoon by me, we stare at one another again and already it's a different staring. It's a want.

'I simply can't comprehend that, Ali.'

My phone beep beeps in my bag and I'm glad of the excuse.

It's Corina.

Sounds great – 8.30pm and I'll bring the pulled pork.

I laugh. She means the family-size bags of Walkers Pulled Pork and Ranchero crisps.

'Here's the Steffi Street bus, I better get the kids into the drawing room …' He is looking out the long high widows of the Beans as he scrapes the floor again, pushing back his chair.

'Yeah, OK …'

'See ya later.' He puts his hand across mine. 'I'm always here if you need an ear, ya know that, without wanting to sound cheesy – and I just heard myself and that really does sound cheesy – but I'm just not sure what to say about Colin, Ali, and I don't want to say anything I shouldn't.'

I've put him in a terrible position.

'It's fine, Owen, it's going to sort itself – maybe the break away will do me, *us*, good.' I laugh, slightly too high-pitched and pick up my soup spoon. He moves away. Suddenly I feel ashamed. I think of my two incredible children and how with one selfish act I can ruin their lives. This isn't me. I'm not that type of person. I'm a good mother. I'm not a cheater. *Definitely*, I think, *I need some type of counselling*. I stare out the long glass window at the roughness of the River Liffey and eat the rest of my well-seasoned lukewarm soup. Dublin is deep into winter as December drops heavier upon us. People hurry past, cupped hands with coat collars pulled up. Flushed faces. Rushing to get indoors quicker. Jade has gymnastics at seven tonight and she needs a new leotard for Friday afternoon's competition. *She is starting to develop*, I think as I add even more salt to the remains. Little buds of breasts. I'm not sure how to approach her about this yet; and I know she is aware of it. I think I'll let it go a while. I can't push her away any further. The more I try to hold her the more she wrestles away and I don't know why.

There is a lot to do if I am to get to Dance World this afternoon so I finish my lunch, rummage in my bag for my vitamin C and zinc tablet, knock it back with the end of my tap water and head back upstairs to my office.

Flopping onto my swivel chair, I awake my sleeping laptop. No word from Colin. Flicking through my emails I spot the mail from Colette and the list of what shows she needs us to attend on Friday night. That means during the day I will be in Amsterdam, on my own. Owen, too.

Butterflies escape in my stomach and hit against the sides like a fly in a glass house. This thing I feel for Owen is actually so physical I can't stop it. It's making me nervous and therefore nauseous.

I open the attachment and scroll down the list – quite a few smaller shows to choose from – I'm mainly looking for smaller production companies whose values and ethos will be the right fit for the City Arts Centre audience. I'm also consciously looking for anything that Owen will avoid. The thoughts of him sitting close to me in a darkened box in Amsterdam are too much for me to take. Scrolling down, I see one. A small theatre company from Haarlem have a one woman show called *Heat* – performed in English. It seems unlikely that Owen will choose this one and it's also a half hour away from where we are staying so I open a separate email and I mail Colette that I'll scout this show. There is no set, it's easy to travel – just one cast member, the lighting designer and the stage manager.

I google more about Amsterdam, it tells me it's often taken over by tourists, there is just so much to do and see and most people tend to take it in as a weekend break. It's also home to the Teylers Museum, the oldest museum in the Netherlands. Colin hates museums, I adore them. I love their smell. I could spend hours and hours strolling around just staring at the history and lives and experiences hanging on a wall or in a glass box. The last time I asked Colin to come we took the kids to the National History Museum. There just happened to be a glass case that was empty and he went on and on and oohed and ahhed at the brilliance of the non-existent piece. He made it all into one big joke and had them in absolute stitches.

Now, while I'm always on for a good laugh, it was slightly inappropriate. He should be encouraging culture, especially home-grown. Not making a mockery of it. Corina again said I was overreacting.

'Ah, come on, Ali, some of it is a bit pretentious, you have to agree?' She had been eating a 99 ice cream with raspberry ripple at the time and I remember watching in awe as she cleverly calculated the ratio of chocolate flake to ice cream and nibbled and licked her way to the end.

I didn't agree.

I hear a commotion outside and stand up to look out my window. Down below I see Owen with his Steffi Street class. He is marching and they are marching behind him. I stand on my tippy-toes and open my window slowly. This is all a part of 'Arts in the Community' that the school and Colette have programmed as part of their fourth-class curriculum.

'Left right, left right, left right – get in step, James Rafter, that's it, we are an art army, we are art soldiers!' He lifts his left hand to his head and flicks out a salute. I grin widely.

'Canna woman bea soldier, sir?' asks a little girl in navy jeggings and a navy hoody, tugging Owen's shirt.

'A woman can be anything she wants to be, Zoe. Anything.' He places his hands on her tiny shoulders and squeezes them

'Now what do we see?' He extends his hands to their urban surroundings.

'Nuttin',' comes a voice from the back of the line.

'Nothing, James Rafter? And why have you come out again today with no coat? Are we still this blind to the nature around us? Please ...' He runs his hands over his shaven head. 'Look harder.' He leans back against the grey-graffitied lamp post.

They all look around, giggling, messing.

'I see a bird, sir,' James Rafter offers now.

'Exactly!' Owen bends at the knees and snaps his fingers on both hands. 'Now what is it doing, James?'

'Flyin', sir.'

He joins James and they both look up into the sky.

'That bird, James, is just like us on this journey through life. We fly together in groups, in gangs, if you want: sometimes one of us is in the front, the leader, but when one tires and falls back, if one is having problems, a new bird takes the lead – they all stick together; they have one another's backs. Just like you guys.'

The Steffi Street gang all nod in unison, in understanding.

I shut the window gently. I return to my seat and I pinch the bridge of my nose so tightly it hurts.

5

Monday night. My kitchen.
After the nine o'clock news.

The country is no longer depressed. The Republic of Ireland football team have qualified for the European Championships in France. My stomach flips a little. This will be the end of Colin around the house all summer. He will be at every game for as long as we carry on through the tournament. This makes me happy and I see long bright nights out on the road with the kids, takeaway chippie chips drenched in salt and vinegar and me stretched out across my big double bed. Peace and harmony. No one to tell me what to do or point out all the things I am doing wrong. Come on, Keano and Martin O'Neill; keep our menfolk away all summer.

Corina is muttering out loud to Facebook, seated in front of our family computer in the kitchen as I take Jade's new purple-and-black long-sleeved leotard out of the plastic and fold it into her gym bag with a face towel. Possibly I should be washing it first, but I'm the type of person who buys new bed linen or towels and uses them immediately. Clean enough for me. We had spent an hour and a half choosing this in Dance World after I collected them from Laura's. The assistant had actually closed the shop and we were still there.

'That's really pretty,' I had said four hundred times as Jade posed in front of the mirror jumping and twirling and testing them all out.

'I'm so bored, Mummy,' Mark had moaned, sprawled out face down on the hard ground.

'I know, sweetie, we are going now.' I pulled him up onto my knee.

'Are you really going away for two nights, Mummy? Jade said you are.' His little lip curls downwards.

I wasn't going to tell him until the last minute as I knew he'd fret.

'We'll see,' I said.

'You are, Mom. Dad says you're going on a trip to Oompa Loompa Land this weekend to visit your Oompa Loompa friends.' Jade falls into the splits, kind of, and it looks sore.

'I want to come to Oompa Loompa Land, Mummmmyyyyyy!' Mark roars and pulls at my jacket.

'Come on, Jade, just get that one, otherwise you are going to be late for gymnastics. Take it off now and, Mark, Daddy's just *trying* to be funny. He's just joking, there is no such place as Oompa Loompa Land.'

'Daddy is the greatest daddy in the entire world!' Jade's bright blue eyes challenge me.

'He absolutely is and you are very lucky children to have such a terrific daddy! Now let's go!' I plaster a wide smile on my face.

As I stuff Mark's football gear into his bag now, I wonder why Jade said that about her dad? I know she adores him, but it seemed a bit out of context. Corina still sits at the family computer, her legs stretched out, barefoot and noisily dips her hand in and out of the family size bag of Rancheros on the desk.

'Gotta love pulled pork … eh, yeah, as *if* that's a no make-up selfie, love!' she snorts. 'Come on, if you are going to do it, do it! Those are double-layered false eyelashes, for crying out loud!' She munches away to her heart's content.

'Who is it?' I approach her and lean over her shoulder rolling Mark's blue and white football socks into a ball.

'Ahh just some girl I know … well, actually, I don't know her at all – we're Facebook friends. In fact, I have never actually met her. Just going through her photos. For some strange reason, I think I saw she liked some post of mine there from months ago and I went to investigate. I always find it a bit unsettling when someone likes a picture you posted years ago, don't you? Are you nearly ready to sit down? I want to see *Gogglebox*.' She licks each bacon-flavoured finger carefully, twisting and turning them to be doubly sure. Tonight Corina is in her comfy velour tracksuit and her Uggs sit at the front door. Her wild red curly hair is all scraped back into a high bun, no bits tumbling around her face. Her eyes free from mascara. She is in fact ready for bed and she looks so young. Her face is line free. Sleep. I put her good, wrinkle-free skin all down to sleep! Corina gets bucket loads of sleep.

'Yeah, sorry, I was so focused on not forgetting gymnastics stuff for Friday afternoon's competition, I forgot about football tomorrow and I'd nothing washed from last week – just ready. I quickly need to pop up to Jade and take the iPad off her.'

'In my day I had a cuppa cocoa made on water with

my Enid Blyton books by my bedside table,' sighs Corina nostalgically. 'Not for the world and Tom Hardy naked sprawled across it would I change that for any iPad. God, the adventures that woman took me on with her Famous Five and her Secret Seven, not to mention Malory Towers and my absolute obsession with Darrell Rivers, and then I moved to St Clare's where I swapped my obsession onto Pat and Isobel O' Sullivan. I devoured them all. I used to pretend I was George from the Famous Five – I'd wrap a black towel around my head, turban style, one of Dad's ties around my fluffy toy dog Max and drag him around behind me as Timmy the dog while I sneaked downstairs for a midnight feast. Which mainly involved me opening a six-pack of Monster Munch and finishing them all, then with my trusty dog I'd hide the empty packets all over the house. Behind the couch, in the overcrowded kitchen drawers. I remember my mother thinking she was getting an early onset of Alzheimer's every time she went to get the crisps for the lunch boxes … Ahh, those were also the days, crisp sambos for lunch in school. Believe it or not I only told her that a few years ago. Actually, come to think of it Enid Blyton and her wondrous midnight feasts are to blame for the start of my overeating! I've just saved myself a small fortune in therapy!'

'Different world, Corina.' I sigh as I leave her and make my way up the carpeted stairs and peek into Mark's room. He is fast asleep. His tiny body curled up in the foetal position with GoGo, his scruffy off-white teddy, under his arm. I love him so much. I feel a huge pang of guilt that I didn't read another story. He'd begged. I had read four. I was tired. Drained. I still had loads to do. But was

I mainly rushing my son to sleep so I could go down and drink wine with Corina? Maybe I was. Turning out his *Cars* lamp, I kiss him gently on his forehead and then pass across the hall into Jade's room. American accents hit my ears through her massive soft pink headphones.

'Time to go to bed, lovey,' I whisper as I lift the left earphone out from her ear.

She nods and yawns and removes the headphones. She's tired. The gymnastics always tires her of a Monday, and the late-night on Friday and Saturday. She hands me the iPad and I click it off. *And you forgot about her and left her up late last night because you were drinking wine.* My guilt, my Red Devil, on my shoulder pokes the black pitchfork into my brain.

Prod.

Prod.

Prod.

'I love you, boo boo, sleep tight.' I kiss her forehead.

'Mom, please ... don't call me boo boo, I really hate it! Even Dad agrees it's too babyish!' She grinds her teeth at me as she says this.

'Sorry, love, I ... I forgot. I won't say it ever again.' I rub her back.

She's just over-tired, exhausted. I leave the room.

★ ★ ★

'Make mine a large one.' I flop on the couch beside Corina, who has now moved into the sitting room in front of my fake, plug-in artificial fire and is watching *Gogglebox*.

She hands me a glass of red from the table.

'That Scarlett girl is absolutely hilarious,' I say as I nod to the TV and raise my glass to my mouth.

'She should have her own show!' I add and take a drink. A welcome bitter bite off the wine.

'So ... I think I may have met myself a keeper of a fella.' Corina makes a wide grinning Cheshire cat face and her tongue does a wild jig outside her mouth.

'What? Go on!' I hit mute, slip off my flats and curl my feet under me and put a cushion over my knees. *Gogglebox* goes on without us in the background. Us watching them watching us.

'Ah well ... I dunno ... I met him in Whelan's last week and we just had a brilliant chat over wet elbows at the bar. He's from Manchester—'

'But we had lunch on Sunday,' I interrupt. 'And you never mentioned him!' I bang the pillow with my free hand.

She tilts her head at me and lowers her voice.

'Now what kinda best mate would I be if I started ranting and raving about a keeper of a fella I'd met and you going through such a bad patch with Colin?' She raises that perfectly arched eyebrow again.

'Are they HD brows, Corina?' I simply have to ask at this inappropriate moment.

'They are. Vanity Rooms in Stepaside, amazing beauty salon, and I can get yours done for free if you want them: I organised the opening for the two Jennifers, Butler and Swaine, the owners, of their newly revamped rooms the weekend before last. It was so much fun, one girl had been growing her leg hair for two years for charity and got waxed ... it was like Toni & Guy at the end of a busy Saturday. Hairtastic.'

'This guy from Manchester ... he lives here, right?' It hits me.

'No ... just over on his brother's stag, the Pimple they call him, he bought me a shot ... Trevor, that's his name, not the Pimple ... I was about to ask him back to mine and then something happened.' She leans forward and takes a long, slow sip of her wine.

'Hang on, I'm confused: is Trevor your guy?'

'Yes! Keep up! Or as my old auntie Betty used to say: shape up or ship out.' She rolls her eyes at me, then she reaches up to her bun, pulls her hair free, throws her head over between her legs and scoops her red locks and redoes her bun.

'Well? What happened!' I throw my hands up at her.

'Well, Ali, I decided to make him wait. Fo' dis.' Corina stands up and starts to do what I think they call twerking. Her bottom is extended and she is shaking it around. It's a cross between looking like she really, really needs the loo or she's just spilled boiling hot coffee all over her lap.

'"Dis" is worth waiting for, no?' Her two index fingers point at me as she is half on the ground now.

'Er ... yes ... it is?' I am starting to shake with the laughter as she is now actually on the ground.

'Giv'us a hand up, will ya?' She winks at me and I pull her up.

We are in stitches as she sits and goes on.

'Think I pulled a muscle in my lower back there. So anyway, I didn't sleep with him on the first date, or on the second or on the third, and I tell you one thing, Ali, this man is falling for me big time! He's like a little puppy who knows there are cooked sausages in my pocket but he has to be patient and keep sniffing around until I pull them out.'

'You have had three dates with him and never told me?' I'm shocked.

'I didn't want to jinx it … that sounds so pathetic, I was all geared up to tell you about our fourth date on Saturday night but then you were in such a bad place I thought it wasn't appropriate.'

'You saw him four times in one week?'

'True dat.' She rolls her shoulders.

'Why are you talking like that?' I ask her.

'Isn't it hip?'

'Not really, just confusing. Now go on … Saturday night, what happened?' I drink a sip.

'Oh, OK, sooooo …' She picks up her glass.

There is a knock at the window and we both jump out of our skins.

'Ffffuuucckkkiinnnggnnnoorraaabatttyyyyy!' Corina spills red wine all down the front of her cream velour tracksuit.

'Who the hell is that?' I turn to the window.

'Are you expecting someone?' She grabs the kitchen roll from the glass table and wipes herself down.

'No!' I stare at my watch. 'It's half nine at night!' I tiptoe to the window and pull back a tiny inch of fabric from the heavy curtains and there, his perfect nose pressed up against the glass, is Owen O'Neill.

I snap the material back. It waves and ripples before falling still.

'Well?' Corina is heavily breathing down my neck. 'Will I ring the guards? I know a detective in Store Street very well … very, very well – too well, the naughty boy.'

I go red from the tip of my toes to the top of my messy bun.

'No … It's … it's a … well … a work colleague of mine.' I open the sitting room door and then stand at the front door. Corina is on my shoulder again.

'You can stay inside.' I urge her, holding out my hand to touch her elbow.

She eyes me up.

'No … no, you know, I think I'll stay with you, just to be on the safe side. You never really know that your work colleagues aren't serial killers for sure, do you? I mean, look at Jeffrey Dahmer. Who'd have guessed looking at him across the office that that sandy-haired boy could—'

'Shuuuush!' I silence her with a long hiss as I slowly open the door.

'Hey there.' I release the word on my breath.

'Hey, sorry, I was just …' He stands directly under the porch light.

'Well, hello there!' Corina pops her head out from behind my body.

He jumps.

'Oh, shit … Sorry, I didn't know you had company. Hey … hello there to you too.' He has moved from under the light now, three paces back into the front garden.

'Come back! Sorry, I'd frighten a blind postman looking like this.'

He moves towards us and then I smell it. Whiskey. Now I know a lot about Owen and I know that he only drinks whiskey when he's tortured. Either finishing a painting or desperately hung-over and looking for the cure. Neither of which I feel are the causes this evening.

'Aren't you coming in?' Corina literally hits me with her hip bone out of the way and pulls Owen inside.

'It's brass monkeys out there.' She winks at him and it's then he knows who she is.

'A-ha, Corina Martin, I presume.' He's chemically relaxed as she nods at me to close the front door and shows him into the front room. I can see Corina can't take her eyes off him either. He's incredibly sexy. Too sexy to be calling to my door at *Gogglebox* Hour with my husband on an overnighter. He's like the Milk Tray man, all dressed in black, black jeans, his black biker jacket and black beanie hat. And apparently dangerous.

'Yes, it is! I'm in your life drawing art class actually. I painted the basketball hoop lady? You said it was wonderfully abstract. I was legitimately trying to draw what I saw, but whatever ...' She raises her perfectly plucked, high-definition eyebrows at me in a way that tells me I need to cop myself on. A what-the-fuck look.

'Huh? Oh, of course, you have met Owen at the City Arts Centre ... in the drawing class ...' I say as I spot an imaginary fly and swipe it away.

She knows me well enough. She mutters under her breath. 'Idontbelievethis.' He won't be able to decipher the mumbled words but I do.

Her words waltz around my mind.

We both stare at him as he removes his beanie hat and runs his hands over his head.

Corina makes a small noise like a mouse is caught at the back of her throat.

'I wasn't aware you guys were so pally-wally,' she winks at me.

Cow.

'Stop, Corina … Eh, can I get you a drink, Owen?' My palms are sweaty.

Corina moves to the couch and is patting the place beside her for him to join her.

'I don't want to intrude …' He is reluctant to sit until Corina pulls him down.

'Have a glass of wine with us, sure the bottle's open.' She leans forward and grabs the bottle.

'Another glass, Ali, if you will? And a damp cloth for my wine-stained tracksuit.' Corina wants the goss.

I make my way into the kitchen and get another glass from the shelf. I cannot believe he's sitting on my couch. He looks taller, bigger, more real. Big presence. I look at my distorted reflection in the silver oven hood. I lick my index finger and run it under both my eyes. I smooth my hair down, grab a wet cloth and I return like this is a perfectly normal situation and hand Corina the cloth and the glass. It's Colin's wine glass, a Waterford crystal one with big bubbles in the glass.

Suddenly the front room door opens quickly and Jade arches her head in.

'What's going on?' she rubs her sleepy eyes and then she focuses on Owen and backs out of the room.

'Sorry, boo— sorry, Jade, did we wake you?' I follow her out quickly and shut the door behind me, leaning my back against it now. My breathing heavy and fast.

'Who is he?' she asks. 'And why is yer woman Corina drinking from Dad's special wine glass? Dad hates her.' Jade purses her perfect rosebud lips together.

'Shush! Thank you, Jade, that is enough! Owen is a work colleague dropping over the itinerary for Amsterdam this week … and Corina is my best friend, and she happens to be very good to you. Please have some respect. Didn't she take you to Miley Cyrus last year?'

I move away from the door and put my hand on the small of her back. It's a few hours' bed-warm so I quickly remove my cold hand. We walk back up the stairs.

'She, like, spent the entire gig on her cell phone, Mom!' She heaves her chest out.

We walk into her room and I turn her pillow over and hold back the duvet. She slides in. I gently cover her up.

I whisper now.

'That's because she can't stand Miley … but she went just to bring you.'

I can't stand what Miley preaches myself, or that tongue!

'She's so fake.' She curls up.

I exhale a slow, long, in-labour-type breath.

'She isn't … just because Daddy says that about her—'

She interrupts me.

'Like, she's so old and isn't even married – that's just weird.'

'You should always take people as you find them, Jade,' I whisper and I kiss her head. 'I love you. They're both leaving soon, so I won't be long.'

She closes her eyes and wraps her left elbow over her face and I leave the room.

Owen and Corina are in full flow as I re-enter the room. They both give me a secretive look as Corina hands me my glass. I sit on the black leather armchair opposite them.

'Just telling him about Jade on the bloody iPad … I'm

so glad I grew up in the eighties: I did so much stupid shit and there is no record of it anywhere! Here … he's never had an exhibition! Like, come on. I am the event exhibition queen – I know all the coolest spaces … Tell him, Ali, tell him he should exhibit!' Her words all blurt out and I can tell she's not so much flirting but giddy in his presence. Can't blame her for that.

'You really should, your work is brilliant.' I take a long gulp of red wine and it's oh so welcome.

'Ah, sure, we'll see … listen, I only popped in as I was passing … to say, er, I won't be back in work this week. Colette's sending me to Belfast tomorrow to an auction of the concept art room at the Belfry Centre. They are closing down, so I'm gonna fly from Belfast on Thursday evening … I'll just see you in Amsterdam.' He sits forward, wine glass cupped, resting on his two knees.

Corina is like a spectator at a McEnroe vs. Connors tennis final; her head is sweeping from side to side, studying our faces. Back and forth. She is onto me.

'Oh, right, that's good, is it?' I hold the wine glass over my face.

'Uh-huh, should be. Should be able to buy some good supplies.' He is starting to look less merry, more twitchy.

Corina now has her nails in her mouth nibbling. Nibbling and staring.

'So have you ever been to Amsterdam before, Owen?' she asks, leaning in to him. I can tell he wants to leave now but she is like a dog with a bone.

'I was there once actually, about five years ago now, a stag, I don't remember that much to be honest.' He laughs, wiping his knuckles slowly across his brow.

'Classic!' she says. 'I've never been, I'd love to go, some amazing things to see I hear.'

'Oh, there are … I was gutted I never went to see Anne Frank's house!' He hits his head with the palm of his hand. 'Idiot!'

'Oh, I'd absolutely love to see that!' I butt in. 'It's somewhere I have always wanted to see ever since I was in school.'

'We'll go Friday—' he answers me immediately, enthusiastic, and then stops himself. The word *we* hangs heavy in the air and as I look to Corina her mouth is hanging open, hand about to go in to nibble on a nail, all her actions seem frozen in time. Frozen in our moment. Her expression is one of absolute puzzlement. Like one trying to work out the word conundrum on *Countdown* with that annoying music in the background.

Owen stands now and says, 'Thanks for the wine but I better be going – early train.' He drags his beanie hat over his shaven head.

'Really great to finally meet you, Corina, properly, I mean. Takes me a while in new classes to get to know students – so many of you, so few of me, you know – but Ali never stops talking about you.' He puts out his hand and she rises slowly and takes it.

'My pleasure, Owen, let me know about finding an exhibition space. Honestly I'd love to help … and listen … enjoy Amsterdam, don't do anything that isn't illegal.' She winks at him.

I will kill her.

He turns to me. 'Thanks again, for the wine, Ali.'

'Fine … anytime.'

'You just made a rhyme.' He laughs.

'And now I'll do a mime.'

Ridiculously I start to do my Marcel Marceau window piece across the room and now Corina is literally paling. Horrified expression.

I stop.

He's laughing. Hard.

'Most excellent!' he says and claps lightly, four fingers to bottom of palm.

'OK, then … see you in Amsterdam, so.' I am having an out-of-body experience and now I am feeling faint.

'Lovely.' He imitates my last move, still laughing at my mime.

Corina slowly zips up her wine-stained tracksuit to the very top. Tight to her neck.

'Oookkaayyyy … Thank you for that, um, fine performance, Ali, and goodbye then, Owen, again. Till our next class.' She offers her hand, again.

'Cool, yeah OK, good luck.' He shakes it briefly and turns and opens the sitting room door.

Should I walk him out or stay here?

An awkward pause ensues.

'I'll show you out, Owen, shall I? I better be heading myself soon too, it is a school night after all.' Corina steps in.

They leave the room and I drop like the scarecrow from *The Wizard of Oz* onto the couch and my hands rise to support my face.

'Arrghhhhhh!' I moan into my hands.

I hear the Chubb lock close with a sharp click and she returns. I stay the way I am. I hear her knees crack as she sits on the leather chair opposite me and I hear her take her glass from the table. The liquid slides down her throat. Still she waits. Still I wait. She sips again and then replaces the glass. A rattle of glass meeting glass. I take a breath in through my nose.

'What the actual fuckity-fuck was that?' she asks. It's a reasonable enough question.

At last.

'I don't know.' I pull my hands down the skin on my face. Eyes straining from their sockets. Showing the red blood in my veins.

'Ali!' Corina slowly shakes her head.

'It's nothing … There is nothing …' My voice doesn't even sound like my own.

'Eh, excuse me? That was like being a bed sheet on the set of *Mr and Mrs Smith* … the sexual tension was off the radar. I want to know everything and I want to know it all right now!'

And then I start to cry.

'Oh no, Ali … What's wrong?' She is off the leather chair and has her arms around me. I smell Jo Malone and Rancheros.

'Sorry, I don't know, Corina, it's Colin … Things are really shit and he's just so nice …'

'It's OK, it's all going to be OK … I promise.' She makes soothing noises and rubs my hair gently. I inhale her and I stay cocooned in the comfort of her arms until I stop crying. I'm crying for loads of reasons and they all swim into each other around my brain. Like those fucking sperms for years trying to penetrate my goddamn egg. I'm crying because I'm a fake, I'm not being honest with my best friend; I'm crying because I don't think I want to be married to Colin any more; I'm crying because I don't want my marriage to fail; I'm crying because Jade is slipping away from me, I miss my little girl, I miss the little girl who wanted me and only me; I'm crying because of how I feel about Owen and it's all wrong. I'm crying because I don't want to be a failure. Corina reaches for the kitchen roll again and tears off another sheet. It's well-earned its more expensive cartoon endorsement option this evening that kitchen roll. Allegedly wood-chipped though it is.

She gets up and pours us both another full glass of wine. She sits beside me and when I've finished blowing my nose and wiping my stinging eyes I stuff the sodden piece of kitchen roll up my sleeve and take the wine she's offering. We sit side by side on the couch.

'I've never been married, I've never been in a relationship that lasted more than three months and I've never been the one to finish a relationship ever. By process of elimination, I am not the one to give you advice, love. However, I am worldly, I have opinions and morals and ideals.' She puts her wine to her mouth and beckons for me to do the same. We both drink. She carefully places her glass back down. 'But, Ali, this is a dangerous game. This isn't wise or clever or even fair on anyone – never mind, Colin – I'm thinking about Jade and Mark.' She puts her hand on my knee.

'There is nothing going on, though …' I break off, there is no point in pretending. I've gone there in my mind so many times now it feels like I have cheated already.

'But you would dearly like there to be, right?'

'But yeah … you're right,' I manage the truth.

'And so would he, right?' she questions.

'I don't know and that's being one hundred per cent honest. I have never discussed it with him, but I get the impression ... that maybe ... yeah.' My voice is small.

'OK, well, at least nothing has happened yet. Thank God I came here tonight – this is our grannies helping with this intervention. What would have happened if I wasn't here?' She blows out air slowly and glugs her wine.

'Nothing!' I hiss at her.

'It's after ten, feck it, pour me another, I'm getting a cab. Is he why you are, well ...' she pauses, 'seemingly, lately, for want of a better turn of phrase, looking for a way out?'

Her voice is soft, but I know it's not exactly sympathetic.

'I'm not looking for a way out, Corina, you have no idea what it's like lately.'

'OK, so we have all the time in the world, tell me ... tell me just how bad your relationship really is, Ali. I want it all: warts, farts, slaps ... whatever it may be, I want to know the whole lot.' She sits bolt upright.

'Oh, it's not slaps, Corina, I promise you that. Colin has never raised a hand to me.' I watch her shut her eyes and blow her cheeks out wide in relief.

'Jesus, thank God.' She blesses herself and raises her eyes to heaven.

I feel trivial in my want of her attention now. I go on because I have to; I've dragged her to this place with me. She only wanted to share a bottle of wine, munch on a few crisps and watch *Gogglebox*. Now here she is bolt upright on the couch in therapy with me again. I am such a shite friend. So self-absorbed right now and that's just not Ali Devlin.

'It's ... it's ... just I don't think I'm in love with Colin any more.' I can't help myself. I plunge her in deeper. Ducking her head below my rising marriage tide. Submerging her in my problems.

She raises her left hand.

'OK, so tell me stuff. Tell me scenarios. Give me specifics of how bad things are in the marriage. Give me actual examples.' She never takes her eyes off me.

'Terrible ...' I whimper at her.

'More. Give me proper examples, Ali,' she demands. 'I want to try and help.'

'OK, well, we just can't get along, and I'm desperately unhappy that the kids are hearing us fighting all the time and I have zero attraction physically to Colin any more ... I told you that, but what I couldn't tell you is that I can't stand it when he touches me. I freeze. How my skin crawls when he wants to make love to me, how I want to scream and run when we are intimate—' My bottom lip is quivering.

'Ali, it's OK ... it's OK ... OK ... it's OK, I get it, love,' she interrupts. Her tone is soft. 'You have no sex drive ... no desire in you ...' She takes a long pause here. 'But you desperately fancy Owen the artist, yeah?' She is pointing out my problem, I see this.

'Yeah,' I admit.

'You wouldn't mind Owen having a grab of your tits now, would you?'

As coarse as this conversation is, it actually feels really good to get this off my chest. Yes, I am mortified, but maybe confessing it will make it go away. Burst its bubble.

'No … I wouldn't.'

'What else is wrong with Colin apart from you not wanting to ride him at the moment?' she asks, before adding, 'I'm just trying to get the full picture here, Ali, I'm not trying to do anything else. I'm no Dr Phil's wife.'

'He's just suffocating. I can't make any decisions – he picks me up on every tiny little thing I do wrong. I'm changing, Corina, and he isn't. Sometimes, a lot of the time, if I'm honest lately, I just don't like him at all.'

'What kind of decisions?' she probes.

'Oh, Corina! I dunno! I mean … I wanna shop in Lidl, he wants to shop in Aldi … I wanna go to IKEA and buy new cutlery – I hate our cutlery – he won't let me, he hates IKEA. It's not green enough and he says I'm wasting money, that our cutlery is fine … I wanna go on a sun holiday and lie on my back for a week reading *Fifty Shades of Tom Hardy*, he hates sun holidays and Tom Hardy. He wants to go on an adventure … outdoor sports. I hate adventures and I hate outdoor sports … I want to tell him that his fascination, no addiction, to Manchester United makes me cringe, and … and … and every single day he makes me feel like I'm a really terrible mother …' I swallow a mouthful of saliva. 'That is what's so wrong with our marriage, Corina.'

My last words get through to her, I sense that immediately.

Her eyes dip to the floor for a brief moment and when she looks back up she says slowly, 'Can't you talk to him about this?'

'No, because every time we try to have a conversation we fight and then he always blames me and accuses me of not being able to hold an adult conversation. That makes me feel even more like a shit mother. Then I back off because I don't want the kids to hear us fighting all the time. That somehow makes me feel like a better mother. Plus, Jade is totally on his side, for some reason, and Mark just gets a tummy ache when we row and then I hate myself even more.'

'Shit.' Corina scratches her head.

'Shit is right.' I scratch mine.

'But you do know, Ali, that this Owen guy isn't the answer to all your prayers. He's not going to fix you.'

'I know that, Corina. I wish to God he wasn't in the picture and that I didn't fantasise about him, but you asked so I'm telling you,' I pant.

'He knew Colin was away tonight, right?' Her HDs rise again.

'I think I told him over a shared lentil soup at lunch.'

'A shared lentil soup?' Her eyes pop out of her head. 'Like off the same spoon? In your place of work! What are yee, Mickey Rourke and Kim Basinger?'

'No! Well, yeah, we shared a spoon, but I bought it. He just tasted it.'

'Oh, for feck's sake.' She stands. 'He's dangerous, Ali. He shouldn't be coming here at night like that with the children asleep upstairs. He should be staying far, far away from you. I'm guessing he knows all you just told me about Colin though, right?'

I nod. 'Most of it, yeah.'

'And I'm guessing he's totally single, free-as-a-bird available?'

Again I nod.

Corina sits back down now on the couch and lifts her

glass from the table. She swirls the dark red liquid as she stares into Colin's huge bubble wine glass.

'Like I said, I can't tell you what to do. But I wouldn't throw all this away without trying to fight for it. And I especially wouldn't have an affair, Ali. Shitty people have affairs, horrible people. That is not you.'

The *Gogglebox* credits roll and we look each other in the eye.

'I better Hailo. I've to be in the convention centre at seven thirty.' She rummages in her bag for her phone.

'I feel like a total tit,' I whisper the words hard at her.

She doesn't look up for a minute and then she does.

'Love is blind, lust is fleeting. The Owen thing ... it will pass.' She stands again. 'Four minutes, gotta love the Hailo app.' She stuffs her scarf into her bag.

I stand and walk over to where she's pulling on her dark brown ankle Uggs by the door.

'Thanks for listening.' I hug her tightly.

'I love you, Ali. God, I only want for you to be happy. If he was hitting you, then that would have been a totally different situation. I'd have you and those kids in my house by now and the guards up Colin's arse. But this is different ... and look, if things can't work with Colin, then so be it, but you owe it to those two beautiful little people upstairs to at the very least give it a try. Couples' counselling, yeah?' she advises again in as many days. She winks at me.

I nod my head and for the first time I feel maybe there is a chance for Colin and me. Maybe just maybe therapy can help us. You always hear the cases, don't you? Of marriages that survived a crisis and became stronger than ever.

'You're right, thanks. What would I do without you?'

'Well, ye'd have a clean liver for one.' She winks at me again.

Her phone rings.

She slides across the answer button.

'Thanks, Rajah, I will be right out.'

We walk to the door and as I open the front door I hold it ajar for a second.

'I never heard properly about Trevor, he sounds great.' I scratch my head again; my anxiety is through the roof.

'Next time.' She seems suddenly tired now as she kisses me on the cheek. I look down; the headlights from the taxi cab illuminate my driveway and her ankle Ugg boots.

I watch her slide into the back seat and I make a mental note of the driver and the registration plate as we always do. Closing the hall door quietly, I make my way through the living room and the kitchen tidying up as I go. The family computer is purring at me so I sit and I log out of Corina's Facebook account and enter my own details. My messenger pops on my screen four new messages, all from Owen O'Neill.

I just presumed you were alone
Sorry
Did I make things awkward for you?
Incredible mime my friend!

I laugh out loud. I can see he's currently on Facebook via the chats so I type back.

Why didn't U call? Send.

Nah Corina's totally fine, she knows the shit I'm goin through with Colin. Send.

He's typing back.

I just called in on a whim
'Backfired'
I type:
No was delighted 2 see U … It's fine. Send.
I'll miss U 2morro. Send.
I sit and wait. He is still active.
I'll miss you more
My breath escapes in a burst of excitement. I can't say anything else. I mustn't. I hover the cursor in the shape of a little white arrow now over the X in the red box at the top of my screen. Then I click it and the page closes down. I go to bed.

6

Tuesday evening. The dinner table. At home.
'Where are my two chocolate eggs?' The hall door slams
with a thud and both Jade and Mark jump up from the
dinner table.

'Daddddddyyyy!' Mark squeals as he runs down the
hall.

'Dad! Oh, Dad, I've missed you soooo much!' Jade
squeals higher. He's only been gone a night.

'My chocolate eggs!' Colin shouts and rattles his car
keys down hard on the glass hall table. Leaping up, I
turn off the heating. I have literally just put the dinner
on the table. Half an hour before work this morning I
spent prepping the beef stew, peeling carrots, parsnips,
potatoes, onions, stripping thyme from its stems (if Jade
sees a stem, she freaks) and slow-cooking it this evening,
and they have just deserted it.

I won't say a word.

I push back my chair and stand at the kitchen door
looking down the hall at this wonderful family tableau.

'Hi, Colin.' I lean against the kitchen door and smile at
my husband. He looks up at me for the briefest of seconds
before turning his attention back to the children and
saying, 'Now which chocolate egg wants their chocolate

egg first?' He reaches into his long dark work coat pocket and pulls out two cream eggs.

'Me ... me ... meeeeee!' They yell in unison.

'They are just about to eat their dinner,' I say. I hate myself already but what choice do I have?

'Mummy, I will still eat it all up ... please can I eat the egg, please?' Mark waves his hands around frantically in the air.

'No Mark, eat your dinner first and then you can have the egg.' I stand firm. He needs to eat better. He needs building up. I know he won't touch the stew if he eats all that; he's a pigeon appetite as it is.

Colin slowly rises from his haunches and starts to unbutton his coat.

'Mummy's right, Mark: dinner first, egg after.'

Colin eases the heavy coat off and finds a spare coat hook on the wall by the hall door for it.

'Ahh, please, Dad!!' Mark pulls at his legs.

''Fraid not, little buddy.' Colin ruffles his hair.

'Please, Mummy ... please ... I swear I will eat all the chew!'

'After dinner, Mark, all right!' I raise my voice slightly to show him I mean it. I really want him to eat meat and vegetables. He's so thin and small.

'OK, calm down, Ali, he's only a kid.' Colin sweeps him up.

I want to say, *Oi Devlin! I thought you didn't agree with us picking up Mark?* But I don't, I let it go, I want to avoid a disagreement so instead I say, 'I know ... I'm saying yes after dinner.' I can feel the anger ripple up my legs into my stomach. I swallow it back down. Squeeze my toes tight together.

Jade sits down again and actually gives me a sympathetic look. She helped me cook this evening; she crumbled the Oxo in and stirred the pot brown, so maybe that's why. She dips her spoon in and tastes.

'It's awesome, Mom, realllly gud … reaalllyyy reallllllllllllly gud,' she drawls. It takes every ounce of strength for me not to correct her American accent.

Colin pops Mark onto his chair.

'Eat up there now … I suppose a dinner for me is out of the question?' He does a double-take at his place at the table where he seems to expect a plate of dinner to be. His attitude towards me was hostile as soon as he walked through that door. He barely looked at me when I said hi. I am just about to sit but I push my chair back in. Deep breath. In through the nose, and out through the mouth.

'Of course there is. I wasn't made aware of your estimated time of arrival home, so I didn't plate you up a dinner, but there is plenty in the pot.' I force a half-smile as I move over to the stovetop. He follows me and stands at my shoulders. I lift the lid and retrieve the black plastic ladle still in there. Colin stares in, and then he takes a step back.

'Ah, yer OK, I'll just grab a sandwich,' he says, his teeth clamped together. No tone to his voice, he just says it. But I know he doesn't like the look of my stew. He doesn't like my cooking.

'I helped, Daddy,' Jade leaps in. Colin immediately softens.

'Did you now? Well, I can't say no to that.' He grimaces at me and I grab a plate and start serving. I bite down on my lip and throw the ladle into the sink when I'm finished.

'Will you watch it!' He jumps back, some of the stew scattered and splashed as the ladle hit the sink and it splashes his dark navy Brown Thomas bought suit.

'Sorry, I didn't mean—' I grab the wet cloth from the sink and wring it out.

He makes a massive deal about pulling off the suit jacket and laying it over the countertop. He grabs the wet cloth from my hand.

'For fuu— Jaysus, I only got this from the dry cleaner's last week.' He rings the cloth tighter.

'Finished!' Mark jumps up. 'Can I have the egg, Daddy, please can I, can I?' Mark hops from one small leg to the other.

I look at his plate and it is all but untouched.

Colin doesn't answer, he is deep into his scrubbing.

'Go ahead, Mark.' I move back to the table and pull my chair out, sit and choke on my own first bite, my appetite completely gone.

'But that's not fair, he barely ate a bite!' Eleven-year-old-should-know-better-Jade says, her spoon resting on the side of her bowl.

'Go ahead and have your egg, Jade.' I wipe my mouth with my paper napkin as she eyeballs me. Blue eyes flashing.

'It's reaaalllllyy gud, Mom … I'm just, like, I'm kinda, like, full and stuuuuuff …'

Oh God.

'Go,' I wearily tell her.

She springs up and Wonder-Daddy takes them both into the front room with their chocolate eggs. I hear snickering and whispering and then the theme tune to *Austin*

108

& Ally. Colin is slagging me off to them, I know he is – it's nothing awful, granted, but I know in my heart of hearts he's saying how clumsy I am and how Mummy is always messing up. Trying to do too much. Wearily I begin to clear off the full plates and scrape them into the bin. Colin immediately returns and closes the kitchen door softly behind him.

'Maia and Donal split up,' he says as he crosses me and opens the fridge his head poked right in.

Maia Crowley, Colin's colleague at Devlin's Designs. The vegan woman I was telling you about earlier. He employed her about two years ago. She drives a plug-in car and only wears mineral make-up. She's nice and all that, just very, very *green*.

'That's nice.' I take my foot off the pedal on the bin and the lid clangs.

Colin gets a fright and bashes his head off the top of the fridge.

'Fuckin' hell, Ali, what have I told you about letting the bin lid smack closed?' He pulls out, rubbing his head with the palm of his hand.

'Calm down!' I hiss. I move to the sink. I know I can't put the dishwasher on now because he's here and he will say it's a waste of energy, think of the planet and wash the few dishes. He will want me to fill the sink slightly with lukewarm water and wash them by hand. He's right, OK, I know. Believe it or not, I do actually care about the planet. I recycle everything I can, I get that it's important, but these days Colin is just way OTT with his greenness. I start to wash the dishes.

'Why can't you close the lid quietly? Look, come here

…' He closes the fridge door, moves to me and takes me by the elbow. He tries to move me over to the bin. I dig my heels in.

'Are you going to give me a lesson in closing a bin lid, Colin?' My temper has materialised in a grand fashion as I yank my elbow away.

'It's not that difficult to do.' He runs his thumb into the palm of his fist as though I've somehow injured him. 'Anyway what do you mean "that's nice"?' he asks.

'Huh?' I flick my fingers quickly under the running tap to check the temperature.

'When I came into the kitchen, after settling the kids in front of the TV, I told you Maia and Donal had split up and you said "that's nice".'

He moves back to the fridge, opens it and removes some items. I watch as he peels back the plastic cheese wrapper, cuts two slices of low-fat hard white cheddar, and then he reaches up and pulls the sliced loaf from the shelf. His shirt rises up out of his suit trousers and I catch a glimpse of his stomach. Taut. The start of a six-pack. He's been back in the gym lately.

'Did you buy white bread again?' He studies the infamously familiar blazing yellow-and-white Brennan's packaging. The whitest of white bread Ireland has to offer.

'It looks like it.' I twist off the water supply.

'God, I hate white bread.' He removes a slice, holds it to his nose and smells it.

'Urgh … have we any cracker bread?' He rummages again before adding, 'Anyway, what's nice about a break-up?'

He finds half a packet of poppyseed Ryvita and sets about making his snack.

'It was a joke ... I'm sorry to hear that, Donal's a nice guy,' I say.

'He is. He doesn't get her though, ya know what accountants are like?' His voice is muffled from the inside of the fridge again.

'Did you not buy ham?' He pops out again. Like a puppet on a string.

'I did, but I've already used it on the lunches for tomorrow. I'm ahead of myself this evening. What doesn't he get about Maia, so?' I continue my job at the sink.

'He only went and bought a brand new 4-litre Range Rover!' Colin tells me, aghast.

Colin is removing items from the fridge and putting them back. His mutterings tell me he's unhappy with the snack choice currently available to him.

'Did you use the whole packet of ham?' he contorts his face. Stubble this evening, I notice for the first time. I wonder why he didn't shave this morning. Colin is a clean-shaven type of guy, especially in the workplace.

'I just got two slices of premium ham at the deli for the kids' lunches.' I leave the glasses to drip dry.

'That's crazy, Ali, you would get twelve slices of Denny's ham for the same price.' He extends his hands out to his sides.

'I'm not buying processed ham any more, Colin. I don't like it, not after all those allegations about it.' I refer to a study that showed processed meats and smoked meats to be dangerous.

'Like we have the money to believe one-sided studies, Ali,' he snorts. 'It makes me laugh, I have been telling you all about the carbon footprint on our planet for years and you don't listen – suddenly a slice of ham is carcinogenic and you are in an all out panic!' Smacking the hands now down by his sides.

What's the point in retaliating? I try to change the subject.

'A brand new Range Rover huh? He must be doing all right for himself, so,' I half chuckle.

'See, that's the fucking worst thing about these arseholes who don't care for our planet, who suck the air out of our planet: people like *you* think' – he puts on a squeaky dumb high-pitched girl's voice and dances his fingers together

– '*Ooohhh, look big fancy car, what a big man he is* ... I mean, how do you think Maia felt when he pulled into her driveway in that monstrosity? She is a manager of Devlin Design's, she was sickened, how could she be with this guy?'

'We all have shit about our partners we don't like but we have to put up with. It's a Range Rover, not a sawn-off shotgun, Colin.' I've had enough.

'Finished, Daddy.' Mark is back with the cutest chocolaty face. I smile at him as he pads across the kitchen in his tiny bare feet.

'I'm a teeny bit cross you didn't eat your dinner, love.' I bend and wipe his face with the tea towel. The chocolate is stuck hard so I lick my fingers, wet the area and wipe again. I'm not cross at him. I am cross at his silly father for showing him chocolate before his dinner. Idiotic.

'Sorry, Mummy ... I love you, do you still love me?' He raises his arms high above his head to me.

I want to pick him up. I want to pick him up. I want to pick him up.

I can't. It will for sure start a real row even though Colin scooped him up earlier. One rule for one.

I pat his head.

Colin sits at the table with his cheese on poppyseed Ryvita. I dump an entire pot of stew in the bin, and hold my foot on the pedal as it releases slowly, its previous clamorousness denied. There is no point in keeping it for tomorrow. No one will eat it.

'I've an idea,' says Colin, 'how about we all watch something together, turn off all electronic devices? I could make a big bowl of my buttered popcorn? We all need some family time.'

'Yes!' Mark skids across the kitchen floor on his knees.

He's just given him a Creme Egg, but say nothing.

'Do you want to pop up and have a bath first, Ali?' he asks me. I recognise he is trying to please me and I follow suit. Maybe we can salvage this night after all.

'No, thanks, Colin, it's OK. I'll light the fire, shall I? Maybe we can all get into our cosies?' I am trying too.

'Now that sounds great, love. Let me finish this and I'll get Mark changed. So what's yer news, buddy? When is the next training session with the Ranelagh Rovers?' Colin says happily to Mark as Jade struts in.

'By the way, Dad, Mom had a party last night.' She puts her foot on the pedal bin, bins her chocolate egg wrapper and gently lowers the lid. It does not bang.

'Huh?' Ryvita pieces crumble from Colin's mouth onto the table.

Balls.

'I didn't have a *party*, love, what are you talking about? Corina came by ...' I huff the words out. It's like

113

someone just kick-started a motorbike in my chest.

'And that man was here too,' she says.

'Yeah … and Owen from work dropped by.' Please don't let me blush. I busy myself wiping the fallen crumbs of food with a wet cloth. They stick. I shake them into the bin and don't let the lid bang. My heart's racing.

'Owen, dropped by our house?' he says slowly.

'And that Corina one was drinking out of your good wine glass from Waterford that Maia got you for your Christmas present last year, the big bubbly one.'

My daughter digs me a deeper hole. I know she is not being malicious, how could she be? How could she know her 'mom' wants to have a rodeo ride on the man she works with? Realllly badly … reeeeeaaaaallly, reeeeaaaal-lllly badly.

'What was going on?' He puts the self-made snack down and pushes back his chair and folds his arms staring at me as I potter around in a panic.

There is only one thing to do here. I go on the defensive.

'Jesus, what? Nothing! Corina called over for a glass of wine. Owen dropped in the itinerary for Amsterdam as he's away until the trip. It wasn't a party!' The kids are staring at me now too. I see the look on their faces: they know this is the start of another fight. Four alert eyes.

I'm way too defensive and his eyes are now blazing.

'Kids, go into the other room,' he demands.

'But I thought you said we were having family night with buttered popcorn?' Mark's little face drops.

'Another night, Mark. I'll be in in a minute. We can watch the end of *Toddlers & Tiaras* OK, Jade?' I say, but she doesn't look back at me.

They are only too familiar with the tone of their parents' pre-fight, and both leave the kitchen immediately and pull the door. I hope Jade comforts Mark when we fight, I really do. The door clicks shut.

'I don't want either of those crazy fuckers in my house when I'm away, got it?' he rages at me.

'No … I don't "got it". It's my house too.' He can go fuck himself.

'I pay the mortgage, I pay the bills—'

'Oh, Colin …' I rest against the sink, my arms stretched out, gripping the countertop. 'When are you going to stop throwing this at me? I can't take much more of it.' I scratch my head.

'Truth hurts.'

'Fuck off,' I hiss, grinding my teeth at him.

'Such a pretty face, Ali…'

We glare at one another.

'So the painter fella called in at what time?' He stands up now, pacing the grey slate flooring.

'I don't know, I didn't clock him in.' My heart is stee-plechase racing in my chest.

'Well, Jade saw him, so was it teatime?' The question is patronising.

'No … Jade was in bed. She came down.' I tell the truth. He'll find this out anyway and my anger is carrying me through this conversation.

'Right, so he called in here late … Knew I was away, did he?' Colin examines the nails on his left hand. He manicures them sometimes, I know he does, but he won't ever admit it.

'Don't be so ridiculous,' I lie to him.

'Show me the itinerary he left then.' He holds his hand out.

'It's back at work,' again I lie, like a butterfly. Easy-breezy words fluttering out of my mouth.

'Work? Yeah, right,' he spits the words in a laugh at me.

'Yeah, work,' I spit it back.

'That's what you do, is it?'

If he's going there, he really wants a full-blown row. I won't subject the kids to this.

'I'm going to bed, Colin. You can put the kids up tonight.' I push my weight off the countertop with my outstretched hands.

'My pleasure. Get lost, liar.'

'No, my pleasure.' I leave the kitchen.

* * *

In a boiling hot coconut-scented bath, trying to drown out my guilty thoughts, I submerged my head under the water for a moment too long. I came up spluttering. The glorious isolation and feeling of being powerless under there was much needed. Drowned out every horrible aspect of my life right now. Drowned out the noise in my head that I am indeed a terrible mother.

I dry my hair and put on my giraffe pyjamas. My mood-killers, as Colin calls them. Or should I say, as Colin used to call them. My Elizabeth Arden eight-hour cream is another passion killer, so I lash it on liberally. My laptop bag is hanging over the upstairs banister and I take it into the bedroom. They are all laughing and joking downstairs and I feel desperately alone. I feel like everything is entirely

116

my fault, but the reason I am up here is so they don't hear us fighting. I am trying to protect them for us.

Removing the laptop, I place it on the side locker as I slide in between the cold sheets and prop my pillow behind my back. I open it and log into my Facebook account. As the site loads, I make a mental note to send a message to Maia about her breakup. I have her number in my phone, and we have texted each other on occasion. I see three little red messages at the bottom of my messenger.

Well ...

Did you request those adjoining rooms yet?!! ;)

Owen. All day I have put him out of my head. I knew Corina was right. Not a text nor a call nor an email nor a social media message did I send him. Nor did I check my Facebook all day. The messages he had sent the other night were the last ones we shared. In fact, I was so busy today I enjoyed not having the distraction of him around the building. I had focus.

At lunch I mingled with some actors from the new Christmas show, *Little Red Riding Hood*, and I got a load of work done. I'm in the process of trying to coordinate an art event in the centre's gallery with the local Old Folks Club at the St Andrew's Resource Centre, as well as trying to get them funding for transport. I have been in to see them about five times now and they are magnificent people. Owen came with me the last time to offer his help to anyone who might want it. Nanny Farrell, who is eighty-five and partially blind, sang out, 'I mightne be able to see good ya know but, Jaysus, I can feel yer vibe, love.' Well, we all doubled over laughing. Owen had given her a huge hug, almost lifting her small frail body off the ground and smacked a kiss on her toothless mouth. Ranging from a sprightly seventy to a naughty ninety-eight-year-old, I have commissioned them all, those who are interested, to draw something, anything, with paint, pencil, crayons, chalk, twistables, whatever. I gave them all sorts of supplies and we are going to have an exhibition night in the City Arts Centre on Christmas Eve with mulled wine. Corina is doing the PR for free. We hope to get enough media coverage to help with our campaign to get the Arts Council to fund a new bus for them. Transport is desperately needed. At the moment they rely on relatives and friends to drop them to the club and collect them, and some even spend a chunk of their tiny pensions on taxis, just to get out to see another human face.

The City Arts Centre is all about helping the community through art. I know my work is important. I didn't need to defend it to anyone. I didn't need to prove it. But right now, even more so after that fight with Colin, I welcome Owen's messages with a warm heart and a terrific tingle up through my spine deep into the base of my neck. Escapism. Owen understands how important the City Arts Centre is to the community and to me.

He added a .gif of a cartoon guy banging repeatedly on a hotel door.

I know he's messing and I laugh as I continue to read.

Belfast is so beautiful, hadn't been up here in years. Colette rang me – there's a residency opening for 6 months at Centre Culturel Irlandais in France.

I gasp audibly. I panic-read the next bit going from the bottom up. I try to slow my mind down and read it carefully.

Is he leaving?

Is he leaving?

He can't be leaving?

Oh my God, he cannot be leaving!

Be a great opportunity for me to tap into the resources of the CCI and the City of Light as well as being an important means of showcasing Ireland's dynamic contemporary culture on an international stage. Hark at me!

He adds a .gif of Boyzone's first appearance on the *Late Late Show*. I laugh despite my shock. Keith Duffy in those big red Budweiser braces dancing around like his life depended on it never fails to crease me up in laughter.

Big application process and deadline end of January, one other thing though, artists must have had at least one solo exhibition work! What do ya know! Tell Corina I want her number after all!

He adds a winky emoji and a .gif of the movie *Manhattan* and the famous Woody Allen art gallery scene.

I don't want him to go to France!

I rest my head back against the softness of my goose-feathered pillow. My fingers wiggle over the keys. Downstairs, I hear Colin's huge pretend laugh. There is no need for him to laugh that loud, he is making sure that I can hear him up here.

I don't want you to go to France. I tap-tap-tap the words.

I linger over the return key then hit it. Enter.

Sent.

The little bubble appears: he is reading.

Why not?

Coz. Send.

Coz is not a word never mind an answer, stand in the corner Miss Devlin.

OK because I'd miss you then. Send.

Bubble.

It's only for 6 months.

What am I saying?

It's a huge opportunity for you I know that. Send.

The city arts is fantastic but I was only supposed to do a residency. Colette just keeps asking me to stay on. I'm trying to think bigger ya know? If I want to make a living from my art I need to be braver.

What is it U actually want? Send.

Bubble.

To be an artist.

You are an artist! Send.

Bubble.

Not a real one.

Yes! A very real one. Send.

Bubble.

Thanks. You're so supportive Rose but I know you just want me to draw you like one of my French girls.

He adds a boat symbol. He needn't have. I got his poorly written James Cameron/*Titanic* reference.

I'll never let go Jack, unless that is I really need to save myself and there just happens to be a massive door floating by.

Winky face. Send.

Bubble.

I never got that before. I am totally Jack and you are the unsinkable Molly Brown.

What do I say to that? Is that a joke or a compliment or an innuendo? I'm not sure. It's so easy to be brave from the comfort of my own bed but I need to rein this is. This is going nowhere safe fast.

I hear the TV go off and the sighs of unhappy children being sent to bed.

Have to go, night night. I press send as I gently fold the laptop lid shut, slide it onto the carpet and quietly switch off my lamp. If he does come into this bed tonight, I will be well and truly asleep. Dreaming. Dreaming of another man.

7

**Wednesday morning. Minus 2 degrees outside.
City Arts Centre. My office.**

I'm not quite as snappily dressed as I usually am for work,
I admit to myself, as I close my office door. This morning
we slept in. I completely forgot to set the bedroom alarm
clock. Of course I did. Totally my fault. We were all late
and I look like I've been dragged through a hedge backwards. You know those rushed mornings: your make-up
doesn't blend, the nib breaks off your eyeliner and you
cannot find a sharpener, you can't find the right coloured
bra or matching socks, the jeans that you are wearing are
too tight underneath, the slide in your hair keeping your
fringe out of your eyes has snapped, and no matter how
many times you empty your overflowing bag there just
isn't another loose one in there.

Colin had been furious. He had indeed slept in the bed
beside me but I hadn't heard him getting in. He had pulled
the duvet down and screamed me awake.

'It's after eight, Ali, did you not set the fucking alarm
clock? I have a display presentation at nine in Dundalk!
Fucking hell! Nice one, thanks!'

He had dressed by the bed in yesterday's clothes, which
were hung neatly over the wicker chair, and run down the

stairs, taking them two by two, grabbed his keys off the glass hall table and straight out the door.

I was also running late for work and had an important meeting and people waiting on me. Even though sons, daughters, grandsons, granddaughters, nephews, nieces, friends and neighbours had agreed to drop the older club members to the St Andrews Resource Centre for ten o'clock this morning and were returning to collect them at twelve o'clock. Even though necessary medicines had been administered before they left to coincide with the meeting. But my time isn't as important.

So it was down to me to get the kids up, breakfasted and dressed, drive them to school, do the whole sign-in-late shit, which drives me potty as it just makes already flustered parents even later! Only then was I allowed to get myself to my work.

I was so late. When eventually I reached work I ran up to my office and gathered all the stuff from my desk that I needed, mainly the release forms to be signed so that we could legally display the work. God bless Corina, I'd texted her at a red light on the way to the school to see if she might be free this morning to help me out of a massive hole. As usual she had my back. She had got there at ten o'clock for me and she was holding the fort. It was a quarter past ten by the time I looked up at my ticking office clock and dashed back down the stairs.

Anyway, I am relieved Owen is in Belfast. He usually sees me looking pretty together. My work clothes are normally skinny jeans and a nice shirt teamed with my black suede ankle boots. I sweep my blonde fringe to the left-hand side, it needs a cut. I usually cut it every four weeks but I've decided to grow my hair longer. Colin loves short hair on me, which I suppose is why I've always had it short.

I wave at Jenny on reception as I leave through the front door of the centre and put my free hand out to hail a cab. The Steffi Street gang are just arriving as I look down the road; Mick the handyman is taking them today, showing them maintenance management. As I stand in the bitter cold, hand turning blue as it waves about for a cab, their noisy bus coughs to a halt and I watch them all emerge. Some without coats, some with hoodies pulled up over their heads. Owen is so incredible with them; he really should be an art teacher in a school. I see Zoe, the little girl Owen is always on about. The one who lives with her granny in the flats in Old Bond Street. Both her parents are heroin addicts, doing time. James Rafter irritating her by standing on her lace that has come undone.

Or maybe that's the look. Open laces. I think of my beautiful Jade. She just seems so angry towards me right now. She has so much to be grateful for but I think all she really craves is for Colin and me to be happy. She's eleven, she gets it, she feels the rows and the anxiety and I hate myself deeply for making her live through this. I know she doesn't have it as hard as these kids, nowhere near it, and I know I can't pop her inside the perfect bubble ending of *It's A Wonderful Life*, but still. Speaking of which, I reluctantly remove my phone and dial Colin's number, holding the phone under my ear with my chin and shoulder. The bitterly cold, hard breeze blowing my fringe into my eyes.

'Yeah?' I can hear an animated breakfast talk show on the radio in his car.

'Good morning to you too.' I am trying.

'Traffic was an absolute bitch, I couldn't even get onto the M50 for half an hour, I'm only pulling in here now,' he pants. 'Thank God for Maia, she was early so I prepped her over the blower and she's in there already.' I hear his engine die. Talk show terminated.

I wave frantically at a taxi with its light on. He doesn't stop.

I gesture wildly to him to turn off his fecking light!

'Can you meet for lunch today? We need to talk. Will you be back in Dublin in time?' I start walking in the piercing cold, heading in the direction of the centre, still eyeing up the traffic for a free taxi.

'Maybe, not in that City Arts Centre though. That food yer one, Patricia, cooks is rancid.' I hear him opening the car door.

'OK, how about the Pepper Palace at half past two, after the lunch rush and that will give you time to get back from Dundalk?' I suggest hopefully.

'Grand. I've a call from Maia coming in here, I need to take it, Ali. See ya later.' He rings off. Hallelujah. A cab pulls in and I wave at a latecomer from the Steffi Street gang, who is meandering down the road as I hop in and give my destination. Sitting back, I try to compose myself. This cab doesn't smell too great, stale cigarette smoke and coffee. Perhaps a vomit or two not properly taken care of. Springs in the back seat stick up into my bottom. I shut my eyes. Deep breathing.

After I'd finished messaging Owen last night, lying there in the dark listening to my children brush their teeth, I was

125

overcome with emotion. What was I doing? Even though nothing has happened or, I hope, ever will happen, this is all wrong. It was one thing to fantasise about him but now I'm telling this man I don't want him to leave, to take a fantastic job in France, flirting with him over Facebook, am I completely off my head? I had listened to Colin putting the kids to bed with a lump in my throat. He is a caring, loving father; he adores his children and they adore him. He works really hard to give us a comfortable life. I listened harder to Mark's very loud whispers.

'But, Daddy, please … I want Mummy to put me to bed, she does nosies,' he'd pleaded with his father.

'Mummy had a very long day, dude. She's very tired; she can do nosies in the morning, little man,' Colin had told him.

My eyes popped open. I hadn't drawn the bedroom curtains because the sky was as black as coal now and it would be the same in the morning.

The stars in the dark sky made a pattern of a giant climbing a large hill. *I have to try and fix this mess*, I promised myself, as my eyes fell heavy, that I would talk to Colin today. I don't know what I'm going to say over lunch later. It's nothing to do with Owen really; I just can't go on like this any more.

'Sort it!' I say to myself inside the cab. 'You are a mother first, remember that. Your own mother did that for you, she put everything else on hold to raise you.'

And she did. Daddy dearest, Paddy O'Dwyer, left Bernie O'Dwyer and me when I was eight years old. He moved to Blackpool to live with his childhood sweetheart, who he had reconnected with through the Thin Lizzy fan club. Over to Dublin, came the pair of them once, by the B&I boat, when I was ten years old, and took me to see *Seven Brides for Seven Brothers* at the Olympia Theatre. I was seated behind a huge white pillar, it was uncomfortable and I wasn't very communicative. Daddy dearest bought me one of those glow sticks and I sat, my hand gripping it so tightly, the mark stayed for days. She was nice enough, Marie, or Mar'eeeee. A slim woman with short curly mauve hair. She'd had a large packet of strawberry bon bons in a small square brown paper bag that she offered me at various times during the show. I declined. Even though I desperately wanted one, I was too shy to dip my hand in. Whenever I hear 'Bless Your Beautiful Hide' to this day I can see Marie, or Mar'eeee, chewing away like a sucky calf.

That was the last time I saw them. As far as I know they still live in Blackpool and run a B&B near the North Pier. Mum wouldn't accept the pitiful offered maintenance from Daddy dearest and never met anyone else either. She wasn't a qualified accountant but she was brilliant with figures and she did people's books from our small three-bed semi-detached house in Rathfarnham. Mum never moaned, never told me her life was shit. In fact, I don't think it really was shit. Hard, for sure, but not shit. I think Bernie O'Dwyer quite enjoyed being a single and independent mother. She was always a mother first. That was her one true gift. She was an exceptional mother. She used to read poetry to me all the time but especially at night when we'd be cuddled up in her big bed. She loved romantic poems. She always read that famous one by Forest Witcraft, but she expecially loved ones by unknown authors. We must have read them all a thousand times.

When she came across a new one she'd enthuse, 'Oh, fabulous … author unknown, how truly poetic and moving that a nameless, faceless person left behind such magnificent art.'

Why can't I be like her? Or is this a part of me wanting to be too much like him? Would a shrink tell me I'm following a pattern? Just as well I don't buy into all that BS. My father isn't in my life and nor will he ever be. Am I damaged by this? No. I'm really not. If I want to go and see him and sit on his knee with yellow ribbons in my hair sucking on a fizzy cola lolly, I know where he is. I am happy to talk out my marital issues with Colin to a professional but I'm not interested in delving back to find the cause in our respective childhoods. I know why: Colin's being a dickhead. Full stop.

'Eight fifty, love, when yer ready there.' The taxi man wraps his arm around the passenger seat as he turns his head. Flat cap and yellow fingers. I hand him a tenner and thank him. The cold fresh air is suddenly welcoming after the stench in the cab. I rush into the resource centre and down to the back into Room 2. The music hits me before I open the door.

'Ohhh, the hokey-cokey-cokey!' I literally do a double take. Corina Martin is in the middle of the floor doing the hokey-cokey as the old folks all make a wide circle around her and put their left legs in and take their left legs out. An iPhone plays the music propped up on a desk against a large jigsaw box.

'Come, come! Join us, Ali!' Corina beckons me into the circle as she puts her right leg in and takes her right leg out. Her knee-length red skirt is flowing and flapping to the beat. I join in. I laugh hard. Corina is dressed in a bright red wrap-around top too, her knee-length skirt is red wool and her knee-high black boots expose a flash of green tights as she hokey-cokeys her legs around. Santa's little helper.

When we are finished Corina runs out to make tea for us all and I ask everyone to relax and take out their pictures. They all place them on the long trestle table at the back of Room 2 and then sit down. Those in wheelchairs or on frames stayed seated and placed them on their knees. I walk around and look. Everyone has tried. Everyone has drawn something. I am proud and I am mesmerised. I am fascinated. I am humbled. Nanny Farrell has drawn herself as a young girl; partially blind now, she managed to sketch from her mind's eye a small girl sitting by the canal and a huge yellow sun beaming down on her. Mary Clancy, seventy-nine, drew in pencil. Mary drew seven stick children and a small box. I question her.

'The box, Mary?' I run my fingers over the sketching.

'Ahh, that's me eighth born, Kathleen, she was took from me when she was three-year-old … TB.' Mary smiles at me a watery smile, her tear ducts now stretched with age and sadness of the memory of a lost child and I reach down and hold her cold hand, bulging blue veins and wedding rings that haven't been removed in years.

'Tell me about Kathleen.' I keep hold of her hand and kneel down beside her.

'Ah she was a beaut, the apple of me eye, so she was, hair as white as snow. She was never well from the day she was born … her chest. She slept in me arms for them three years. I miss her today the same as I did the day the good Lord took her from my arms as we both slept …' Huge fat tears drip softly and slowly down Mary's face. She doesn't wipe them, it's as though they are a part of her face.

'I never forget it, Ali. 'Twas the start of spring and the seagulls were bleating outside. The room was warm and bright. She was nestled into me. I didn't want to move as I was happy she was gettin' sleep, her breathin' had been so bad the night before … up all night me and her were. Walked the floor with her I did till the sun came up. I lay there for over an hour but little did I know she left me durin' the night. It was only when I tried to move to go down and put 50p into the gas meter for the breakfast … only when I seen her little face …' Her chin wobbles and her nose starts to run.

'C'mon now, Mary,' says Eileen Kilkenny, an eighty-one-year-old leaning on a silver frame, placing one slow orthopaedic navy lace-up shoe in front of the other toward Mary.

'Won't she be waiting for ya with her little arms raised when you leave this world?' Eileen reaches Mary and puts her hand on her shoulder. Then she leans on the frame, panting.

'She will, Eileen, an' yer right a'course.' Mary's face lights up. The tears rest in the deep crevices on her face. She doesn't feel them. Mary unclasps her old-fashioned bag and removes her rosary beads, she knits them around her old fingers and becomes lost in prayer.

I stand up. There is nothing to say.

Brian Drennan, eighty-one years old, has drawn a river

and what appear to be a lot of machines or cranes high in the skyline.

'The docks.' He blows his red thread-veined nose loudly into his clean white linen handkerchief. 'Fifty year I spent on dem docks, man and boy.' He examines the contents before he folds it away up into his sleeve.

'It's great, Brian, thanks,' I say. 'Have you been down there at all recently?'

'Sure I can't get around anywhere with the hip. Only me daughter runs me here. I'd be looking at dem four walls, day in day out.'

I will take him down the docks in the New Year. Nothing surer than that.

Kitty Tead, eighty-four, has drawn a large cross and coloured it in perfectly, all in black.

'A cross, Kitty?' I ask.

'It's for my Lord, I give thanks every day for what he did for us. I hope you go to Mass and bring yer chil'er'dren?' She wags a bony finger at me.

'I try … and that is wonderful, Kitty,' I add. Her faith is inspiring. No fear of death. Awaiting reunion with past loved ones. Amazing.

Corina bursts back in.

'Tea is up, my party of spring chickens!' She is holding a round silver tray with a huge old-fashioned silver teapot on it. The old-school one, you know, the one with the really long narrow spout. Like a baby elephant's trunk. Behind her a young, petite Asian girl, Shirushi, is carrying cups, with matching milk jug and sugar bowl designed with brown-and-orange stripes along with a box of Jaffa Cakes on a large wooden tray. We break for tea and Corina hands me a cup. I walk around and look at the drawings as I sip my hot drink.

How can Colin say this isn't important work? These are our people, our elderly, that can be so quickly forgotten, but they have so much to say and to offer and to teach us. I want them to be heard and seen. Generations should be fussed over not forgotten. One day we will all, if we are very, very lucky, be them. There are various pictures I can't wait to show Owen. He will be fascinated! By the time twelve o'clock comes and family members and friends arrive to take them all home, we have had another round of the hokey-cokey, Kitty Tead sang 'Paddlin' Madeline' and everyone had a chance to see each other's pictures.

'That was a lovely morn'nin',' Kitty Tead tells me as I help her to her son's car. He's double-parked, hazards flashing and stressed-looking, speaking loudly on his phone. A builder, I see by his clothes and hard hat. He's in a hurry to get back to work. He shouldn't have had to leave. There should be transport provided for these people.

'Will we be gettin' 'nother project to do, love?' Nanny Farrell pokes her wooden cane into my shin.

'You bet, this is only the start of it. If we can get the funding for the bus on a weekly basis, you can all come over to the City Arts Centre and we can do loads of stuff there. Have a whole plan of activities for next year,' I shout into her good ear, as Nanny is also almost stone deaf.

'No need to shout, I'm not deaf, ya know.' She bangs the cane on the ground as it supports her move to the car.

When they are all gone, I walk Corina down to her car.

'I'll drop you back,' she offers and I accept. It's bitterly cold again and sleet has started to fall.

'What have you on now?' I ask as I pull my seat belt across in her little car, blowing onto my cupped hands.

'Oh wait for this: Masked, the dating service, are launching their new app. I have been working on the event last few weeks and the owners are rather weird. A married couple with a lot of quirky outlooks on life. They want everyone to come today in masks and I'm, like, eh, no press are interested in masked faces: those pictures will not land anywhere. They are literally making my job impossible.' She turns on her engine, checks her mirrors and indicates to pull out.

I laugh and I turn to her. 'So ... 'ows Trevor, chuck? Eh? Eh?' I put on my best *Coronation Street* accent.

She stares straight ahead, the windscreen wipers speeding up as she pulls out.

'Not interested.' She tries to pretend her visibility is bad and shifts forward in her seat closer to the windscreen.

'What?' I ask her.

'Nope, I dunno, Ali, I really don't. Like I told you, I held off sleeping with him, played the good girl card. We got on like a house on fire ... had amazing sex and then nada! There's obviously something very wrong with me.' She shifts up into third gear.

'There isn't ... What did he say?' *Idiot*, I think.

She indicates again and turns down the quays.

'Are you ready for this? So we had sex, really great sex, he stayed the night. I got up early, did the whole Kristen Wiig in *Bridesmaids* routine on him, re-did my mascara, brushed my teeth, rolled on deodorant, Jo Maloned myself,

133

fixed my hair and snuck back into the bed. I gently woke him. We chatted and kissed, but I dunno, I immediately felt he wanted to get out of my bed. Which he quickly did. When I offered to make him a fry-up he said he had to get to work. There were no more questions about me, or what I liked and all that previous stuff. He was monosyllabic. I told him I really liked him and that I'd had a great time. He didn't say anything back to me except, "Where's my watch, d'ya know?" In a strange sort of defensive tone. Anyway, then he hurriedly left and just said, "See ya," but me being me – oh, wait for this, Ali, Corina Martin strikes again! I texted him a few times during the day and when he never replied to any of them, I left it until after I left your house to call him but he didn't answer. Then in the taxi I swapped to private number – don't judge me, I was drunkish and feeling very suspicious. Just as I thought, he answered and when he heard my voice, he was like, "Yeah, what d'ya want?" I was tipsy and said a few naughty things to him, and then he said, "Look I have a girlfriend, it's serious, so ya know … that's that, love. Don't call me again or I'll block your number." And he hung up on me.'

'Oh, Corina!' I exclaim. She is driving faster and I have to hold onto the tiny handle above the passenger's window. We drive in silence.

'Shouldn't have rang him after him not texting me back all day. Will I ever learn?' she says eventually as she pulls up fast outside the arts centre and pushes on her hazards.

I shake my head.

'No, probably not, love … but you know what: better to know he was a waste of space, yeah?' I click my belt.

'I guess … I just feel … I dunno … used … again! He made such an effort to get know me, like, seriously spent ages asking about my family, my job, he wanted to know it all … my favourite film, favourite food, and for what?'

'He's a prick,' I say.

'Like, was it his mission just to ride me and then just dump me?'

I shake my head at her.

'*C'est la vie*, eh?' she says. 'I'm … maybe I'm just not long-term loveable, Ali.' She winks at me but it's a slow, drawn-out wink. Her eyes aren't dancing behind it.

I stare at her gorgeous splattering of freckles.

'I don't know that I've ever met anyone as loveable as you, Corina. You are an amazing woman and any guy would be so blessed to share his life with you.' I mean every single word.

'I better fly, I have a mask to buy. Oh, shit, you aren't going to do a mime now I said that, are you?' she slags me.

I shut my eyes tight and hover my hand over the door handle.

'What are we like?' I say.

'Like two big bloody eejits.' She flicks off her hazards, indicates and looks in her mirror. I get out and slam the door, and she pulls away.

I have so much work to do before I go to Amsterdam on Friday. I head into the centre and up to my office. I look at my desk – it resembles my brain: shit everywhere. I focus on tidying up my space first, recycling paper as I go, and then get to work on my city council and Arts Council applications for funding the St Andrew's Resource Centre transport. *I'll work on the Steffi Street kids' new learning*

135

sign language programme after that's finished, I think.

Before I know it, it's coming up to two o'clock. I save my work on the applications and grab my coat from the back of my chair. I look out the window. Dublin is dull and dark. Huge black clouds hang low. I make my way out of the arts centre and turn left down Moss Street towards the Pepper Palace. It's a lovely cosy cafe run by an Australian couple, Samantha and Daisy. They were recently married and had their wedding reception in the cafe. Owen and I popped down with a card and had a glass of bubbles with them. Pretty cool ladies. The sleet is starting to come down very heavy now as I push open the door and see my husband sitting in the back far left corner beside the painted Santa window and the white, flickering Christmas tree. His head buried in a menu and he's still wearing his coat.

'Hiya, so cold, isn't it?' I slide into the white plastic seat opposite him and pull myself in. He smiles at me.

'Yeah, a bit, I suppose. I've mainly been in the car, how's things?' He puts the menu down.

'Yeah, grand. Sorry about the alarm, Colin,' I offer my apology as I unwind my scarf slowly and peel off my coat. I stuff the scarf far down into the sleeve. I'm always losing scarfs. I turn and hang the coat off the back of my chair.

'Anything good on their specials?' I pick up the long, slim menu.

He shakes his head.

'I'm not hungry today at all for some reason. Must be the big meal you served me last night. I'm just going to have a bowl of soup, it's butternut squash, Daisy just told me.'

I ignore his jibe. The mention of soup springs a vivid picture of Owen into my head.

'You badly need a haircut, Ali,' Colin says now as he removes his coat.

'Do I? Do I really, Colin?' I say very dramatically, it's all a bit Hannibal Lecter-sounding, as I lean my chin in my hands elbows on the table.

'What is up with you lately? Honestly this PMS thing is really out of hand, Ali, you are like a psycho all the time. You jump on every little thing I say.' He pushes the stainless steel salt and pepper pots away from my elbows towards the window. Maybe he is right, maybe this is all hormonal, because the hair comment has me raging inside and I don't know why. I need to calm down. Right on cue Daisy approaches.

'G'day, how are you, Ali? Getting set for Christmas?' She pulls her small red pencil from behind her ear and takes her dog-eared notepad from the pocket of the white apron tied tightly around her slim waist.

'Nothing even started yet, I've a business trip away this weekend, so I'll be into all that when I get back,' I tell her.

She nods. She has recently come back from a trip back home Down Under. Her skin is golden brown, her hair sun-bleached and she looks so relaxed. Oh, Vitamin D. How I need thee. I see myself do Marcel again. Horrific.

'Just two butternut squash soups, please, with brown bread,' I tell her.

'Wholemeal, rye or sour dough?' she offers, licking the nib of the red pencil and writing down our order. Samantha bakes all the bread in here the night before.

I look at Colin, he shrugs his shoulders.

'Surprise us!' I laugh, 'And two tap waters too, thanks.'

Colin is on his phone now. I study him. His dimple deep and so familiar. I close my eyes and hope when I open them he has disappeared. For the second time in as many minutes I wonder whether it's all me. Why would I want my husband to disappear? The cafe door opens and two office workers with accreditation badges swinging around their necks come in, shaking out their cold hands and take a free table. I lean in and with my index finger gently push his phone out of his hand down onto the table.

'We need to talk, Colin,' I say in a low serious tone.

'OK, go on.' He looks at me curiously as he puts the phone down.

'Things aren't good, Colin, ... between us, I mean. Like, not good at all, are they? I think—'

'What is wrong with you, Ali?' he interrupts, leaning in now too in hushed tones.

'What is going on with you? I can't figure you out, you are so miserable all the time, you are so snappy.'

All I can hear is his accusation: *YOU. YOU. YOU.*

'I'm not, Colin. You ... you, you pick on me all the time ... I—'

He interrupts again. 'What are you, twelve? Jade's more mature.'

'I mean it. I can't seem to do anything right in your eyes.'

He genuinely looks shocked.

'Give me an example?' He says.

'Well, take Sunday for example, you had a problem with me drying Jade's leggings in the dryer ...'

He scoffs.

'Yeah, because putting a single pair of leggings into a dryer is stupid. Sorry, but it is. It's costly and so bad for the environment.' He tilts his head at me. 'Next?'

'You tell me how to wash dishes.'

''Cause you really don't know how to wash them and I know when I'm not there you put the dishwasher on for a few dishes and again that's costly, Ali, and so bad for our environment. Next?'

Daisy is over with the soup and I lean back to let her place them down. She has brought a mixed bowl of breads. We thank her. This conversation is going nowhere fast. I don't mean it to be tit for tat. I need to make him understand how he is making me feel but more importantly the effect it is having on our children. He dips his spoon in, raises it to his mouth and blows. I watch the liquid quiver.

'When was the last time you said something nice to me, Colin?' I don't touch my cutlery. I sit still. Poker straight. Poker face.

P-p-p-poker face, p-p-poker face. Mum-mum-mum-ma.

'I tell you all the time how much I fancy you, Ali, you know I do. I honestly don't know what you want from me any more. OK, so I'm passionate about not wasting energy and you don't get that—'

Now I interrupt.

'I do get that, Colin. It's just I'm not obsessed with it and you are, it's not my number one—'

'Well, it should be,' he jumps in. He just won't let me finish a sentence. 'You should be, it's our children who will suffer if we don't take care of our planet.'

'That's all very Maia Crowley,' I scoff now.

His eyes dart up at me. The dimple pulsates as he pushes his long, floppy, light brown hair back from his baby-blue eyes. We look at each other before he goes back to his soup. I dip my spoon in but just swirl it around. I wish Owen was here to taste it, his lips on my spoon.

'Look, Ali, things are tough, I get that. *We* are trying to hold down jobs and bring up two children; it's never going to be a bed of roses ... I really don't know what you expect? This isn't one of your Hollywood movies with that freak Tom Hardy, it's real life.'

When he says '*we* are trying' this riles me again. I'm the one working my job around the kids, and pick-ups, and dinners and shopping and gymnastics and football and art classes and weekend parties. Colin goes to work, he drops the kids on his way and that's it.

'It's like you think life should be one long romantic movie. It's not. It's graft and hard work. That arts centre has you all full of crappy romantic notions.' He twists an inordinate amount of black pepper onto his soup. Usually meaning he doesn't like the taste.

'Are you happy?' I ask the question before my brain tells my mouth it's OK to do so.

He puts the pepper down slowly.

'Define happy, Ali. Am I happy to work to provide for my family? Yes. Is my wife giving me a hard time every second of every day? Yes. Does this make me happy? No. Do I want to lose her? No ... No way.'

I'm shocked. It's the nicest thing he has said to me since I went back to work full-time.

He puts the spoon down now and I watch the orange

liquid slide from it and melt into the cracks in the old wooden table.

'Find your smile. Go off this weekend on your holiday and enjoy yourself,' he says.

'It's work. Not a holiday, Colin,' I say, even though I know I shouldn't, he is reaching out but I can't help myself.

He raises a half-smile. A smirk.

'Of course it is.' His eyebrows raise and drop as he lifts a piece of heavy-looking brown bread and dips the bread in the bowl, bending his head over, then eats it. I bite my lower lip. His black suit from yesterday is still sharp with the grey tie; he always dresses for the office like he's off to a very trendy wedding. He still has stubble this morning, I suppose because we overslept and it suits him. He always was the best-looking boy in the school. Colin Devlin, with that cool khaki bag.

'Oh, I'm booking my flights today for the Irish games in June, just so you know,' he chews.

And that's why his humour is good. Something to look forward to. Football. The lads. I risk this one.

'Are you taking Mark? He will be thrilled! I've a hectic calendar at work in June.' I tear a piece of rye bread in half and dip it in.

He takes a few seconds to answer.

'No, I'm not taking my five-year-old son on the Irish Man U lads' trip to the Euros, are you mad?'

'I am mad, Colin, mad as fuck!' I glare at him as I raise my voice on my curse word. He thinks he can just swan off whenever the hell he likes and leave me with everything. Why can't I swan off whenever I like? Fuck that.

'Oh, here we go.' He reaches for the purple paper

napkin and wipes his mouth. He pushes back his chair and looks out the window.

'Here's Maia, saved by the job … I have to go, we can finish this later. Get some Valium, will ya?' He grabs his coat and moves away towards the door.

I look out the window as the green Honda Fit EV 2013 pulls up. Maia rolls down the window, her blinking hazards reflecting in her eyes, and gives me a huge happy smile. Maia is early thirties; she has a dark, wild curly bob haircut, kind of 'Scary Spice circa huge Spice Girls success'. She is always saving energy. Her car is lease only, she had told me last time at a business dinner for the company in L'Ecrivain restaurant. 'It ranks as the single most efficient electric car you can drive out of a dealership today. You can't buy it though, Ali; it's lease only,' she enthused into my face.

I wave back like a crazy lady. Smiling, waving, happy, happy, happy. I watch my husband fold himself in beside her and they drive away.

'Will I bring the bill, Ali?' Daisy asks as she clears the table, expertly balancing soup bowls and the mostly untouched bread plate along her left arm. Her hands, claw-like, holding up the two glasses.

'Please, Daisy, thanks,' I say. I rummage for my purse in my bag and realise I've left my phone at the office. I pay and head back to work. I bump straight into Corina at the reception desk.

'What are you doing here?' I say and fall into her embrace. 'And you are unmasked, my friend!'

We laugh and hug.

'I was calling you.' She's changed and now looks like

something from the movie *White Christmas*. White coat, white bobble hat and white leather gloves.

'Sorry, I left my phone. What on earth are you wearing since I saw you last?' I stare at her get-up.

'Like it?' she twirls. 'I got Fierce & Furry to sponsor today's launch for the Masked app at the very last second. They do mainly kinky fur stuff, like furry handcuffs, and furry knickers, big ears, tails ... For people who like the furry stuff, y'know.'

I stop her and pull her away from reception where a courier is looking at her strangely.

'People who like the *furry stuff*?' I'm totally confused.

'Ali, where have you been? It's all the rage in LA, on dating sites and apps ... people want to have sex with people who are dressed up as furry animals. You know, Furry Dating ... they are called Furries? Tell me you know what Furries are? Anyway, Colette wanted to meet me about next year's schedule, see what PR we can drum up, I'm going to be taking over the Facebook and Twitter pages here too.'

I'm still trying to digest the Furry info.

'I'm lost, Corina. I hope to stay that way, tell me no more about the furry shit ... but that's great news about Colette's call. We love having you based in here,' I tell her.

'You have a few messages,' Kim the receptionist informs me. It's a shared job. Jenny B. does the mornings and Kim does the afternoons. I take the yellow Post-It from her.

'Thanks, Kim,' I smile at her.

'Time for a coffee after I see Colette?' Corina asks.

'Mmmm ... could you get a take-out from the Beans and come up to my office? I've a city council and an Arts

Council application to finish today, if at all possible,' I ask her and I pull my purse out of my bag.

'I don't want the money! Yeah, no probs, I'll bring us up two extra hot lattés when I'm done.' She is already moving away. I shake my head. I'd like a stiff drink but really better not fall down that road. I'm bad enough.

I go through my messages as I walk up the wooden staircase to my office. Nothing important, but one makes me laugh, a Mr A.M. Sterdam called, asking me to call him back. I recognise the number immediately: Owen's. I crumple the Post-It in the palm of my hand. The guy's mad.

I get straight back onto my application for the bus and then the Steffi Street sign language programme as I wait for Corina and get quite a lot done before she returns.

'What took you so long?' I stretch my arms high above my head and find a huge, deep yawn.

She kicks the door closed behind her, puts the lattés on the desk and sits. She removes her Polar Express outfit and pulls out a giant bag of Maltesers, pulls the bag apart and leaves them on the desk between us. She pops one in her mouth and sucks before she answers me.

'I need chocolate so badly.' She eats more. 'You know how they say people in love glow? Well, people out of love grow!' she tells me.

She holds a Malteser between index finger and thumb and nibbles the chocolate all around it. It's like watching a small dog gnash on a bone. She pops the rest in her mouth and looks at me.

'Ah, you weren't *in love* with him ... but I get it,' I say.

144

'No, I don't suppose I was, but I wanted him to want to see me again. Is that too much to ask?'

'No.' I smile at her.

'How did lunch go, then?' She changes the subject and sucks away on the chocolate as she removes the lid from her latté.

'Ahhh.' I lean back in my office chair. 'Ended in a big fight, yet again.' I take my coffee up now and feel the warmth from the paper cup heat my cold hands. I twist it around several times in my palms. The City Arts Centre isn't exactly centrally heated. It ain't no Google offices, that's for sure. We each have a small oil radiator in our offices.

I fill her in as she sips her hot drink and eats the entire bag of Maltesers.

'I want to talk to you about Owen and your trip this weekend,' she says when she's finished licking her fingers.

I look at her. Then I tidy the already tidy pen tray.

'Stay away from him, Ali, he is the disease not the cure.'

'Ahh, come on, that's not fair, Corina, you don't know him.' I'm upset with her for the first time since we met.

'It's not him I'm worried for, it's you, Ali, and you have a marriage to concentrate on, kids to think about. It's too important to lose out to lust. Is it worth risking everything you have for a ride?'

'You have no idea how bad things are between me and Colin, Corina.'

She moves and sits against my desk, holding onto the sharp edge.

'I do! I really do. I know you are going through a really bad time, but it will be OK, you need to talk—'

'That's why I just met him for lunch. I am trying … to talk. It's impossible.'

'So tell me what? Do you want to end it then?'

I roll a red Bic pen beneath my hands and feel the hard groves.

'I honestly don't know,' I admit.

'I told you: you just need to go out and get some really sexy underwear – you need to feel sexy yourself – and then seduce him. Sex makes everything better,' she says matter-of-factly.

'I don't fancy Colin at all any more, Corina. I have tried to tell you this. I can't stand the thought of having sex with him. I try, but when he touches me I completely freeze, it's awful.'

I am composed and matter of fact; she, however, is speechless.

'But Colin's an absolute ride, Ali, like, a total hottie. How could you not fancy him?' She tucks a strand of loose red hair behind her ear. I know she hasn't really understood what I said.

'I just don't. I don't know why but I don't fancy him at all any more. There is zero chemistry, Corina, it is gone.'

'Flipping hell,' is all she has.

'This is what I have been trying to tell you!' I say as the sound of my desk phone ringing brings us back to the present and I pick up. It's Colette asking me for the proposed teacher profile for the sign language funding proposal and can she see it before I submit. I tell her it's on the way and hang up.

'I have to get back to work,' I tell my best mate.

She slides off my desk and crouches down beside me.

'I didn't know it was this bad, Ali, I'm sorry. I just thought it would pass, that it was the usual seven, twelve-year-itch stuff. I was looking stuff up and …' She rises and gets her phone from her bag. She taps it and the light comes alive, she taps some more.

'Here … I found something on the internet I think may help you. His name is Mort Fertel and he helps people create extraordinary loving relationships. There are seven relationship skills you need to know by all means.'

I clear my throat in a way that says I'm not exactly convinced.

She flops back down onto her chair and says, 'Two minutes … listen, don't mock the power of the internet, Mr Mort has the answers to all your problems. He even covers the "What to do if you find yourself attracted to another man or woman" and "Two monthly acts that will restore the passion between you".'

'Spare me the American fix-it Mort man, please,' I sigh.

'OK, this won't take long, I promise, I'm going to give you a quick quiz. These are the main warning signs that your marriage will end in divorce, humour me if you will?' She winks at me and raises her HDs.

'Whatever,' I sigh harder.

She sits up straighter.

'Number one, do you and your partner spend hours together under the same roof, at social engagements or performing routine errands yet rarely engage in meaningful conversations?'

Has the Mort man been spying on No. 13?

'Yes. All the time. Next?' I sing the last word.

'Number two, do you feel your every action is being

147

watched and criticised by your partner? Can you do no right in their eyes?

'Tick. Next!'

'Number three, are your arguments becoming routine with all the same issues and no resolutions?'

'If I had a buzzer, I'd keep my hand on it. Next!'

'Number four, is there a considerable decline in physical affection—'

'I'm interested in this one,' I interrupt her. 'Is there a solution to any of these, by the way, from Mr Magic Mort?' I laugh sarcastically.

'Indeed, he has answers for them all, Ali, that's what I'm telling you, but, eh, you have to buy the audio book, I'm afraid … hold on …'

Her eyes scroll down. 'Here, he goes on a bit about this particular one, yeah: "Intimacy is the act that allows us to bond as husband and wife, if your partner is showing no or very little interest in intimacy with you then they are showing little concern for their emotional bond with you as husband or wife."'

He's saying I am the one to blame here, I am the one who has lost interest in sex, therefore I am the one showing no concern to Colin's emotional state as my husband.

'So if I buy his audio book, he will fix me and Colin. I'll suddenly be Samantha from *Sex and the City* every night, will I?'

'Meh.' She drops the phone onto the desk. 'All I'm saying is there is help if you want it. OK, maybe not Mort, but it's out there.'

'I've done some research of my own on married people, Corina, I've googled … Sure, lots of couples go through these phases all the time and come out the other side …' I pull my chair in and linger my finger over the keys on my laptop, I really do need to get back to Colette soon.

She stands and gathers up the empty latté cups.

'Just promise me you won't do anything silly with Owen this weekend. He isn't the answer. We'll figure it out when you get back, yeah?'

'I promise,' I say, but I'm crossing both my big toes over the next ones and I don't know why.

8

Just a normal Thursday. Or so I thought.

Worked hard all day and got loads done. On the walk back from Merrion Square, I feel contented with the applications I have put in. I always send an email attachment application and have a bound hard copy hand delivered. I like to work like that. No confusion. No electronic mix-ups. No: 'This didn't attach or that didn't attach.' No: 'I didn't get that.' Because it's all backed up by a silver paperclip in black-and-white in a brown padded envelope. I have no idea if Colin will be home.

I pop into Centra to grab a small bag of microwavable new baby potatoes; there are some chicken breasts and carrots in the fridge – I will do a little mini casserole for us this evening. As I come out of Centra I spot the bridal lingerie shop, Ideals, on the corner. I check out the window display for a split second before I dash through the traffic, push the door open and go in.

* * *

Colin's car is in the driveway as I open the front door. I haven't got the kids from Laura's yet, I still have half and hour. I usually make a quick coffee, get the dinner on and then run down the road. As soon as I open the door I hear my family.

'Muuummmyyyyyy!' Mark speeds down the hall and attaches himself to my legs.

'Hello, baby! Did Daddy collect you from Laura's, pet?' I bend down and hug him tightly.

'Hey there, Mom.' Jade swings her slim body on the doorframe of the front room. She's wearing a tweed cap on her head, with thick blonde locks tumbling out of it around her face, with her school uniform. On her feet, they may need to be surgically removed, her trusty Uggs. I take them over the high heel any day, but still. The main thing I can say about the Uggs is they aren't sexy, and I'm all for any clothes that are in fashion for eleven-year-old girls not being sexy.

During the summer Jade had begged and pleaded with me to buy her one of those revolting children's bra and knickers set from Penney's. 'Absolutely, categorically no way!' I had told her. There was no debate but we clashed for a long time over it. Karen had three sets in all different colours, she'd shouted at me as we drove away from the shop brown-paper-bagless. She never really forgave me, I guess.

'Come in here!' She drags me back to the here and now and believe it or not she is smiling brightly. Her words leave her mouth fast and I can't hear her American drawl either. Praise the Lord!

I take off my coat and carry my laptop bag and the small bag of microwavable potatoes into the kitchen. The table is laid with cutlery, condiments and plates with a massive cardboard pizza box in the middle. A bottle of wine is open and two wine glasses sit beside it. On the CD player Billy Joel sings about his Piano Man. The heating is on and my home is warm.

'What the …' I drop my bags onto the floor, completely blown away.

'Hiya, love!' Colin, in his black Adidas tracksuit, chequered tea towel slung over his shoulder, is at the oven.

'Hi.' I look at him quizzically.

'Garlic bread is just ready.' He bends and opens the oven and the smell is mouth-watering. He flaps the tea towel at the emerging heat. Then he comes over and takes my bags up and puts them on the counter.

'Well … this is a pleasant surpr—' I stop myself. I don't want anything that can be misconstrued coming out of my mouth.

'Thank you, Colin,' I say.

'Mummy, I don't like garlic bread, can I just have pizza, can I, can I?' Mark asks tugging at my shirt.

'Oscar got like another black mark on his card today, you know what he did, Mom? He like totalllllllllllly messed up …' Jade is talking so fast I can hardly catch any words. The young American has returned.

'Mummmmyyyy, can I? Daddy says I have to try the garlic bread.' Mark pulls at my arms now.

'He was like giving crap back to teacher and teacher was, like …' Jade speeds up.

'Mummmmmyyyyyyyy, can I? Can I?' Mark pulls and pulls.

'Kids! Stop! Let your mother get in the door, now go and wash your hands. Mark, you don't have to try the garlic bread; Jade, save your story about Oscar to tell us all over dinner.' Colin moves to the table and pulls out a chair for me.

'My lady.' He bows.

I smile at him and sit as he pushes my chair in. His hair is freshly washed and still damp. He is freshly shaved and smells of shower gel and Hugo Boss aftershave. He takes a piece of my new Winnie the Pooh kitchen roll and places it softly across my lap. Then he pours me a large glass of red.

'Wow, are they like that every evening? Now relax, Mrs Devlin.'

He is gorgeous, of course he is, I can see that. I think of the new expensive sexy underwear in my bag as I lift my glass. My nose automatically dives in and I inhale cherries and a bitter sweet euphoria. I take a long gulp. The kids come back and Colin serves the garlic bread and pizza at the same time. It's a Hawaiian pizza, my favourite but not Colin's – he doesn't even like pineapple yet he got this for me. Colin rolls his yellow-handled pizza cutter through the dough and he puts generous slices on all our plates.

'Whoever wants the garlic bread just tuck in.' Colin sits at the head of the table.

Jade recounts her story of naughty Oscar in her American accent as I plop a huge portion of mayonnaise on the side of my plate. By all accounts Oscar told teacher that he has no right to put his hand on his shoulder. Jade's hair is now piled up in a messy bun, she's still wearing her grey school uniform but she's one of those girls that can wear anything. Her white shirt collar is turned up on one side, deliberately yet casually wrong, the tie perfected

153

ever so slightly loose. A uniform suits her because she somehow makes it her own. I'm suddenly reminded of Colin in his school uniform, they are so alike. I love her so much. I want us to be closer. I want us to be best friends and I don't care if that's all sorts of wrong. I want all of her. Maybe I should have got the vile bra and knickers set, she'd love me so much more.

'Mummy, can I get Dark World Lego for my birthday?' Mark asks with the longest string of cheese pulling away from his mouth still attached to his slice. I want to say mind the uniform but I don't. I never ever allow them to eat dinner in the uniforms because I'm the one who has to wash them. I choose to say nothing.

'Isn't Dark World for over-eights?' The mayonnaise covers the base of my slice as I dip more and I bring it to my mouth. Hunger suddenly hits me and this is to die for. Is it possible that I am relaxed?

'Well, yeah, but, no … but, like, it's so deadly!' Mark's tomato-covered face is pleased with me. 'And Daniel has it and he's not even five till after Santie comes!'

'Daniel has older brothers though, that's probably why.' I lift my glass and warm it between my palms before I release the magical end of argument, the two words between mummy and son: 'We'll see.'

That's pleased him no end. He nods and smiles and tucks into another delectable triangle.

'Karen's family sit down like this like every night … like, her mom is, like, everyone has to eat together at five thirty. I used to be, like, "Urgh, you mean you all have to sit together while you eat dinner?" But, y'know, this is kinda nice, right?'

'It really is, love,' Colin says and it's not a dig. It's a fact. I get it.

★ ★ ★

We have a lovely family meal with so many laughs and we all get on famously. Colin has made a huge effort, I know that. It isn't going unappreciated. The kids are still eating but I'm carbed out now so I turn to him.

'Thanks for this,' I say softly.

'No bother at all.' He smiles.

'Did you finish early?' I keep my voice jolly.

'Well, sort of … not really … Maia took my last appointment.' He runs his index finger around the edge of the pizza box gathering the leftover cheese.

'That was nice of her,' I say.

Colin licks his finger and takes the slice I have left on my plate and I watch him peel the pineapple off.

'To be honest I think she's happy of the extra work now that she and Donal have split, she's a bit lonely I think.' He raises the slice to his mouth. I sip my wine. He chews, swallows, dabs his mouth with Winnie the Pooh and then says, 'I've put the emersion buttons down for you, so a bath should be ready to run after you have that glass. I've emptied the school bags, washed the lunch boxes and I will start with them on their homework.' Colin wipes his mouth now, and I catch him looking closely at the Winnie the Pooh print on the more expensive, less eco-friendly kitchen roll, but he is saying nothing. I could say it's Thursday and Jade needs extra help with her after-school Christmas art project on a Thursday, but I don't. I could

155

say he needs to go through Mark's hair with the fine-tooth comb after another letter home about nits in the classroom, but I don't.

I say nothing except, 'Thanks, Colin.'

★ ★ ★

When I emerge from my glorious soak, all coconut smelling, I go into my room to dry my hair. I stand again in front of my slightly opened wardrobe mirrored doors, both reflections stare back at me.

'It's going to be OK,' I whisper to both of me. 'Tonight you are going to put on some sexy underwear and make passionate love to your husband,' I mouth to the shocked reflections. Opening the bedroom door I pad quietly downstairs to grab my bag. They are watching *Tangled* and I can hear Flynn Ryder enquiring about Rapunzel's day. I sneak back up. If Mark hears me, he will run out. I close the bedroom door and drop my polka-dot robe. I study my body. It's in good nick – tummy a bit flabby but as I said I'm OK with that. I haven't been eating much at all lately either so I have lost a few pounds. My breasts are becoming slightly saggy, no longer the pert pair I once had. I am unshaven and wonder should I have shaved. It's tidy enough but a spot of landscaping wouldn't have gone amiss. I look at my face. I smile widely. Lines. A lot of small creeping lines. Laughter lines I suppose. Lived-in lines. I take my right hand and slowly pat the skin underneath my chin. I don't like the look of this. Sagging. Growing an additional chin, it would seem. Like Mother Nature has now decided one isn't enough. I stretch my neck up and out as I open my mouth and examine my teeth. Just like Owen I am the proud owner of characterful teeth, I suppose. Front two perfectly straight (just as well, as my mother never had the money to send me to a dentist), others slightly overlapping. I step back and look at my feet, Cherry Bomb has now gone from numerous toes. I need a repaint. Turning, I open the Ideals bag that's laid out on my bed. I remove my purchases; they are wrapped up lovingly in soft gold paper sealed together with a discrete gold sticker that bears the name of the shop. I unwrap the black lace quarter-length bra top and then the lace high-rise boy shorts; I remove the suspender belt and the barely black stockings. I stare at them. It has to be done. I dress in the garments quickly and slide my feet into my black patent Red or Dead high heels before I turn to look in the mirror. I wonder how I will look? I turn slowly and open my eyes.

'Oh, whoa! Not too bad,' I whisper to myself. I look damn sexy, if I say so myself. The underwear sucks me in in all the right places and I've blow dried my hair into a short but sleek ponytail because it is getting longer and I know Colin likes it back off my face. I'm kind of uncomfortable and on edge but I'm making the effort and that in itself feels strangely right. I'm doing the right thing. I want him to desire me, of course I do, but I wish I could desire him back. I think of Corina's call after she'd left my office.

'Hey, it's me again. I was thinking: OK, sex is a funny one … sometimes we need a little … well, assistance with it. Would you not think of watching a sexy video with Colin? Do what I said, buy the underwear: it will make *you* feel sexy and then suggest a little blue movie. He's a man, he will love the idea and it might just turn you on a bit more so that sex with Colin is good.'

I was blushing from head to toe on the other end of the phone. I'm not one to discuss my sex life, never have been, even with Corina who on the other hand is more open than that Dr Ruth.

'Will you try that for me?' she panted as she walked to her next appointment.

'He tried that the other night, showed me some horrible porno, a really young-looking girl; I couldn't stop thinking of Jade. I was really uncomfortable with it …' I shook my head to remove the image.

'So you choose something, something that you like.'

'I will try, OK … and I do appreciate your friendship, I know I must be a pain in the hole right now.'

'Ah, stop, it's life, Ali, it throws curveballs. But you need to be sure you can catch it or else duck, ya know? I might not have the greatest body in the world, or have the face of Cara Delevingne, but I make the best of what I've got. Man, the gear I got online to wear the first night with Trevor, it was top-notch sexy! I felt top-notch sexy in it! That's my point, I think.'

'I'm walking too, off to the Arts Council offices on Merrion Square, let's walk and talk?' I had said and we'd had a great chat on the phone and arranged to meet up next week for coffee and lemon cheesecake at the Pepper Palace when I was back from Amsterdam.

Kicking off the already uncomfortable heels, I leave them by my side of the bed. I grab my polka-dot robe and pull it around me. Tying the belt tight, I flick off all the lights upstairs, saving energy, and head down.

Mother is singing about how she knows best as I slide onto the sofa beside Colin. He isn't watching with them, he's on his iPad. I see the red, white and black colours of Manchester United's website. I wish he could watch the film with the kids and be in the moment. Jade doesn't like it any more, but it's the only compromise that she and Mark can come to. Colin refuses to get a second TV so I'm faced with their 'she wants, he wants' TV arguments day in and day out.

'Mmmmmm, you smell great.' He leans in.

'Shush, Daddy, this is the 'cary bit!' Mark shuffles back and settles himself between my legs.

'He'd climb back inside you if he could,' Colin whispers in my ear.

The knickers are riding up my bottom and I shift on the couch. I could do with another glass of wine I decide, and I push Mark gently up the rug and I excuse myself to get a 'drink'.

'Almost bedtime, lads,' Colin tells them.

I open the kitchen door and I audibly sigh. It's in bits. The leftover pizza box and dinner dishes are still uncleared from the table. Dirty plates and glasses piled in the sink. Homework copies and pencil cases scattered all over the place. Sexy momma gotta get her cleaning on. I don't moan, I just get on with it.

As I hand-wash the last glass and leave it to drip dry, Colin has taken the kids upstairs. It's late for them on a school night, it's after nine and they are still hyper. I remove the knickers from my bum with my middle finger, I now feel all sweaty in them and stiff. Colin comes back down.

'I gave Jade half an hour on the iPad … Oh, I'd have cleared all that up.' He looks around.

'It's fine, I don't mind,' I lie through my teeth. Spying the clean but empty colourful lunch boxes on the counter I go to the shelf and remove the wholemeal sliced bread and go about making the lunches. At least the lunch boxes have been emptied and washed. Colin seems satisfied with that as he sits at the table.

'Maia thought you looked really well today, by the way.' He wipes crumbs with his cupped hand and scoops them onto the floor. He gets up and gets the sweeping brush from beside the pedal bin. As he sweeps I say, 'I so didn't look well today, I hate rushing out the door, my make-up was crap and I felt wrecked all day … but totally my fault!' I add quickly.

'Are you all set for Friday, the business trip?' I swing my head to him but he's concentrating on a piece of dirt on the floor. He is barefoot now.

'I am – I'm looking forward to it actually.'

Honesty.

'Are you? Can't say I ever look forward to business trips away.' He rests his finger in his dimple looking at me.

Be nice, Ali.

'Mmmmm,' is all I say. The charcoal clouds are gathering. A storm is brewing.

'Ali, I'm glad you like your job, I really am …' He props himself up, leaning on the sweeping brush. 'But I will be honest, I would prefer if you were here for the children after school every day. I can't help how I feel. That's just me.'

'That's so unfair, Colin.' I put the butter knife down. 'I am doing my best.' I scratch my head.

'I'm not saying you're not, at all … I just want you to understand where I'm coming from. When we agreed to have children, it was my understanding that you were going to look after them.'

My breath releases on a high note.

'I *do* look after them! What is that supposed to mean?' My heart rate is speeding up. Adrenalin activated.

'Calm down, I thought we were going to talk … this is called an adult conversation, stay with me.' He lowers his voice and replaces the brush beside the bin. Bending, he gets the dustpan and small brush and picks up the dirt.

He is so patronising. I turn back to my bread.

He walks over and stands beside me.

'How nice was that? A family meal and be honest?'

'It was lovely … but it took the effort of you getting home early also … also I do eat with them every night, you know?'

He holds his hand up in front of my face.

'I get that, don't be nitpicking …' He wags his finger at me now. 'I try my best to get home for dinner every night, sometimes I'm just not able, but I'm talking about weekends too.'

'A-ha, you don't like me going to lunch on a Sunday with Corina.'

'I think it's selfish, Ali.' He shrugs his shoulders. Nonchalant.

'But I work all week, like a dog – both with the kids, the house and in my job!' I'm losing it now.

'A *job*, Ali, is supposed to bring money in, your *job* doesn't do that. All it does is pay for a stranger, who, after seeing her this evening wrecked out of her brain, is

161

definitely far too old and incapable to watch our kids after school … I'm not sure how you think that's OK? Don't yell, that's all I want to say.'

I slide the butter knife through the softened butter and scrape it onto the bread. His words ring out in my ears. I'm making holes in the bread I'm so heavy-handed with the knife.

'I love my kids more than anything in the world … more than you …' I whisper to the bread.

He leans against the fridge door. He didn't hear me. I continue.

'I love my job, I love getting out of the house all day, I love watching work being created, dance, theatre, art, whatever. I love working with the inner-city community … with the elderly and the disadvantaged kids …' I am trying desperately to explain myself once again.

'Or, you could be watching your own kids growing up.' He gives back.

'I am watching them growing up, what are you saying?' I grip the knife so tightly now my knuckles are protruding from under my tight white skin.

'Well, aren't they disadvantaged too by not having their mother here after school?'

'Oh, please, Colin …'

He interrupts me. 'And aren't you missing Jade's gymnastics show this week?' He straightens his back against the fridge, pulling the zipper on his tracksuit top up to the neck and back down again.

'Yeah, I am … God, how will life go on, Colin?' I slam the butter knife down now. Holes in the bread. Holes in the marriage.

162

'I'm just pointing out that I think family should come before "the arts", that's all.' He uses quotation signs with his fingers as he say The Arts.

So I'm supposed to hop into bed with this guy and ride him sideways in half an hour. I can't stand being in the same room, I can't hold back any longer. I have to tell him.

'I don't fancy you any more, Colin.' My words release on a shaky breath.

He is standing over me now, fridge rocking slightly from where he has pushed his body off it.

'What?' his voice croaks.

The sweeping brush falls over with a bang onto the grey slate tiled floor. I go on.

'You want us to have an adult conversation, well, there you have it. I … I don't know why … I just don't.' My lip quivers. I can never take this back and I can't believe I have started this conversation with the children in the next room.

'You sure you're just not frigid, Ali, because it's been some time since I ever imagined that you fancied me. That's not breaking news, love!' His baby-blue eyes are blazing in temper. Colin is very angry now.

I need to make sense of what I am saying. I grab his Adidas tracksuit top in my fist, twist the material and in hushed tone, I say, 'I *want* to fancy you … I *want* to desire you … I can I think, if you would just stop … just stop … talking.'

It's ridiculous. My reasoning is ridiculous. I stare at the missing Cherry Bomb. It's like me, neither here nor there.

'Stop talking? Have you lost your fucking mind?' He

163

grabs my hand roughly and pulls his tracksuit top free from my vice-like grip.

'Stop irritating me, I mean … here, look!' I pull open the belt on my polka-dot gown and hold it wide open. His eyes widen.

'I bought this for you … for us … for tonight … and after the pizza and your help, I was so keen to try and get us back … but then you say the shit you just said about me as a mother and my job and frankly, Colin … I hate you right now …' I do. I really do.

'Well, I hate you back, you stupid fucking bitch!' he screams at me, white spittle escaping and landing in my face.

'Dad!' Jade is at the doorway. 'I heard a crash … I'm – I'm … sorry …' She turns, runs down the hall.

My hands fly over my mouth and I go to move.

'Happy now? Leave her! We aren't finished … Has this lack of desire for your husband anything to do with your little fancy artist gobshite pal?'

'Where's Jade gone? Why are you fighting again? I hate when you always fight.' Mark rubs his eyes at the kitchen door now, his bottom lip covering his top. His little chin wobbling.

'Answer me!' Colin shouts into my face again, flecks of spittle all gathered at the sides of his mouth.

'Don't be ridiculous.' I move away towards Mark and usher him back inside whispering nothings into his ear. I close the door.

'Because all this shit started when he joined that fucking spastic zoo.' His face is blood-red with temper.

This can't be happening, my beautiful eleven-year-old

and tiny five-year-old cannot be subjected to this. I hate myself so much. I need to stop it. Now.

'Sorry … I'm sorry. I'm so, so sorry. Please stop screaming. Listen, it's me, I dunno … maybe it is hormonal, maybe … I'll get checked out by the GP …' I'm begging with every part of my being.

'Maybe you need a shrink!' He moves to the table and pours more red wine from the bottle into my half-full glass.

'You need to cop on to yourself or you are gonna be sorry.' He holds back his floppy hair from his eyes.

'Meaning?'

'Meaning … I'm watching you.' He necks the glass of red before continuing. 'I tried hard this evening because I thought after lunch today that was what you wanted,' he says now.

'It is and I do.' But it isn't and I don't. The children. I lower my voice.

'But I do this every day and night, Colin. Every day I do the school stuff and every night I collect them and I make their dinners, and I do the homework and I watch a movie with them … You ordered a pizza, and it was lovely, don't get me wrong. But I'm not giving up my job, Colin, because you ordered a pizza mid-week, why should I?'

'Did you not listen to one word I just said? Because you are a *mother* first and foremost, I know your own mother was a workaholic—'

I jump in.

'How dare you! My mother worked to keep a roof over my head and food on the table and made sure I got a good education!'

'And look at her now swanning, around India, not paying a blind bit of notice to her two grandchildren,' he scorns.

'She doesn't have to … and she always talks to them on the phone. She has her own life to lead, she's reared her child. She has no interest in raising her grandchildren and that's her perogative!' I am shouting now.

He is on top of me now and grabs my arm, not too tightly but I'm alarmed slightly at the colour in his face he has paled now completely.

'I don't know why you are trying to break us up, but you are – and if you keep this up, I swear to God you'll be sorry.'

'Is that another threat?' I gulp.

'It's not, it's me telling you to cop the fuck on … I'll do couples' counselling or whatever it is we need. I didn't come from a broken home like you and my kids won't either. Now go and flit around Amsterdam with your arty pals, look at blobs on a wall, or people throwing shapes in a dark alley, look at old rocks and ooh and ahhh over them, whatever. But you better come back to your real life with a different attitude.'

'That doesn't make any sense, my attitude is fine. You want me to give up my job and I won't.' I dig my heels in. They won't be seeing the Red or Dead black patent high heels again tonight obviously.

'You know what, Ali?' He is looking me up and down now, like I'm piece of shit on his good shoe.

'What?'

'I don't know who you are any more.'

I throw my eyes up to the ceiling.

166

'I'm going up to see our daughter.'

'Please, Colin … Can I go, please?' I am clasping my hands together, prayer like, begging him.

'No. You better get packed, aren't you leaving early.' He walks out of the kitchen and shuts the door. I hear him take Mark up from the front room.

I haven't smoked since I found out I was pregnant with Jade but right now I want a cigarette so badly. I want to scream. I neck some wine from the bottle and grab my phone from my bag under the table.

I pull out the chair and pour the rest of the bottle into Colin's glass.

With shaking fingers I open Facebook and message Corina.

Just told Colin I didn't fancy him any more. Send.

The little bubble with the dots appears. She is active and reading.

Oh shit. Are you OK?

No. Send.

What can I do?

Nothing. Send.

Are you still going in the morning?

Yes. Send.

Will I call you?

No. He will be listening. He's upstairs. The kids heard all the fighting again, I feel so terrible. Send. I choke back the burning tears as I type.

As I type my phone lights up.

A Facebook Messenger message from Owen O'Neill.

I open it.

Three words.

I have to scroll down.

Adjoining rooms baby.

He has added a .gif of the famous restaurant scene from *When Harry Met Sally*.

I message Corina back that I'm going to bed, I will call her from the airport in the morning. I stare at the Facebook message from Owen. Then I do something absolutely insane. I stand up slowly on the kitchen chair. When I have control on my balance I hold the phone in my right hand, extending it out as far and as high up as I possibly can. I unwrap my polka-dot robe and let it slide to the grey slate kitchen floor. Then I take a selfie of me in the sexy underwear and I send it to Owen.

9

Friday sunrise. Dublin Airport.

Not surprisingly I have a new Facebook message from Owen, which I cannot bring myself to open. I sit on the hard airport seat at my gate and sip a lukewarm latté, holding my passport and boarding card tightly between my knees.

This morning at four fifteen tears fell down my face as I kissed both my babies.

I'm an utter disgrace.

How could I have done that? Sent a picture like that? That's not me. I don't know who I am any more. How do I explain that one to Colin? To anyone in their right mind? It's torture. The fear has me paralysed.

I stand up – the gate area is still empty as I checked in so early and I'm not boarding for another hour. I put my passport and boarding card safely in the zip pocket of my bag and I walk to the toilets. Urine, bleach and heady perfumes hit my nostrils as I look in the full-length mirror. A pretty air hostess in a green-and-black uniform moves away, drying her hands on some hand towels. I'm dressed in a black suede skirt to my knee, black tights and high black leather boots. I have a white shirt on and my long red winter coat. I take out my messy make-up bag and smear on my Clinique

Dramatically Different moisturiser, then I edge to the side of the mirror so I'm not blocking the other women. I apply a light Mac Face & Body foundation and then lashings of mascara before I run a soft dark black kohl pencil several times on my lower lid. I'm not in a cat eye mood. When I'm happy I remove my phone. I walk outside and sit away from my gate. At an empty gate. Everything about me is empty. I slide across the bar and open his message.

Wow.

One word. That's it. I look at the picture. Oh my good God. I am so embarrassed. Humiliated. Cringe. Beyond mortified. Who am I? I have to call him. I just have to, before I see him face-to-face, I know that. Suddenly the phone rings out in my hand and I jump on it. It's Corina.

'I've put on half a stone in two days, how is that even possible? Good morning, how are we this morning? Are you checked in? What's the craic? Are you OK? I'm up for an early breakfast meeting. Holy crapola.'

I press my phone to my ear.

'Yes, at my gate now and you always look amazing,' I tell her.

'Trevorweight, I'm going to call it.' I hear her opening her wardrobe and rummaging between the clanking of hangers.

'Fecking Trevorweight is going to see me have to buy new clothes. Eh, hello! What the heck happened last night? Spill!' she orders me.

So I spill in hushed tones until I get to the end. To just before the selfie. I pause.

'So the underwear was a waste of money then ... Oh, Ali, you guys really do need to go and see a marriage

170

counsellor as soon as you get back. I'm so sorry the little ones overheard that. I used to hear my parents at each other's throats all the time and although kids are way more resilient than you think, it is still shit. Counselling saved their marriage. You know what I might do? I might try go see Jade in her gymnastics competition later if I can slip away. You said they are in rehearsals from eleven o'clock right? Maybe take her to Eddie Rockets for a strawberry milkshake on her lunch break? Would I be able to do that?'

'Oh, don't worry, Corina!' I say, knowing Jade won't want her there, as kind as she is to offer. 'There is more.'

I swallow hard.

'Well, what do you know, my grey culottes from Marks & Spencer's still fit … Praise me, a button that reaches across and fastens … Trevorweight needs to go! Sorry, now what else?' She puffs and pants down the line.

'I took a picture of myself, a selfie if you will, in the sexy underwear, after Colin stormed out and I sent it to Owen.'

I cough, gently putting my hand over my mouth even though there is no one around me to contaminate. Across the way I can see my numbered gate, which is now filling up with early morning passengers. I hear the creaking of a bed. Corina tries to get her voice out. It breaks several times. She clears her throat again.

'T-T-This … this is so not good, Ali. Why the—? What the—? What did he send back?' I can almost picture the look of pure horror on her freckled face.

'He just said wow,' I say quietly, placing no emphasis on the word.

'Dear Lord above …' I can hear she has now totally flopped back on the bed, it creaks under her.

171

'So there ya have it.' I exhale.

The tannoy announces the boarding of rows one to twenty and the imminent departure of my Aer Lingus flight EI 778 to Amsterdam and Corina hears it also. Aer Lingus are on the ball this morning. Looks like this flight won't miss its slot.

'I'm … I'm sorry. I need to think about this, Ali, I don't know what to say … Call me when you land – fly safely. Love you.' She rings off and I move down to my gate and sit apart from the heaving queue of eager passengers. I remain on the edge of the plastic seat until the last person goes through the gate and then I board my flight.

I love flying. Once I get over the initial panic attack I always have about the reality of where I am, I can enjoy it. I cannot remember the last time I travelled anywhere just on my own.

I stow a guidebook on Amsterdam in the seat pocket in front of me, the net straining to keep it in, and order a coffee and a cheese-and-ham toastie when the air hostess passes with her trolley. I thank her, and place them on my grey-coloured extended table top as I stare outside. The world looks perfect through my small oval- shaped window. Big blue sky with scattered fluffy white clouds, it coruscates with flashes of bright and beautiful sunlight and I lean my head against the thick glass while my coffee cools. The world is serene and quiet and I feel almost out of my own body. As though I have somehow escaped something. I have no control right now. No control over anything. No way of knowing what is happening in my world right now. It's strangely relaxing on this morning when I feel forty-five not thirty-five. I unclench my jaw. I loosen out my shoulders.

The fear still has a tight grasp on my heart over me sending such a terrible picture to Owen. I'm a mother of an eleven-year-old girl and a five-year-old boy; it's inexcusable. I did it in temper, I know, and the timing had a part to play, but I did it nonetheless. I sent a dirty picture of myself to another man. The fear crushes down on my heart and it gallops at a million miles an hour. *OK, Ali,* I say in my head. *You did it, it's done, all you can do is apologise to Owen and tell him the truth as embarrassing as it is. The truth shall set you free. Forget all this Owen nonsense. You can do good work this weekend, programme a really great show for the centre and go home and fix your broken marriage. Everything happens for a reason, right? Maybe this is my rock bottom.*

Carefully I peel the white plastic lid from my coffee, steam billowing out. It's still scalding. I open my cheese-and-ham toastie; the plastic is also boiling and sticks to the bread.

As soon as it cools, I peel it off, then I eat and drink, and feel somewhat better that I have decided to tell Owen the truth.

I draw my guidebook from the confines of the thick grey net. There is so much to see and do and I plan to see and do it all. This will possibly be the last trip I take on my own for some time.

Maybe I do have to seriously consider giving up the job, as much as I love it, we can't carry on like this. Perhaps I could do something from home. The thought of letting it all go, of rediscovering my normality, of simply giving in, actually mellows me out.

Putting my seat back just a fraction, I sip my coffee and wade through my guidebook until I come to our hotel, Hotel Falcon Plaza. It's a three-star in a great location, situated on Valkenburgerstraat. I thumb the pages, reading about the surrounding area.

Like I told Owen, I've never been to Amsterdam before. I'm excited. A new city for my eyes to behold. The added buzz of seeing two new shows reminds me how much I adore being in the theatre. Colette is on the afternoon flight with Michael and she wants to meet in the hotel bar at six o'clock for a quick drink and a chat before we all disperse to go and see our various dance shows, theatre shows, art exhibitions. *No idea what Owen booked to see*, I think, as I nibble on the end of my toastie, head buried in my travel book. I mark off some sights I'd like to see as a tin tube flies me through the skies at a million miles an hour.

10

Late morning. Room 141. Hotel Falcon Plaza. Amsterdam.

The flight takes less than an hour and a half and the taxi transfer is twenty minutes. In the black taxi cab I take in every view. Every street. Its people. The city has fifty-one museums, fifty-five theatres and more than one hundred and forty commercial art galleries, I'd educated myself on the plane. The canals whiz by as I stare at the bridges and bare trees that accompany them. This is one busy city with the most incredible architecture. I check my phone, I have no messages. As we pull up outside my hotel and I pay, I'm feeling all right. Excited even. I like that Ireland switched to the Euro, a shared currency, it makes me feel as though I belong in every city I visit, even though I still love the tradition of the pound. Christmas is all over Amsterdam and especially the hotel. Red-and-green lights twinkle at the reception desk and a huge real pine tree sways slightly in the breeze at the entrance. There is no sign of Owen in the hotel lobby, I'm relieved to see. I check in and then dash to the gold lift as fast as I can. I'm on the third floor, room 141, so I hit the button and it lights up red. The doors close and a deep voice informs me first in Dutch, '*Omhoog gaat*,' and then in English, 'Going up.'

I travel up. Locating my room, I take the key card from its white folder and slide it into the door handle slot. Red. Access denied. I try again. Red. Access denied. I miss keys. Last try or I have to go back down to reception. Green. Entry permitted. The door to the room next door creaks opens.

'*Goedemorgen, mevrouw.*' I hear the accented voice.

Owen steps out onto the narrow corridor on the hotel carpet. I notice it's navy, speckled with white stars.

'*Hoe gaat het?*' he says very seriously.

His accent is so funny, I can't help it, I burst out laughing. He is shirtless in navy jogging bottoms, drawstring loosely tied and in his bare feet. He laughs now too, leans in and pulls his room key card from the wall as his door clicks shut and he approaches me.

'Here, let me grab that for you.' He takes my small case and we step inside room 141. I don't even see what the room is like because I immediately turn to him. I can feel the colour exploding in my cheeks.

'Owen, I need to explain the picture,' I blurt out.

He puts my case on my small bed and sits on the edge. The room is not spacious. A single bed near the window, a table and lamp and a desk with TV. He says nothing. I stall. He looks so amazing.

His hair is freshly washed, I can smell almond shampoo. He looks bed-ready. He talks first.

'Ali, look, I know you're married and I know things aren't great, but I was thinking, after last night … how about we park all … all the shit for this weekend only and just live in the moment? Drink beer, see some works, see the sights and, feck, maybe even eat a hash brownie. Let's

176

not discuss Colin or analyse anything for two whole days. What will be will be. The last thing I want is for you to feel bad about what you did. It's not a big deal.'

The room seems so small and I can smell him so close and I am honestly in a way in love with him. I can't stop looking at his bare chest. It's intoxicating.

'It's not a big deal?' I tilt my head at him and scratch my head.

'Nope, it's just a picture. A very beautiful one granted, but I know you. I know you will be beating yourself up over it, so I think we don't ruin our weekend by analysing it. Let's just forget it ever happened.'

'You sure?' I ask.

'Hundred per cent. Now ...' He pushes his hands palms down between his legs and pushes himself up.

'Let's just savour this time together. Let's go and enjoy ourselves and this city. I hope you brought a pair of runners, did ya? 'Cause we have six whole hours before we have to meet Colette and Micko before we go see our shows tonight. I'd love if you spent them with me. What'ya say? *Ja? Nee?*' He rubs his hands down his bare chest. Then he stands in front of me and opens his arms out wide.

'*Ja*, you lunatic!' I say and I step into him. We stand in the moment. I feel completely alive. My head is light and my senses on high alert. He steps back and takes my face in his hands.

'You'll figure it all out in time. Right now I better get dressed, be back in five minutes.' He lets out a long slow breath as he opens my hotel room door. It shuts behind him.

I won't think about it.

I take off my red coat and hang it over the back of the chair. Opening my case I take out my white Nike runners and my blue jeans. My shirt is fine, I think, as I unfold my brown leather jacket.

I grab my phone and fly off a text to the kind mother who is collecting Jade and to Laura, just reminding them to still text or call Colin if they need anything but that I have now landed in Amsterdam, in case they need me. They know that already but it's more for my peace of mind.

I move towards the bathroom as Owen knocks on the door. Opening it, I let him in.

'Two seconds.' I grab my clothes to change in the bathroom.

'Sure I've seen it all before.' He bites his top lip and his smile runs along his top teeth.

'Seriously, piss off! I thought we had forgotten about it? It's still way too sore to be funny.' I half-laugh, though.

I shut the bathroom door and lean my back against it. *Everything's going to be fine.*

11

Late Friday morning.
De straten van Amsterdam (The streets of Amsterdam).
We elect to go see Anne Frank's house first, as Owen and I are both fascinated with her life story. Owen tells me it's only a twenty-six-minute walk to Prinsengracht from the hotel or we can grab a cab and be there in fifteen. I choose to walk. I want to see it all. Connect with the city physically. It's cold but crisp and early Christmas shoppers rush past as we tourists gaze around in awe.

'The museum is open on Christmas Day, that's mad, isn't it?' Owen says as he reads and walks. His arm rubs against my shoulder. 'Right, that's not bad for a poor artist, nine euro in. You know the way the Anne Frank House is made up of the former business premises of Otto Frank, including the secret annex, together with the new building next door? We are gonna get to see that annex, Ali,' he informs me in an amazed tone as he takes my elbow to manoeuvre me out of the way of a bicycle who's rider is ringing his bell. I tremble at his touch.

'The original building has as far as possible been kept in its original state; imagine that, Ali?' Owen holds the book down and looks up at me. 'It's still hard to get your head around, isn't it?'

I nod. It is.

'How can a world so beautiful be such a revolting, dark, murderous place?'

We have often had these conversations about our world, about the war-torn twentieth century all the way up to the present. Murder. Genocide. Terrorism. High school shootings. It's a scary place. To be sitting at your desk at 8.46 on a sunny September morning and have a commercial aircraft flown deliberately into your place of work. To be sitting in a cafe in central Paris, eating a warm pain au chocolat and a frothy cappuccino, only to be shot in the head. To be a child born in Syria. To be the parent of that child, trying to escape terrorism, knowing you face drowning in open waters. Wrong place, wrong time. We haven't come as far from Anne Frank's world as we might like to think.

'The museum has quotations from the diary, photos, films and original artefacts illustrating the events that took place in the hiding place. You know I was telling the Steffi Street kids as much as I could about Anne before I left for Belfast. In a weird way they could relate to it. James Rafter hid under his bed for two days when his da' was in hiding from the police for robbing the post office in Balbriggan. I must see if I can bring home something for him from the museum.'

We avoid another bell-ringing cyclist.

'You'd have made a brilliant teacher,' I tell him and I link his arm. It feels wonderful and I feel so completely free. His body heat immediately warms my cold hand. I'm free of all my responsibilities for two whole days. *My responsibilities.* It hits me. I can't think of my children right now because if I do I will burst into tears.

'I would have loved it but all I really want to do is paint, Ali, as shit as that is for me and anyone I may ever have to support or contribute financially to. I called Corina, did she tell you?'

My heart skips a beat.

'No, why?' *Am I jealous?*

'The exhibition, I'm finally going to do one. Apart from the fact I have to have one to apply for France, I think I'm ready to put myself out there to be judged. I have about four pieces I need to finish, which I'm planning to do after Christmas, and then I'm good to go.' He raises his eyebrows at me.

I nod.

Why didn't she tell me he'd called?

'And Corina's going to do the event for you?'

'Yup, and she said she won't take a penny! I insisted, of course, so she said if I sell anything on the night she will take her fee out of that sale, otherwise the deal's off. There's something so familiar about her, like I've known her all my life. She's deadly, isn't she?'

'She is.' We stop at the lights and I unfurl my arms from his. I turn him towards me.

'Why don't you have a girlfriend?'

He does a double-take. 'Where did that come out of?'

The crossing lights make a piercing beeping noise and we cross.

'I … I have … well, I suppose I'd never met anyone I wanted to be with day in and day out. A girlfriend isn't just for Christmas.' He smacks his lips together.

'Hmmm,' I say. I don't want to think about him leaving to go to work in France.

We walk along the river in silence until we reach the museum. Throngs of people are looking up, taking pictures on their cameras and iPhones. I get a chill immediately. This poor girl. This pretty average, middle-class Jewish family who tried to escape the horrors. This was the place it all happened. I cannot take it lightly. I stare at the plaque on the wall.

Anne Frank Huis.

My breath rises as the weather seems to turn colder. The secret annex was beyond incredible, I think as I look up. A true miracle. I know what Kitty Tead would say. The hand of God.

'Shall we go in?' Owen asks back with the tickets, waving them about in his right hand.

I nod. He is as emotional as I am. He takes my hand in his.

The warehouse is on the ground floor. We go up a short flight of stairs and into the office area. I can feel the hairs on the back of my neck rise as we study the various pictures together. I wish I could explain the smell to you but I can't. It's so unfamiliar. We move down, and in front of us we see the office of Otto Frank, then we take a right up another flight of stairs and there in front of me is the bookcase that I had read so often about, the bookcase that hid the entrance to the secret annex. One steep staircase and I am in her world.

Anne Frank was here.

Anne Frank was *here*.

I am completely overwhelmed. I think I am overwhelmed for lots of different reasons. I know the story, of course I do, so does every living person on this planet I imagine. As I stare at a chart on the wall recording the children's growth, a lump the size of a golf ball chokes into my throat and I find I can't swallow.

Selfish. I don't know who you are any more Ali. Selfish. The words hop around my brain.

I should be at Jade's gymnastics.

Should I?

Am I selfish? Or am I just a working mother?

Slow tears drop and Owen sees me and quizzically looks but he just hands me a crumpled up tissue. Here were parents who did everything for their children to protect them, to give them life. I try to compose myself as we move into Anne's bedroom, her pictures on her wall, her writing desk, her diary. It's all too much for me and I turn to Owen with free-flowing tears and sobbing runny snot.

'I have to get out of here.' I turn and he follows.

He puts his arm around me. Protecting me.

We push past the tourists and out into the air. He cradles my sobbing head into the crook of his arm and we walk, straight down the road and into the Two Swans, a bar and cafe. Owen leans over the bar.

'*Toiletten alsjeblieft*,' he says.

The woman points to the back of the bar and I go. I can't stop crying. I must look a complete mess. I enter the toilet and grab a roll of yellow toilet paper, tear some off and wet it in the sink. I dab my eyes. I miss my children so much. I've a physical ache in my tummy now. I want them to have a happy life and if that means me giving up my job and making my marriage work with Colin then so be it. Decision made. I take my phone out of my brown leather jacket's inside pocket and I text Colin.

Colin, I don't want to fight any more. I'll hand in my notice at work.

I send the message and watch it go and I clean myself up a bit more. I feel better already.

At the back of the bar Owen has secured a free low table and two drinks.

'You all right?' He jumps up.

'Sorry, yeah. I'm so sorry … I ruined Anne's house for you.' I pull out the small wooden three-legged stool and sit down.

'No, you didn't, I promise. Here, I got us a whiskey each, and there's water in the jug if you like?'

'I think I'm going to give up the job, Owen,' I say as I sniff and sip my smoky whiskey. It burns my throat and the pain feels great.

'What? Why?' He slides off his motorbike jacket and I take in the tight black V-neck T-shirt he's wearing under-neath it. He tugs at the sleeves a bit.

'Because I'm a shit mother and my children will have shit lives if I don't.' I take a sharp breath in through my nose to stop any more crying.

He reaches across and takes my cold hands.

'You're a brilliant mother, Ali. I've seen you with the kids, you talk so proudly about them all the time, why are you saying this?' He runs his thumbs across my knuckles.

'Because the main thing Colin and I flight over is this job: he doesn't want me to work outside the home,' I explain.

He doesn't jump in, he just removes his hands from

mine, sips his whiskey and swirls the golden liquid around his glass.

'I won't … I can't comment on your marriage, Ali, I'm just not that type of guy. That's your personal business, you and him, but you are my friend, and you are exceptional at your job, and like millions of mothers all over the world you do both jobs amazingly well. I think you are incredible.'

He raises his glass and I raise mine and we clink.

My phone beeps. I grab it out from the inside pocket. It's not Colin, it's Corina. The text is a reminder. I never heard it beep.

Hey. I'm going to go over early to Jade's gymnastics competition so don't fret I'll send you some videos and loads of pics so you won't miss a thing.

God, she's wonderful.

'OK?' he asks.

'Yeah, Corina's going to go see Jade's gymnastics rehearsals.' I push the phone into the back pocket of my jeans now. It's strange Colin hasn't replied to that text.

Owen pushes the jug of water out of our way.

'OK, this is a bit out there, but it's still early and we have till six p.m. I propose we go to a coffee shop, have a little smokey joe and then take our raging appetite for a slap-up lunch of tagliatelle and linguine, or seafood, whatever, with some great red wine.'

I make a face.

'Oh, I dunno, it's been years since I smoked a joint … and even then I only tried it once at Croke Park seeing U2 because someone handed it to me. I'd nearly be afraid. It is a work trip, after all?' I wince. I'm not good at being out of control.

185

'Tell you what, you eat a little brownie and I'll have a little joint. We will ask for something really light and mild and fun, because you know what, Ali, you really do need a laugh.' He finishes his whiskey and places it dead centre of the square beer mat.

'I really want to go and see the Teylers Museum today too though, I don't want to waste a minute of this city.' I bend over to the floor and pull my travel book out of my bag and flick through the thin pages.

'Promise we will do both. Have you ever been to a museum stoned?' He reaches out and takes the book from me just as I locate the marked page.

'No!' I shake my head wildly, my ponytail coming loose so I shake my hair out. I run my fingers through it, its gathering some length and I like this grown-out crop. It makes me feel younger. I'm not sure what it looks like, but I don't care. I push my fringe to the side.

'It's amazing, trust me, Ali.' He reads the page in front of him on the Teylers Museum.

I pinch the bridge of my nose lightly. I feel a bit weak at the knees again. It's the way he says the words *Trust me, Ali*. Like, I hear in them a romantic intent.

I stare at him holding my travel guide, his amazing big brown eyes darting over the pages and I'd still love to strip him naked and ride him like Seabiscuit, but I can't and that's just the way it is. This might be the very last day I ever spend alone with Owen O'Neill. I knock back my whiskey. I am only thirty-five. Can you prefix thirty-five with the word only? I don't know. I don't know how old I'm supposed to feel. I still feel young, and today I'm going to have some fun. I've made my decision: on Monday I will hand in my notice to Colette and as soon as she can replace me I will be a full-time stay-at-home mum. This is somehow feeling like my 'hens' weekend: after this weekend I'm no longer a working mother.

'Shall we?' I stand, determined to enjoy these next two days, and outstretch my hand. He stands and takes it. Skin on skin.

'Yes! Come on, let's have a bit of craic!' He lets go and hands me back my guidebook and I stuff it down deep into my bag as he shoves his arms back into his biker jacket.

We stroll outside and hail a cab.

'*Smokey coffee shop alsjeblieft?*' He tries his best with the accent, in fairness.

The car speeds off and we knock our heads together as we roar laughing.

12

Friday mid-afternoon. Smokey's. Amsterdam.
Smokey's is nothing like I might have imagined inside.
It's very civilised and quiet, and cool-looking people
lounge around, not fall around, chatting and laughing.
A lot of people are drinking coffee and eating snacks.
It all seems so normal and not choked with smoke like
I had expected. There is sawdust on the old wooden
floor and the bright yellow walls are hung with various
pictures. A strange sweet tobacco scent is in the air. We
take a seat on the soft fabric-backed chairs and look
at the smoking menu propped up in front of us. It's
incredible that all this is legal. A waiter with dreadlocks
approaches us, about the only cliché I can spot in here.

'English?' he asks in an English accent as he stands
beside us.

'Irish.' Owen says.

'Deadly buzz.' He imitates our lingo and we laugh.

'So you need any help with the menu, mate?' the waiter
asks Owen now. Londoner, I'd say. East End.

'We do actually. I'd love a light, happy smoke and for
the lady a light, happy hash cake?' Owen looks up at him.

'Just something chilled with the giggles, am I right,
mate?' He wipes the table with a dark cloth.

Owen nods.

'Right, we have hash which is solid or weed which is grass and we charge by the gram – I have pre-rolled joints available.' He replaces the menu and turns to me.

'Well, darlin', I'd advise if you're not a regular marijuana user, just half a hash cake first – just to say, don't be tempted to eat the other half if you don't feel anything after fifteen minutes, the drug can take a while to work its way into your bloodstream, it can also dip in an hour and come back, so you know the effect can be mildly hallucinogenic and often disorientating so just make sure you guys are all comfortable with that, we don't serve alcohol and smoking regular cigarettes is illegal, we have hot drinks, sodas and snacks available though too.' He says all of this very long sentence without taking a breath.

'OK, I'll happily take your advice,' I tell him.

He removes the menu again from the table and points out different options to Owen. His nails are longer than would be usual on a man. Owen orders a pre-rolled grass joint promising a happy, giddy, mellow buzz and also orders two black coffees.

'I'm a bit scared,' I confess. It's warm in here and I remove my brown leather jacket and open the top button on my white shirt. Owen remains in his jacket.

'I promise there is nothing to be scared of and that you will thank me. You need a release so badly. You know that your shoulders are literally sitting up under your ears?' He does an impression of me. He looks like Benny Hill.

'They're not,' I say, and then I check them and they so are. I try to release them down; the shift in posture feels great. No wonder my neck has been sore a lot lately. I rub my shoulders with alternating hands.

'Will Colette and Michael not see we're stoned?' I ask him.

'We won't be stoned by then, we're aren't getting bombed out of our minds, Ali, just a little light stimulant to make us relax and laugh. Then we'll go see the museum with open minds and we will have had a huge feed and it will have worn off. You do know Michael is a regular marijuana user for his MS?'

'Really?' I didn't know that.

'Medicinal. Prescribed,' he informs me.

'I don't have many conversations with Michael,' I tell him.

'He's more of a man's man, as he puts it.' Owen scrunches up his perfect nose.

The waiter is back and places my hash cake in front of me. It is cut into two halves on a normal plate sitting on a normal white napkin. It looks so innocent, like any slice of cake you'd get anywhere on a Friday afternoon. Owen takes his joint, a long, fat, white cigarette with twisted paper at the end. He strikes a match from the free strike-anywhere matches that are on the table, cups his hands and lights the fat end. The waiter places two huge yellow mugs of coffee in front of us.

'Milk and sugar's on the table, enjoy,' he says as he takes his leave.

'*Bon appétit!*' Owen says. 'I didn't learn that one in Dutch sorry.'

He inhales deeply and holds it in, his mouth shut tight.

I take a tiny bite and a huge sip of coffee straight after,

so I can't really taste the cake. It's amazing the weight I feel lifted off my shoulders, thinking how happy Colin's going to be to get my text. Happy Colin equals happy kids.

Owen exhales slowly. 'Nice.' He laughs through a bloom of smoke. 'So if I go to France and you give up work, doesn't look like we will see each other for a while anyway, hey?'

He inhales again.

'No.' I take another bite on its own this time, it tastes like spicy chocolate. Still, I don't feel a thing. I take another bite and drink more coffee.

'I suppose the thing is, I simply can't live a happy life if I feel I'm doing wrong by the kids, ya know?' I lick some cake that is stuck to the prongs of the fork.

'Yeah, I get that,' he says.

We sit in comfortable silence for a while.

'It's like my happiness is fuelled by their happiness. Maybe when they are eighteen or when they want to move out we can meet in here and run away together, start a new life somewhere … hot, on a beach preferably? Laugh our heads off day in and day out.' I eat a bigger piece now. It's actually really good. Or as Jade would say, *reaaalllyy reaaaally reaaaally gud*.

I stop. I didn't have a panic attack thinking about Jade just there.

I eat two huge spoonfuls. Chewing quickly, swallowing the calmness down. I try to think of the kids now but my brain is taking me somewhere else. I can see a golden sandy beach, blazing sun and coral blue skies. Where is that?

Owen exhales smoke all around me.

Oh, it's a painting on the wall near the toilet. I laugh as I look around at the different paintings.

'Do you believe in the one, Ali?' he asks.

'The one what?' I ask trying to focus.

'The one person for everyone out there. Your lobster. Your soulmate, get it?' He drags hard and holds the smoke in again. 'S. O. U. L. mate?' he spells the word and chuckles as a burst of smoke erupts from his moth and out down through his nostrils. He coughs and splutters.

I swallow and take a drink of my coffee, not really minding him.

'I do. What a comedian you are. I'd say Peter Kay is shitting himself! I used to believe in the one … I don't know now. Nah … I don't think so. I'm definitely the wrong person to ask right now.'

'Colin was the one once.' He isn't probing, he's just interested.

'Yeah, of course he was, Owen, but I was so young. I didn't know who I was, let alone who he was … I had no comparisons, ya know?' I try to explain.

'Got it.' Owen removes his biker jacket now and I am drawn to the tight black V-neck T-shirt and the body I saw underneath it this morning.

'What do you get from relationships then?' I ask him. 'You are too clever to commit, you did the right thing staying single. I haven't really known you to go on a date in the last six months. Have you?'

'Oh, Jesus no! I don't do dates. Awful things!' He physically shivers.

'So what if you like someone, and you want to get to know them better?'

'I join an arts centre and feck off to Amsterdam with them for the weekend.' He clicks his tongue off the roof of his mouth.

'Got me there!' I laugh as he talks at the exact same time.

'Gotcha!' He blows smoke of the end off a finger gun he's pointed at me. I laugh now. I have a sudden vision of Owen in a suit, driving to his office, kids screaming in the back. I dunno why, but it's really funny to me.

'What's so funny?' he asks and I tell him. His expression changes.

'I'd have liked to want to wear a suit and to drive a Lexus. I'd have fitted into this world easier. It's not easy to explain to people that you are a poor artist hurtling a little too fast toward the big Four Zero with no partner, no house, no mortgage and no kids. Well, especially to family members,' he tells me.

'But who says that's what we should all strive to have? Granted I wouldn't change my kids for anything, ever, but I'd prefer to be single with them … Right now anyway,' I add.

'Would you really? Could you really see your life without Colin in it?' He holds the joint between his first two fingers and I see his eyes are a little misty. I take the last bite of my first half. Still I feel nothing. I must have got a dud. Dud is a weird word, isn't it? In fact words are weird, aren't they?

'If you are asking me right now, right in this very moment, then yes. I don't feel like I'm in love with him any more. I don't fancy him, I don't like how he speaks to me, I don't get that he doesn't want me to be happy, but I'm willing to keep trying for the sake of my kids,' I tell him.

'God, do you know how beautiful you are, Ali?' He leans in and balances the joint in a groove on the lip of the astray.

My jaw drops.

'Stop … I'm not …' I put my fork down and lick my teeth with my tongue. *He thinks I'm beautiful. He thinks I'm beautiful. Don't say anything stupid*, I tell the numskulls running my brain. *Don't speak at all.* I can see the little people from *Inside Out*, Joy and Disgust and Fear, controlling my mouth and I'm relieved to see them with black gaffer tape gags on. I am safe.

He is still talking.

'You really are. You tick every box for me, Ali, every box – physically and intellectually … God, you are so easy to be around. I know it's not … we're not … Colin doesn't know how lucky he is.' He scratches his neck.

I don't scratch my head, instead I feel myself relax. I feel his words wash over me like warm seawater. I am thermal inside. I perceive our chemistry to be unique. I allow myself to feel it all. He looks to me to speak next.

'That's so nice of you to say. It's just all so complicated now.' I pause. 'Life, I mean. It used to be so simple.'

We have controlled eye contact.

'It shouldn't be complicated all the time, it should be enjoyed. We are here for a good time not a long time.' He picks up his coffee.

'In an ideal world, yes, but when you have a marriage

and children it is work, Owen. It's not always a party.' I lick my dry bottom lip.

'Work should be work and life should be life. It can't be all work, Ali, where's the enjoyment? I'm not saying it should be a party either, but it certainly shouldn't be a funeral.'

'Don't they say nothing worth having ever comes easy?' I sit up straight on my stool, push my fringe out of my eyes and I think. I really think for the first time in months. He's so right. Where is my enjoyment? The children obviously bring me a unique and pure joy, but, yeah, I will admit to myself, here and now, they take work. It's hard work being a mother. So what else do I enjoy?

I raise my hand to Owen to signal I am still very much in deep thought. He relights his joint catching his fingers on the match as he does so. He shakes his slightly burnt hand repeatedly.

Work. I enjoy work.

But that's causing so many problems, it's becoming tainted. Corina! She pops into my mind's eye, waving, winking, chatting, laughing, eating, drinking, dancing.

'Corina. Our once-a-week Sunday afternoons. I love them! I enjoy those few hours so, so much.' I clap my hands together.

'Do it twice a week, so,' he exhales.

'Ha! Are you having a laugh? I barely get that one Sunday afternoon with her, and there is always an atmosphere when I return. In fact, Colin wants me to give up the Sunday afternoons too … He thinks we should all be sitting down to a family dinner on a Sunday.'

I know I'm not exactly painting a brilliant picture of my

husband to the man I'm getting stoned with, to the man who has just told me I tick all the boxes for him, but it is the truth. Owen starts to hum. I know the tune. I listen. My hearing is heightened, I can hear various conversations around the room also. It's that Taylor Swift song that Jade plays over and over. It's Karen's ringtone on her phone – another bone of contention between Jade and me, Karen being allowed an iPhone. Owen's still humming but I know the name, what is it now? Oh, yeah. 'Shake It Off'.

'You're right.' I start moving on my stool as the song spins in my mind. I spotted a jukebox in the corner at the entrance of the bar as we came in.

'I wonder,' I say and my voice sounds very high-pitched as I pull my purse out and get up. Over at the music-making machine I flick through the titles, and there she is. Madam Swift. I am way too old for Taylor Swift, but right now I don't give a damn. I wanna hear this song. I punch in my selection, R and 2, and push down on the red button. It springs to our ears. Owen laughs from the end of the room. I start to move towards him. I'm not walking, nor am I dancing. I'm prancing: I'm on a catwalk and it feels wonderful. Strutting now, as Taylor hits the chorus, I raise both my hands and brush myself down just as Taylor does in her video. This song should be the national anthem. The lyrics are so good. I hit our table with both hands and Owen jumps up. And then we dance.

We dance around our table like two silly, carefree teenagers. He seems to know all the words, I know a few, enough to get by. He takes my hands and twirls me and I spin. I spin and I spin.

So many haters in the world, she is right. So many

people who don't want the best for others. So many people who want to hurt one another. My fringe is in my eyes and I throw my head back and let the music wash over me. The music is just so intense.

What great advice for one so young. Shake it off.

Shake it all the fuck off!

Who knew I was such a good dancer? It's been so long. I feel incredibly sexy as my body gyrates to the music. Owen is playing air guitar now and then I start to laugh. This is all so absurd so I laugh more. I snort laugh. I start to laugh so hard I have to hold onto my stomach. It aches. I am doubled over. I wish it would stop. It's so funny, I'm sore. Owen's just staring at me, hand in the air waiting to strum his imaginary chords but then he looks down at his non-existent guitar and he starts. His laugh is so contagious; he slaps his knee when he laughs and suddenly the two of us are literally crying with laughter, our heads thrown back, standing up, tears rolling down our cheeks. This is the best chocolate cake I've ever had in my entire life!

'Everything all right here, guys?' Our waiter is back. 'Good stuff, mates, yeah?' he enquires, his eyes narrowed at us both.

'Brilliant, sorry, apologies, mate. They were playing our song.' Owen holds up his hand and wipes the palms of his hands across his wet eyes.

'No need to apologise, it's a happy house! Belly laughs are greatly encouraged, they keep us in business.' He removes the empty yellow coffee mugs. 'Refills?' he asks.

'Please,' I say. My stomach aches. I try to catch my breath and sit down holding my upper torso up straight.

I'm actually sweating. There are two little wet patches under the arms of my white shirt.

'Oh, man, I haven't laughed like that in years … like, not since I peed myself on the headmistress's floor for drinking the communion wine,' I pant.

'Ahh, me neither, that was brilliant.' He sits back down now too. He inches his stool from across the table to beside mine. And when we settle, he says, 'I meant what I said though.'

I sweep my fringe to the side, trying to keep my arms tight to my body. He takes my hand.

'I know you did and I feel the same way too, but there's nothing I can do about it. Not while I'm still married. And I have to try and stay married for the kids.' I'm deadly serious.

He nods slowly, removes his hand from mine, reaches in and picks up his tiny joint from the ashtray. He holds it between his thumb and index finger and puts the flame from a match to it. Then he puts it to his mouth and drags.

'Just my luck, huh? I wait and wait to find the right one and when I do she's already married … already met her lobster.' He blows the smoke, pillowing out, high above my head.

'I dunno about that.' I stop as the coffees arrive. I take a chunk from the other half of the cake, swallow it down and then another.

'I didn't delete the picture by the way.' He tries to hold back his breaking smile. His incisors creeping over his bottom lip.

'I'm too stoned to be embarrassed, so this is a good time to talk about it. I have to be honest: I was wearing that for

Colin, to see if I could try and fix our awful sex life … It didn't work. I should never have sent it to you, it was very wrong of me.'

'That didn't work? Is he fucking blind as well as a dictator?' Owen coughs on his exhale.

'Delete it please, will you?' I ask.

'I will, I promise.' He drags hard on the butt and on the exhale, he speaks.

'Oh, if I had you in my bed in that gear. I can't … I can't tell you, buddy …' His voice is low and husky.

'What?' I'm stoned as hell again now and brave as hell, I realise, as the marijuana hits me and my whole body tingles. I feel a rush from the tip of my toes to the top of my head. My heart is thumping; like, I can feel it's every beat, but I also feel so calm.

'Huh?' he says through closed mouth, holding the end of his smoke deep into his lungs.

And then I think of Colin and how he speaks to me and how he treats me and how he doesn't deserve me.

'What would you do to me, Owen?' I ask seductively, staring into his gorgeous face. I can tell he's confused.

'Come on! I can't go there … I won't be able to stand up to go to the bathroom!' He laughs and pushes back his stool. When he's gone I look all around me. How did I not notice how beautiful this room was before? The bright yellow paint on the walls like a magnificent sunrise, and the small windows where the light creeps through stained glass, like in an old church. I look at my hands. What a creation they are. I wiggle my fingers, these things, these fingers that move … All the things they can do … Amazing. How could we do stuff without fingers? My engagement and wedding rings look so shiny. The phone beeps in my back pocket and I take it out and marvel at the technology of it all. I turn it around in my hands. This slim machine joining the world together. Technology is a genius. I hold the phone at arm's length as I find my focus. A few missed calls from Corina. Two texts. Must have been while I was dancing. How is it possible that we can speak to each other in different countries? It's unbelievable when you really think about it. How can I type letters on my phone and those letters then appear on someone else's phone somewhere else? Astonishing. Beautiful, wonderful, Corina. I open her message first.

CAN'T GET YOU!!! YOU NEED TO CALL ME IMMEDIATELY!!!!

She is so good, she wants to tell me all about Jade I know. I hope that Jade got a medal for participating. They do that these days. No one is a loser, not like my day when I always came last in sport. I flick up and there are pictures from earlier she has sent of my beautiful daughter. She looks great in her new leotard. A selfie of herself and Corina. I stare at their faces. Jade's beauty is exceptional. Corina winks at me. That's mad! How did she do that?

'Hello?' I speak to the picture. Nothing. Then I open Colin's reply to my last text.

GO TO HELL YOU STUPID BITCH.

Whatevs, I say to him in my head.

'All right?' Owen sits. I can smell the bathroom soap from his hands. It's like banana and something else. I sniff the air. It will come to me. I click the button on the side of my iPhone 6 and the screen goes dark. Colin can't upset me today, he can't rile my temper today, I just won't let

200

him. So long, sucker. Life-blood sucker.

'I'd love a big fizzy pint of beer and some cheese-and-onion crisps?' I slide the phone into the side pocket of my bag and drop it to the floor. My mouth is very dry.

'No beer here. Wanna finish your cake and I can get you beer and food at the Teylers Museum? Your little book said there is a really nice cafe in the Garden Room "with a delightful view of the museum's courtyard". It said, if we look carefully, we will see an "art tree" here. Hand me that book again, will ya?' He holds out his banana-smelling hand.

I pull the book back out as he flicks to the marked page again.

'Yeah, here it is … the art tree. "A lime tree standing on five feet, made by the artist Sjoerd Bu … Bui … Buisman in 1948." Like you can only get to this cafe if you are a visitor to the museum. I really wanna see that. Seems fitting for us today, don't you think? We still have a few hours.' He runs his hand carefully over the cover of the guidebook.

I find the movement extremely erotic. I push myself closer to him.

'I just want to smell you,' I tell him and I lean my face into his neck and inhale him. Is the other smell pear? We sit this close for what seems like an age but could only be minutes and I smell and smell. Precious minutes. I will never get this close to him again.

'This is sooooo nice,' he moans as he leans his shaven head against mine.

I just listen to his heart beat and his breath.

Ba-boom.

Ba-boom.

Ba-boom. Everything as it should be.

'OK, let's go, Ali,' he says eventually. I don't want to go, I never want to leave this bit of heaven on earth. But I do.

'Thanks, man.' Owen gets down with the waiter's lingo as we pull on our leather jackets. Owen pays our bill and we head to the door. On the way I spot a Ms Pac-Man machine.

'Oh, Ms Pac-Man! One game please!' I pull Owen to the machine, nearly tripping him as he tries to zip up his jacket.

'A euro, have you got a euro?' I ask. 'I used my last one on the jukebox.' I'm so excited. This was my favourite game as a kid. He rummages in the front pockets of his jeans and pulls out a handful of coins. I flick through them in the palm of his hand and find my euro and slot it in.

Beep-beep. Beep-beep.

Ms Pac-Man comes to life. All the yellow dots start winking at me as I negotiate the hungry, circular, open mouth around the screen.

'There … there's a ghost!' Owen shouts at me and I laugh hard as I wiggle the stick and move my body to escape the menacing ghosts. Then all of a sudden I see myself in the machine.

It's me.

I'm Ms Pac-Man.

I mean, there's a small round yellow ball with a red bow in its hair but it's me. My face. My hair. How did I get in here? I know what I've gotta do: I've gotta get the hell out. It's a sign. I yank the leaver down vigorously and drag myself around the screen, swallowing all the yellow dots as I move, just as they turn into Colin, eating them as I go. Eating every Colin I see.

'Let me out,' I say to myself from inside the machine.

'I don't want to be stuck in here any more. I need to be free!' Ms Pac-Man me shouts.

'I know you do,' I tell myself.

'What?' Owen asks me. He has been staring out the window in a daze.

'I need to be free!' I get eaten by a ghostly Colin.

'Fuck. Give me another euro!' I jam my hand this time into his front jeans pocket and he gasps under the rummaging of my hand.

'Are you OK?' He looks at me, his eyes totally glazed now.

'A few more games, that's all … I think the universe is talking to me through Ms Pac-Man.'

Owen seems somehow to understand and he goes back to staring out the window. I slot the money in.

Beep-beep. Beep-beep.

And I am off. Where is she? Where is that little red-bow-haired me? A-ha, there I am. This time I'm my normal self. I'm not Ms Pac-Man; it's just me, Ali Devlin, in jeans and a white shirt, eating the little yellow balls. No longer Colin, just balls. I stare at me. I've changed. Now I'm wearing a fantastic full-length ballgown. It's a skin-tight red halter-neck with a long flowing skirt. I turn. It's backless. My hair is so long. It's all curly and tousled. I look incredible.

'You look amazing,' I tell myself.

'It's all a show,' I whisper out from in between a maze of yellow dots.

'Are you OK?' I ask myself into the dark glass of the game.

'No. I'm trapped within myself,' I tell myself.

'I will set you free!'

I play the greatest game of Ms Pac-Man I have ever played and at the end the computer asks me to input my name, I have done so well. There it is: Ms Ali Devlin, number seven on the leader board.

'That's pretty impressive stuff,' our waiter tells me.

'Ready now?' Owen is trying not to laugh.

I grab my bag from him.

'That was absolutely mental,' I tell him as the freezing December air hits me and my head comes back to normal somewhat. My thinking is clearer again. We walk in stoned silence until we hail a cab at the end of a wide, tree-lined street. It's very welcome, the heat of this taxi, as we sit very close together.

'Teylers Museum … Haarlem … eh … er … please … damn, I've forgotten all me Dutch!'

Owen reaches down for my hands and I give them. He warms them between the palms of his own, taking them to his mouth and blowing hot air on them. We look out the window at the darkening December afternoon in Amsterdam. Bicycles criss-cross in the traffic and we don't talk. My head is calm now. There is no anxiety for the first time in so long. I can tell you now, it's just as well I don't live here – not only would I be twenty stone, eating all that cake all day, I'd be stoned every day. If this is being stoned, then I like it. My shoulders seem looser than they have been in months. Flickering Christmas fairy lights twinkle on buildings and shops are decked out with festive trees in every window.

204

'You OK?' He's still rubbing my hands.

'Mmmmm.' I smile at him and he laughs at me.

'What?' I ask.

'Nothing … Just don't think I've ever seen you so relaxed.' His words come out slowly.

When we pull up at our destination, Spaarne 16, the Teylers Museum. I'm all ready for it. I want to see things that will stay with me for ever. A large red flag flies above the entrance, waving wildly at us in the wind. I can hear the wind flap it about. We enter hand in hand. Ridiculous and risky, I know, and as we enter I inhale that museum smell. Those smells of history. Of time passed. We release each other as we walk around and gather various information leaflets. Owen pays for our tickets.

'That was my twist: you got the last tickets and the bill and the taxis.' I *tut-tut*.

'I want to pay for you, please?'

I hand him some information. Crowds throng in. It's a busy day.

'Oh, look, the Real Winters exhibition, perfect for us here in the depths of winter. "It's an exhibition of the most beautiful nineteenth-century Dutch winter landscapes and winter scenes,"' he reads and is very excited. He unzips his leather jacket. It's all very surreal now, kind of an out of body experience. I try to swallow but I am absolutely parched.

'Follow me,' Owen says and we walk across the echoing foyer and up the stairs. We walk through an oval-shaped room and up another flight of stairs to the first-floor balustrades. Then we enter the library.

It's breathtaking. I love it all. I stand and do a 360-degree turn, taking it all in as I close my eyes and inhale the smell of the old books. My head's still muzzy. From this spot we can look around the entire library. I move carefully across the old wooden floor as it creaks beneath another new visitor.

Owen walks ahead, his arm outstretched like a little boy as his fingers gently feel the throngs of books squashed together on the shelves. Brown and red old covers, flaking, fading but still very much alive. The light that comes in through the magnificent ceiling reflects the gold binding of the books.

There is no noise, I notice, apart from footsteps and squeaking doors.

I don't think I'm terribly stoned any more. I think I'm halfway between sober and stoned. A lovely place. Mellow. Fully in control and all my senses wide open but no anxiety. I walk slowly away from Owen and stand in front of a large book on a wooden lectern. An atlas. A map of the world.

I'd love to bring the kids here someday. Teach them about the world. I raise up the flyer in my hand to read it. The museum was established in 1778 originally as a museum for art and science. I want Jade to be interested in this, not Seven Super Girls or bra-and-knickers sets from Penney's. I guess it's up to me to make that happen. She can't love what she hasn't seen. She can't want to be where she's never been. I want to be one of those mothers who shows her children important things … things they pass on to their children. Like this museum, which will be here long, long after my grandchildren and great-grandchildren.

We tour on our own and I like that. I'm ecstatic with the non-anxiety. I watch him walking around staring at the art and the books and he's totally content.

'Come here, look at this piece.' He gently takes my hand in his again as I move to stand beside him. He places me in front of it, then he stands behind me, his banana-and-pear-scented hands firmly gripping my shoulders.

It's a painting of winter. But the sky is painted with light oranges, pale pinks and light greys, so it looks warm in a way. There is ice all over the ground and people in winter coats and hats skate across what I now see is a frozen river; fishing boats lay destitute on top of the ice; trees bare and two windmills at the back of the painting stand tall.

'It's exposed, isn't it?' he asks me.

I don't claim to understand art – I just like it.

'To me ... it's cold but there's warmth about it. Hope?'

'A change will come, would you say?' He squeezes my shoulders, massaging deep onto the knots I have been holding onto. I moan softly under his touch.

'Yeah, a change will come: winter will pass and the ice will thaw and it will be a new beginning. Fishermen will fish again and the trees will be in full bloom ... Life goes on. Without hope there isn't life.'

'Snap! That's exactly what I see.'

'So I'm right?' I'm incredulous.

'There's no right and wrong in art, Ali, not as far as I'm concerned anyway – it's whatever you take from it and maybe you take nothing at all. Maybe you simply admire the brush strokes or the colours or whatever.' Owen lets go of my shoulders and comes in front of me.

'Hungry?'

'Oh, I'm so hungry, seriously it's not even funny, and I am absolutely gasping for water!' I peel my tongue away from the roof of my mouth. I seem to have zero saliva.

'Me too. I'm on it … and I've an idea. We hydrate you first, but then shall we take some red wine to look at the art tree, madam?' He puts his left arm on his hip and I link mine through as we make our way to the cafe.

I see people looking at us. I like the fact that they think we are a couple. We make a nice couple. My phone beeps away in my bag but I'm not answering it. Yet. It will no doubt be Colin feeling bad for telling me to go to hell. Retracting it. We enter the cafe but it's heaving.

'Are we brave enough?' Owen points to a small round silver table outside with two chairs sitting over the gardens.

'Oh, I dunno it's baltic!' I shiver at the thought.

'They have blankets though, see?' And there in a wooden trunk by the exit lie plenty of thick-looking, colourful blankets.

'OK, let's do it.' I push the exit door open. If I don't get a drink I may die.

It is indeed balticly baltic as I sit.

'Hang on, hang on, I was in the scouts. Up! Up! First, a blanket down on the cold chair: protects the kidneys from getting a chill.' He bends and takes one of the red blankets we took from the trunk, shakes it, then folds it over, before putting it on my chair. I sit again. Then he takes another and places this one around my shoulders and a third over my legs and knees and I hold this one up.

'I need water, Owen.' I suck the words out.

'Shit!' He turns and enters the cafe and I see him go to the counter and take the huge jug with lemon and two glasses. I have to say I feel as snug as a bug in a rug. When he returns I literally drink four glasses in a row.

'Is there anything worse than thirst?' I ask.

'Starvation doesn't even come close, does it?' he agrees and downs another glass himself. Then he bites at the lemon and winces.

'Well, I wouldn't know, thankfully,' I say as the waitress appears and we order a bottle of Malbec with two glasses.

'I'm feeling the vibes from the art tree,' he says. 'Now I know how Bono got his muse from the Joshua tree.'

'Are you not using a blanket?' I ask, dumbfounded.

'No.' He shakes his head and he then runs both his hands several times over his shaved head. It's been a few days since he went at it with his shaver. Little dark specks of regrowth lay across his scalp. Makes him look younger.

The red wine arrives and I'm the designated tester. I swirl its richness in my mouth a few times and swallow. I smile my approval at our waitress. Lovely temperature, warm but not too warm. I wrap my hands around the glass to heat its flavour. God, I love wine. This is kinda all sorts of weird, I think now, as Owen dips his nose into his wide glass. I drink. Me and Owen, drinking red wine at the Teylers Museum of a Friday afternoon in December. I drink more.

I might be coming up again. Is that the correct lingo?

'Did you ever see *Indecent Proposal*?' he asks.

'With Demi Moore and Robert Redford?' I can't stop drinking this wine. I refill my glass already. In fairness, the waitress only poured me a dribble. Not an Irish mummies' measure at all, at all.

'Yeah, where he pays the husband, Woody Harrelson, one million dollars to sleep with his wife.'

'Yeah, great film.' I push my fringe out of my eyes again to focus on him.

We look at each other.

'Is it De-mee or Demi?' I could care less but I'm not sure where he's going with this. The ambience of the moment is all too sexy. I drink.

'If I had a million, I'd offer it to Colin, right now.' He bangs the table gently with a fist.

My mouth falls open. I compose myself.

'You, Ali Devlin, make me want to paint.' He says this as though it's a revelation. Perhaps it is.

'I can think of better things you could do with a million,' I say, flattered and slightly brave again as I think of Colin's last text.

GO TO HELL YOU STUPID BITCH.

And this man in front of me would give a million dollars for one night with me. Ha! This man in front of me likes talking to me. This man in front of me never gets on my last nerve. This man in front of me never riles me to the point where I lose control and then I hate myself.

No. You go to hell, you stupid arsehole, I think.

'Money can't buy me love, right? Just as well, as I don't have any.' He smirks.

We both refill and drink.

'You will one day. You will sell wonderful, meaningful paintings to the rich and famous. I'll open a credit union account and save for years, just for a piece of your art—'

He interrupts me.

'This is starting to kill me, Ali, I …' He shuts his eyes tight.

I know what he's about to say and I don't want him to

admit it. I don't want him to say it out loud. I put the glass down.

'Oh, don't go there. I thought we weren't—'

'I have to, I didn't want to say this when we were so stoned, but I'm ...' He stops and shakes his head from side to side. 'Arghhh!' He throws his head back and looks up to the dark winter sky, then exhales very, very slowly, gathering himself.

'What I want to say is that ...' He slaps his forehead with the palm of his hand now, 'OK, try again, arsehole.' He laughs.

He's not the arsehole. Colin is the arsehole. I should stop him but I don't. I drink.

'I can't get you out of my head ... I painted two pieces last week because of where my head is with you. From the moment I laid eyes on you in the Beans eating spaghetti bolognese I was like, wow, look at that girl. It was that really hot Friday in June when Colette was showing me around. You were wearing a white vest T-shirt and a denim mini-skirt with black flip-flops. Your hair was cut really tight and you were the only person I could see in the entire cafe. You were illuminated in my mind's eye. I couldn't stop looking at you. The first thing I asked Michael was your name and what you did. All he told me was that you were married with kids and I deflated. And then I got to know you ... It's the first time I've ever been so entertained and challenged by a female friend who I wasn't trying to impress, and you're just amazingly kind and care about people. That's a rare quality. I know we can't be together but I wanted to tell you that anyway.'

I lean my head in my hands but my eyes are still on

him. He pulls the collar of his leather motorbike jacket up. My very own Danny Zuko. Draining my wine glass, I'm aware of this feeling, this feeling I haven't had for so long. I feel alive again. This is dangerous. The cake is rising.

'That's so nice.' I take my head from my hands and sit up straight.

GO TO HELL YOU STUPID BITCH.

After I told him I'd give up my job, just for him. Just to make him happy.

All the horrible things he's said to me over the last few days repeat slowly in my mind. The scenes play out in black-and-white inside my head, as if on a shaky old projector. The way he mocks me for daring to be friends with Corina, the way he tells me I'm a bad mother. I see him twirling the faulty apple in his hand and scorning my purchase before throwing it at the bin, missing and leaving me to clean it up.

Life is so hard for you, isn't it poor Ali?

The film is shaky.

Enjoy your gossip.

I see his hand clapping together, mocking my time with my wonderful friend.

Crazy winky woman.

I blink and the projector ends. Lights come up.

'Maybe we pretend we made a payment into Colin's account of a million dollars or euros, whatever, and we go back to room 141. We have permission … imagine?' I giggle

Fuck it. I want it. I may as well be honest with myself.

There's no red wine left.

I think he thinks I'm joking. I am and I am not.

He looks very confused, and then he says, 'Right … that didn't last long.' He waves the empty bottle in the air. 'Well, we gotta … get … we gotta get outta here, grab something to eat at the hotel or something to walk with maybe?' he says looking at his watch but I now see his eyes are heavy with desire.

I don't care.

I don't care.

I don't care.

I don't care about anything or anyone any more, only me. I only care about me. Fuck it. When was the last time I cared about me? About Ali Devlin? Previously Ali O' Dwyer. I give no time to myself. I don't even know why. I like Ali Devlin. She's a nice, decent person who deserves to be happy. All she wants is to be a great mother and have a job. It's not a lot. Don't judge me right now, because I'm angry. I'm lost. I'm desperate to find an answer to all my problems. But not right now. I'm doing this. What have I got to lose?

Everything.

The little voice is suddenly back. My conscience poking at my maternal brain. My numskulls are sitting bolt upright. *Absolutely everything.*

You have two kids at home! It snaps at me. Biting at my decisions. I shake it off. I hum Taylor Swift. Leave me alone, guilt and responsibilities. This is a one-off. No one has to know. Ever. Our secret. A stolen afternoon of pure passion. Just like in the movies. And then I adopt the philosophy of 'what you don't know can't hurt you', am I right?

We hail a cab from a long line right outside the museum. As we arrive back at the hotel, Owen tips the driver.

'Stop here, please … eh … *alsjeblieft*.' He pays again.

As we exit, I implore, 'Will you stop paying for everything!'

'Soakage.' He points into the distance.

He takes me by the hand and pulls me towards a street vender selling hot dogs and coffee.

'What?' Is he serious? Street food? I want to eat him! I stop in the middle of the street angering pedestrians who walk into the back of me. Bicycles swerve to avoid me. Amsterdam is just too busy for my nonsense.

'Hot dogs … off the street. Are they safe?' I ask.

'You need another cake!' He laughs.

He's right. We buy two hot dogs and stand on the corner. It's just buying us more time.

★ ★ ★

'I have never tasted anything like this in my life. I am sooo hungry,' I say, face splattered with mustard and ketchup.

'Me too,' he mutters.

He reaches over with his little white square paper napkin and wipes my face.

'There you go.' His hand lingers for a moment too long.

Our eyes pour into one another. There is no need for words

'I want you to have a breather, some food … Let's just think about this, shall we?'

So he is on the same page.

'Are we really going to do this?' I say and I can't look at him now. We are going to have sex.

214

'I hope so … I hope not … oh, Ali, I dunno.' He breathes heavily.

I look into his eyes now. No words needed.

'Let's go,' he says.

We dump our unfinished hot dogs in the nearest bin and Owen takes my clammy hand. We walk fast but in silence the short distance to the hotel. I'm excited yet sick with nerves.

13

Early Friday evening.
Amsterdam. Inside room 141.

As we enter the hotel I linger by the twinkling reception desk and Owen does a quick spot check. I take a sly sniff at my previously wet armpits, not too bad. He beckons me and I hoof the strap of my bag over my left shoulder as we take the stairs up to the third floor two at a time. The lift is too risky in case we bump into Colette or Michael. We look tousled, unkempt, lived-in! Both of us are still giggling as I find my purse and remove my key card. My hand is shaking. Owen steadies it with his and the green light appears as key card clicks its approval of us and the heavy door to my destiny swings open. Green to go.

The room is warm and the light is fading outside.

I stand with my back against the closed door now. Owen walks ahead towards the window.

Turning, he removes his biker jacket, never taking his eyes off me. He throws it on the bed. The zips rattle along with the loose change in his pockets.

Slowly he walks towards me and starts unbuttoning my brown leather jacket. It seems to take for ever. His hands are cold and the buttons in fairness are hard to undo at the best of times. He fumbles.

'Y'ok?' he whispers to me.

I nod. I swallow hard. He prises opens the last button and slides my hands out from the safety of my jacket sleeves. Then he lays my jacket carefully over the back of the chair, on top of my red winter coat.

He leans his forehead against mine. His breathing is paced but hot and heavy. We are conjoined by foreheads. Then he takes his right hand and pushes my fringe from my eyes and tucks it gently behind my left ear. He lowers his forehead. Our mouths are inches apart. Agonisingly slowly he drops his hand and unbuttons the two top buttons on my white shirt. His fingers feeling the material as he goes. Our breath is synchronised now. Inches from my mouth. He lifts my chin with his right thumb, he tilts his head and as he is about to lock his lips on mine, I see it all.

They say your life flashes before your eyes if you are in a life-or-death situation. If you are on a runaway tractor say, with failing brakes, heading towards a treacherous cliff. It's not your life in pictures. It's not memories. It's your brain finding moments like these for reference. Trying to figure out what to do, what memory helped you the last time you were in a dangerous situation? How did you survive? *Flash! Flash! Flash!* The images gallop towards me.

Colin.

Colin.

Colin.

And they are beautiful. The khaki bag. The loose school tie. Our engagement party. Our wedding day. Pregnancy. Holding Jade as a newborn. Holding Mark as a newborn.

The first times. Smiles. Tears. Laughter. Love. My children. Jade. Mark. My world.

I push Owen away. Hard as I can. He goes flying and stumbles back onto the bed.

'I can't do this!' *I can't do this!* I throw my hand over my mouth. I actually think I'm going to throw up. Bile rises into my mouth as I swallow it down hard. I can't breathe. I bend over and put my head between my legs.

'OK, OK, OK, it's fine ... Relax, breathe, Ali, it's OK ...' He is over to me. 'I understand, I get it ... I should never ... This is ludicrous.' He is beaten.

I stare at his runners.

When I lift my head up after several minutes I walk away from him and stand in front of the mirror. Sexy, I am not. Hair all messy, panda eyes, huge sweat stains and my shirt hanging open fresh from aborting the biggest mistake of my life. I could have ruined it all.

But you didn't.

You didn't.

GO TO HELL YOU STUPID BITCH.

What have I done to deserve that? What could I have possibly done to make Colin hate me so much?

'Can I make you a coffee?' Owen appears behind me in the mirror.

'Please,' I mouth but the word doesn't make a sound.

He slips back the mirrored wardrobe door and pulls out a sliding tray with a kettle and cups on it. He rummages for a moment before saying, 'Ahh, you have no coffee sachets either ... neither did my room.' He moves to the phone on the desk and picks up the receiver.

'Hi, this is room 141, we have no tea or coffee, can

we get some up, like, right now? We need to leave for a meeting soon … Great … Yes, both please … Also, I have no coffee in room 142 … Great … Oh, can we get extra milk? Thank you, *dank je*.' He replaces the receiver.

I flop, flat on the bed and kick off my runners and peel off my sports socks.

'Don't lie down!' he says softly. 'We will need to start getting ready for the meeting down in the bar soon.'

'I'm up, I'm up!' I sit up.

'Sorry, Ali.' He sits on the edge and I roll towards him as the bed dips under his weight. I edge away.

'It's completely my fault,' I say and I mean it. It is. He's not married. I am.

'Probably wasn't the best of idea for us to get stoned,' he mutters.

I shake my head.

Shake it off.

'No, probably not. You know I fancy you, Owen, I know you fancy me … I shouldn't have come on this trip at all, especially not after me telling you my marriage is in a crisis state and then sending you half-naked pictures of myself, I mean, what did I expect?' My two hands shoot up and cover my panda eyes.

'It takes two to tango, Ali, I'm as much to blame. I never thought I was this kind of guy either. But look, maybe this needed to almost happen, maybe now we can forget this chemistry thing and just go back to being friends?'

'Yeah.' I remove my hands and give him a milky weak smile.

'Right, come on, straight into the shower with you,' he says and he gets up and moves into the bathroom. His tone is cheery but I know he is feeling like crap too. I hear him turning on the shower. There is a soft knock at the door.

'Coffees are here,' I call, but he can't hear me over the gushing running water so I pad barefoot across the room and pull the heavy door in towards me. For a moment it feels like time has stopped. It takes me what feels like minutes but in fact are nanoseconds to process the fact it's Colin, standing in front of me at the door. Colin Devlin is here. He pushes me inside. The door slams behind us.

'W-w-w-what the—?' I stutter.

'Where is he?' Colin screams as he spins around the bedroom. Owen emerges from the shower, shaking his wet hands. It all happens so fast I cannot even make a sound. Colin grabs him by the neck and flings him back into the bathroom. Owen tries to fight him off but Colin is too strong.

'You fucking prick … you're fucking my wife, are you?' He drops Owen to the tiled floor and kicks him in the stomach. Owen grunts like an animal with the impact. I still can't scream. I move. I grab Colin from behind, pulling at his winter coat as I try to drag him across the room. He shakes me off. He's too strong. Too angry. Owen turns onto his knees, rocking on all fours as Colin's foot comes up and kicks him hard in the stomach. This time Owen vomits everywhere. Huge chunks of red undigested hot dog all over the floor.

'I'm going to fucking kill you!' Colin grabs him up now and drags him into the bedroom, by the bed, and presses him up against the wall. Colin's elbow is across Owen's throat.

I finally find my voice.

'Please, Colin, stop … stop … it's not what you think! Nothing has happened!' I beg him.

He turns to me, his right arm still pinned across Owen's throat. Owen's eyes beg me for help. I am helpless.

'Nothing? Here, is this nothing?' He still has Owen pinned to the wall as he removes his phone from his back pocket with his free hand. He has a screen grab of me in my sexy underwear.

'Always log out of Facebook, you stupid cunt!' He spits in my face.

Oh, this can't be happening.

'Fucking prricccckk!' His temper goes again but this time Owen ducks out of Colin's hold and hits him smack on the nose with a head butt. Colin's nose explodes open. Blood sprays everywhere. My white shirt is dotted. Blobs on a canvas. I am paralysed watching this unfold. They fight. A proper punching battle. I find some sense and grab the phone and try to call reception. I press every number, nothing. Then I run out into the corridor and scream for help through the fire doors.

'Help, help, help! Third Floor. HELP!' I run back but Colin has Owen in a headlock outside the door. One hand on the handle of the door and the other again around Owen's neck. Then I watch in slow motion, the next horrors unfold as I listen to Owen's screams.

'Paint this, you prick!' Colin drags Owen's right hand and puts it into the jamb of the door. Owen fights to pull his hand back but it's too late. Colin slams the heavy door shut on his fingers. Owen howls in pain and slides to the ground screaming and writhing just as three uniformed police run down the corridor towards us. Owen still has his hand pinned in the door jamb. Bile rises in my throat. I swallow.

The police grab Colin and push him up against the wall. They are shouting in a foreign language we cannot understand. I drop to my knees to Owen. He is writhing in pain, his hand still jammed in between the frame of the door. Bizarrely I look for fingers on the carpeted ground but I see none. Impossible? Gently I pull it free. His index finger seems to be barely hanging on by skin and blood oozes in a puddle around us. It's hard to tell what state the rest of his fingers are in, there is so much blood.

'*Hospitaal*,' a policeman says to Owen before he turns to me.

'*Waar kom jij vandaan* … where are you from?' His approach is gentle and he places his hand on my lower back.

'I-I-Ireland … I—' I say. Then I rant: 'That is my husband and this is a … a guy … a man I work with, we are here to see shows …'

His eyes tell me he understands nothing about this situation, it is all lost in translation.

'We will take him to hospital.'

I nod as another policeman helps Owen up and they get his jacket from the room, wrap a white towel around his bleeding hand and leave through the fire door. I don't say a word to him. I can hardly offer to go with him.

'Happy now, Ali? Got what you wanted?' Colin turns to me, his hands now pinned behind his back in handcuffs.

'Colin … please believe me, nothing ever happened. The picture, I can explain—'

'Oh, explain it to the lawyers, Ali. And when you come back the locks will be changed. You won't be getting back into my house, *ever*.'

'You can't do that!' I am petrified.

'I can and I will.'

'It's against the law.'

The policeman who spoke with me approaches us.

'I will need you all to come to police station to give statement. Hotel property damage also.'

Colin speaks. 'Yeah, no problem, this is a domestic case. I'd say if I requested a drug test you'd literally shit your slutty bought knickers, Ali.'

I shut my eyes tight. How can he possibly know that?

'Where are my children, Colin? Who is minding them?'

'Don't you fucking even go there!' he roars in my face like a maniac.

'Please, no shouting, this is a hotel,' the police officer says as he closes the door to my room.

The hotel manager appears and speaks to me in English with a different police officer by his side. This police officer takes pictures of the bloodstained carpet and then enters room 141. I can hear the camera clicking away.

'We will need you to vacate both rooms, yes, all your property must be removed now, yes?'

I nod. Like a robot I walk into my room and pack my barely unopened case. When I emerge a big crowd is standing around.

'Can we go?' I say and we are all led away. Downstairs two separate cars wait to take us to the police station.

14

Early Friday evening. Police station. Amster-dam.

After two hours of waiting on a hard cold bench and then into questioning I am told I am free to go. No charges will be brought against me. How could there be? I did nothing wrong. I'm reading a card with information that tells me the Dutch legal system is a 'civil law' system, which was also explained in plain English to me by a female police officer.

'The other man, Colin Devlin?' I ask the police woman who in fairness has been very pleasant to me, taken my statement and given me water. I was not attacked and I have no reason to press charges. She shrugs her shoulders.

'I do not know,' she tells me matter-of-factly as she holds her hand on a buzzer, pulls open the door and I have no choice but to leave through it.

It's freezing outside and I try to hail a taxi. None come. I can't physically stop shaking. My brown leather jacket offers no heat. My head is thumping now. Putting my head down against the cold, I walk even though I have absolutely no idea where I'm headed. How quickly things turn. How quickly life can just bowl you right over. *Strike!* I take out my phone, twenty per cent of battery left. I call

Colin. His phone is turned off, straight to voicemail. The happy tone of his voice message sends a shiver right up my spine. Then I call Owen. He answers.

'Hi,' he says quietly. 'Are you OK?'

I stand in the doorway of a shoe shop called Clogs. I can smell the fresh leather from the open door. My sense of smell is still bizarre.

'Yeah, where are you?' I ask in rushed words.

'I'm at the airport, Ali, I'm on the next flight home.'

'What?' I lean my head against the freezing cold wall. 'So quickly? What did the doctors say? How is your hand?'

'Not sure till I get home. I won't lose any fingers, that's the main thing. I managed to curl most of them up tight before he slammed the door closed on me, don't ask me how.'

I wince.

'I refused the offer of surgery at the hospital: I've no medical cover, Ali, no VHI, Layla-whatever insurance, no anything. They saw me immediately, threw a few stitches into my index one which is by far the worst, bandaged me up and released me. I got morphine tablets from the paramedics; they splinted all the fingers, two are possibly broken, they think. I need to get home, fast. My brother is going to loan me money. The police interviewed me at the hospital so I didn't have to go to the station.' He doesn't even sound like Owen O'Neill any more. He sounds like a little boy.

'I can't believe this ... I'm so sorry. I have never seen him like that before,' I say.

'No ... well, what did we expect? He's been into your Facebook account, he told the police. All our correspondence, he had it printed out: the adjoining rooms and all that joking we were doing, he thought it was true. He wants … he wants … he's looking for evidence of adultery, Ali.'

'There is none!' I cry out. The rain is coming down now as a crowd of carol singers have set up and are singing the Dutch version of 'Jingle Bells'. Sounds like the English version but then it switches into Dutch: 'Jingle bells, jingle bells, *in de arreslee.*'

Oh, what fun it is to ride on a one-horse open sleigh.

'Did you press charges?' I ask. Trying to focus.

'No … but I might have to take a case against him when I get home, to cover medical expenses. I can't afford to fix this, Ali. You know Kieran, my brother, is a guard; he said I have a case, mainly to pay for my medical bills, Ali, under section 3 of the Non-fatal Offences Against the Person Act 1977. I'm going to need you to give a statement, evidence he did this to me …'

I can't take much more. I roll my back down the cobble-blocked wall and the pain is a relief.

My kids. It's nearly Christmas. 'Jingle bells, jingle bells, *in de arreslee …*' The rain is driving down harder now. I get that feeling I sometimes get in a small lift, I can't breathe, I feel faint. My heart palpitates.

'My stand-by flight is boarding soon, I got a seat … I can't talk, Ali, I'm in too much pain … You … you mind yourself, OK? This isn't your fault. I'm so sorry.' He ends the call.

What am I going to do? I can't leave till Sunday. Oh my God, Colette and Michael. The show. My job. Owen's job. They must have heard about this by now; the room is booked under the Danker name. The humiliation. I try Colin again. Still switched off. With shaking hands I dial Corina's number.

'Corina!' I cry heavily when she answers.

'Is he there? Is he there? Are you OK? Ali, I tried to warn you … oh, what's happened? Oh my God, I've been out of my mind with worry!' Corina is crying now too.

'How did you know?' I manage to sob the words out.

'He came to get Jade at gymnastics rehearsals at eleven. I was there, at the early rehearsals. I was taking her picture … sending it to you … He smashed my phone on the ground – he shattered the glass, the bastard – and dragged her away in front of the entire class and teachers. He called me awful names, you should have heard him. He was insane! You never logged out of your Facebook account on the family computer in the kitchen, Ali! He shoved our Facebook messages into my face. He knew I knew about Owen from them all. He has them printed! He screamed that he was going to find you. God, poor Jade, what she must think, she looked terrified. A parent had to ask him to leave. I called and called and called … re-dialled for hours but you didn't answer … I didn't think to call Owen … till now… I had his number… Oh why didn't I think of that? I knew Colin was going to the airport.' Her sobs are heavy. 'Then I was too afraid to call any more in case he answered.'

'Where are the kids, Corina?' I beg her.

'I don't know, Ali,' she says through shaking breaths. 'But that Maia, the green woman, was with him all po-faced and giving me filthy looks. That bitch stood by and watched him abuse me in front of Jade!'

'I need to wake up. This has to be a bad trip,' I say. I

move off down the street away from the carol singers, the rain slamming me in the face and I tell Corina all that has happened. Still on the phone, I find a free taxi back to the hotel. As I push open the door to the hotel, Colette and Michael are standing at the reception desk. I tell Corina I have to go and Colette comes straight over to me.

'Are you OK?' is her first question, but I can see she is beside herself. She wrings her hands repeatedly in front of her. Michael moves away to the end of the reception desk.

'We have to pay three hundred and twenty euros for damage to the room. The television is broken, as is the shower door and the bedside lamps. The carpet is stained with blood in your room and in the corridor. We are a government-run centre, Ali. If we lose the support, we are closed down. We rely on state funding—'

'I'll pay it,' I say, my chin is quivering and I am dripping wet.

'I think you should leave this evening, Ali. Michael checked the last flight to Dublin: it's at ten. The desk will call you a cab. I can't see another way to deal with this. We will talk about this on Monday, OK? How is Owen?' Her expression changes now to one of concern.

'I don't know for sure yet … He's gone home,' I manage, my hair drips water into my eyes.

Michael approaches with my case and leaves it at the hotel door beside the Christmas tree.

'That's all your stuff,' is all he says and then I see his eyes widen and he seems to stumble. I follow his eyeline. It's Colin. He walks straight to the reception desk.

'Hi, I lost my wallet earlier? I was involved in that fight, room 141?' he says very matter-of-factly.

Has he seen me? I can only see his side profile now, his nose bloody, unbandaged, swollen and cut.

'Yes, Mr Devlin, we have your wallet.' The receptionist in the navy blazer with gold buttons looks less than impressed as she bends under the counter. She stands with his brown wallet and extends her hand. The one Jade bought him last Christmas from TK Maxx. Colin takes it.

'Thank you,' he says and as he turns he sees us. Collette has moved closer to me.

Suddenly I feel really, really sorry for him. What have I done to him? His face is a mess and he looks so sad.

'Colin …' I move towards him.

'Ali.' He shoves his hands deep into his winter coat pocket. A coat that should be hanging on our coat peg in the hall right now, not here, not in this situation. It's outlandish.

'Nothing happened, I swear on the children's lives,' I whisper to him across the busy lobby.

'It doesn't matter any more. You've broken me, this is over.' His voice is low and calm.

I can't speak. There's nothing to say.

'I have a flight to catch. I need to get home to my children,' he says.

And he's gone.

15

Friday night. Corina's living room.
South Circular Road. Dublin 8.

Corina parks illegally at Arrivals in Dublin airport to meet me and sweeps me home in her little car. Colin hadn't been at the airport in Amsterdam when I got there at eight o'clock – he must have been on the seven thirty out. Dublin mocks me with its twinkling Christmas lights and jovial atmosphere. 'Tis the season to be jolly. People in colourful Christmas jumpers under heavy coats walk in the middle of the road, invincible, determined to do the twelve pubs of Christmas. Everyone is merry.

'I want to go home, Corina.' I start to cry again, my eyes are actually sore now.

'Oh, not tonight please, Ali. Let the dust settle … Not tonight. You need to regroup, think about this with a clear head.' She never takes her eyes off the road.

'I need to see my children!' I scream at the top of my lungs. 'You don't get it! I need to see them now!' I bash my hands onto the dashboard. Still she remains perfectly calm.

'Arghhhhhhhhhhhhhhhhhhhhhhhhh!' I scream so hard I hurt my throat.

'Scream again!' she says and I do. I scream over and over and over. How her ears aren't deafened, I don't know. She drives carefully. When I can scream no more, I collapse back into the passenger seat. I lay my head against the soft headrest. Only now can I smell the potent BO coming from me.

'Oh, I stink. Can we drive by the house then, that's all?' I ask in a small voice.

She's in her pyjamas with her long ankle-length fawn Next coat covering them and a pair of black Uggs. We drive straight to my house but the place is in total darkness and Colin's car is not there.

'Where the hell does Maia live?' I whack the dashboard again and wrack my brains. Somewhere in Castleknock but I have no idea where. I've tried calling her too but, like Colin's, her phone has been off for hours.

'Let's just go back to mine, it's late. Tomorrow is a new day. Even if Colin was there with the children, or we found them at Maia's apartment, do you really think they need to witness you both face off tonight?' Corina says in the most sympathetic of tones.

I shake my head. More reluctant than I have ever been in my life. The want to see my children a real physical ache in my belly.

'Fucking hell, Corina,' I say. 'What the fuck have I done? What the fuck am I going to do?'

'We'll see ... we'll figure it out ... Let's just get you home.' She drops her foot harder down onto the accelerator.

* * *

Back at her house Corina makes me take a hot shower, puts me in a pair of her flannel Lenor-smelling pyjamas

231

and makes me sweet tea and hot buttered toast. I drink the tea but the toast sticks in my throat. Her fire-in-a-bag is blazing now, and we both sit cross-legged in front of it.

'I better try ringing him again.' I go to get up.

'Leave it now, Ali. It's after midnight, tomorrow is Saturday … I'm off all weekend, we can go over together in the morning. I'd say he's at that Maia's house, she must have agreed to take the kids on a sleepover to let him go to Amsterdam. He won't expect you home tonight.' Corina leans in and pokes the fire. The flames rage higher.

I nod.

'Your place looks lovely,' I tell her in a very small voice and it is. She has the best taste in Christmas decorations, always does. It's all pale blues and silvers. It reminds me of the cover of Disney's *Frozen* storybooks. What I wouldn't give right now to be reading that to Mark. I'd read the whole book five times over if he asked me to. I'd read all night long and act out every page. There is nowhere else I'd rather be. I'd walk Jade over to Karen's myself and go back and collect her in a hour, any night no matter how dark it was. No bother. Sure, I'd enjoy the time we would get to spend together on the walks.

I tilt my head to breathe in the smell of pine from her tree, which is sitting in the corner beneath her television with white twinkling fairy lights and pale blue decorations. Minimalist.

'So,' Corina says in a tone that tells me she's just trying to take my mind off things, 'I found out Trevor doesn't really live in Manchester, he lives in Dublin. I bumped into the Pimple at a lunchtime event in the Dillon hotel I was doing, for that new men's magazine, *All About Men*.

He'd had quite a few of the potent free cocktails. Anyway, among other things, the Pimple told me, "Trev just tells girls that so he can get away from them easily". Unless they are brain-dead like me and have already planned their move to Manchester,' she guffaws.

The mention of Manchester brings Colin to my mind. His khaki school bag with all its Manchester United graffiti. His love for that team. Is it really that bad that he has an interest? I'd happily watch a match now. I'd go with him to Old Trafford if he wanted me to. It isn't really such a big deal.

'Did you like him that much?' I ask, dragging my focus back to my friend. I curl my hands around my huge mug of sweet Barry's tea.

'Yeah … I kinda did. Thicko.' She raises her perfectly shaped HDs at me.

'Sorry.' I lean over and rub her thigh. The light from the flames bouncing off her sweet, freckled face.

'Holy shitballs with Colin though, what?' She lets out a long, slow breath. She looks shattered, poor Corina.

'Yep. What a massive tit I am.'

Corina looks like she is about to say something, but just nods her head. Agreeing with me. And all I can do is accept it.

16

**First thing Saturday morning. Corina's house.
South Circular Road. Dublin 8.**

I didn't sleep a wink. I have black bags under my eyes and the lines on my face seem more pronounced this morning. I look every day of my thirty-five years. I dreamt all night about Jade and Mark being in dangerous situations. I tried to save Jade from falling down the stairs and when I tried to grab her my arms wouldn't move. I was paralysed. I tried to tell Mark his bike had no stabilisers, to slow down, but my voice wouldn't work. He was heading towards a main road. No matter how hard I tried to shout I just couldn't scream loud enough. I couldn't warn him. I woke in a dripping sweat.

Corina is up. I can hear Sunshine radio in the kitchen. Carly Simon, 'You're So Vain'. I can also smell rashers.

I reach immediately for my phone, no messages. I turn on my back for a moment and admire the beauty of Corina's spare room. She's done it up beautifully. All pale pinks and pastels. A vintage dressing table that she stripped down and sandpapered herself sits under the old ash window. The original floorboards have been sanded and painted in a dark oak-coloured paint. The house is old and a little draughty but it has enormous character. It's all hers. This little place off South Circular Road. I get up. I dress in a cream hoody of Corina's from the clothes horse in the corner and I pull on my jeans. It's just after eight.

'Morning!' She smiles at me, as I make my way into the kitchen. She pulls her pan to one side.

'Rashers and mushrooms on toast OK?' she enquires.

I nod. I really have to try and eat.

'You're so kind, thank you, Corina,' I say.

She winks at me, before saying, 'Look … I couldn't sleep for hours, as I imagine you couldn't. You didn't do anything wrong, per se.' She is straight to business, holding her hands out, palms facing upwards, as though she is weighing what she's about to say. 'Yes, you shouldn't have been in a hotel room together, it looks mega crappy, Ali, but the fact is nothing happened and Colin's reaction was way over the top. I think the first thing we need to do is to get you to talk to a solicitor. I know it's a Saturday but I have a friend, well, an acquaintance, who might do me a favour and see you for half an hour. What do you think? Will I text her?'

'Are you serious? You think I need a solicitor?' I feel sick to the pit of my stomach again.

She jerks her head back to me. Her HDs are nearly meeting her hairline.

'Eh, yeah, a hundred per cent. You need to know your rights, where you stand.'

'I just want to see my kids, Corina,' I say wearily as I take a seat at the table. She has the table all set. It's so sweet. A small, white tea light candle flickers in a teacup-shaped holder in the middle. Salt and pepper set are embracing one another in a cute hug. Ketchup and brown sauce, HP, Colin's favourite, and napkins.

'Ali, it's your kids I'm thinking about. We don't want to upset them any more than is necessary. They don't expect you home today anyway. Colin's not going to say anything—'

I interrupt her.

'He has a broken nose, I'd say! How's he going to explain that?' I stare at the flickering flame.

I wonder if Colin will remember Mark's football game. The Ranelagh Rovers Under 6s are on a winning streak. Mark has yet to be called off the bench but he goes religiously week in, week out, never deterred by the obvious lack of faith Erik Clancy, the manager, has in him.

She folds the tea towel on the counter.

'This is ready.' Toast pops and she removes it and puts it on a plate. The familiar smell is comforting.

'God, he was an animal, a total animal. It was like he lost his mind in that hotel room ...' I recall the fight again to her.

'Please don't think I'm giving that bastard a pass here, Ali, but I think we have to try and see where Colin was coming from? I mean, how did you expect he would react in that situation?' I watch her as she dishes out the rashers and dabs the oil from the mushrooms with kitchen roll as I think of the answer to her very good question. *What did I expect?* She takes the plates to the table and then sits.

'He saw a picture of you in sexy lacy underwear that you sent to a male work colleague, you were in a hotel room with the aforementioned ... looking, as you said yourself, half undressed and him running a shower! What Colin did was beyond the pale – to Owen, how aggressive he was with me – but he did it out of hurt and anger and embarrassment. Not that it excuses...'

'But Owen may never be able to paint again? It was just so malicious ...' I shake the ketchup bottle with vigour.

'Ali, focus! Yes, it's absolutely awful what Colin did to Owen, but right now I'm concerned about you. We need to consider where all this leaves Ali, and what it all means moving forward. It's done now, isn't it? We are where we are. We can go back over it and over it and analyse the brutality, whatever, but it's not going to change anything, this is where you find yourself today ... let's move forward.'

A too big blob splatters over my mushrooms.

'Let's just eat ... This is great, thank you.' I can't afford to piss Corina off as well.

We eat in silence, and I study Corina's life-drawing of the old woman who really does look like a basketball hoop she has now framed on her kitchen wall, and somehow I can't find it funny. It just seems sad. Hard to imagine I will every really laugh again.

Forcefully I throw the food down my throat, washed down with tea. Corina texts her friend and with regret I agree it's the right thing to do this morning.

* * *

Anita, the family law solicitor, has agreed to see us in her home on Sorrento Terrace in Dalkey. After I've washed up, at my insistence, and Corina has showered and dressed, we make our way out on the coast road to Dublin's homes of the rich and famous. The day is cold but clear and crisp and the drive is soothing. All the while I constantly call both Colin's and Maia's mobile phones.

Now I regret not letting Jade have her own phone.

'This is the road,' Corina says as I look out her side at the most magnificent houses I have ever seen. Anita's house is a towering mansion. We park in a space right outside and knock twice on the Jacob Marley-type door knocker.

* * *

'So do you know where your children are right now?' Anita sits behind a huge mahogany desk in her front room office, chewing on the sharpest pencil I've ever seen. She looks like one of the *Desperate Housewives* of somewhere or another. Her colour can only be described as orange, fingernails as long as Stanley knives, hair that is just too still to be real. Not one trace of the legal eagle about her. Corina has filled her in on all my escapades in Amsterdam yesterday.

'No.'

'Have you tried again this morning to contact your husband?'

'Yes, by phone. His mobile has been off since yesterday; we don't have a landline.'

'What is it you want from me exactly?' Anita nibbles the wood.

I look to Corina. I don't bloody know.

'Well, advice, Anita, if you can, and we really appreciate you seeing us. Like I said on the phone, I will send you over some more of those untested Botox home kits from Latvia you liked.' Corina leans her elbows on her knees.

'Could you? Can you get them to me soon?' Suddenly

she seems a lot cheerier. I'm not sure if she's smiling or not. She plops her pencil in a glass vase.

'Tomorrow. So where does she stand? What happens when she sees Colin? What if he won't let her into the house? Can she ask him to leave?' Corina belches out questions.

'Oh, I don't want him to leave!' I am amazed at her questions.

Corina holds her hand up, waves it around to shush me up.

'Let's hear all our options, Ali.' She winks at me. I scratch my head.

I want my mummy. I haven't wanted my mummy for years but right now I do.

'Well, I have a few questions too. I'm presuming the children are children of the marriage?' Her teeth are blinding white. Comical almost.

Corina and I both nod.

'I'm also presuming you own the house jointly?'

Why would anyone want teeth that white?

We nod again. Like two bobble-headed dogs in the back of a car.

'Right, well, in that case you have equal legal entitlement to live in that house – Ranelagh, you say?'

The bobbing dog heads nod again.

'Unless there is a court order which says otherwise, be that a barring order under the Domestic Violence Act, or a Decree of Judicial Separation or Divorce, making a court order in respect of the family home—'

Corina makes a noise and Anita stops and looks at her.

'OK, sorry, sorry to interrupt you, I get all that, thanks,

but what if Colin had the locks changed on the house, last night or this morning?'

I scratch my head aggressively. *Oh, please. Make this stop.*

'Well, Colin, Mr Devlin, cannot change the locks to prevent Ali from entering or indeed living in the house. It's against the law.'

Even though Colin has threatened to do this, I hadn't ever really thought he would until Corina just put it in my head.

'In relation to the children, both you and Mr Devlin are joint guardians and custodians of them. Meaning you both have an equal legal relationship with the children and have equal rights to make legal, medical, educational and religious decisions in respect of the children – you also both have primary care and control of the children. Neither party can remove the children from the jurisdiction without the other's consent. If you are concerned about your children at this moment in time, with regard to them being in Mr Devlin's care, we need to alert the CRI—'

Now I interrupt Anita.

'I'm not worried about them, he would never harm them!'

'What's the CRI?' Corina talks over me.

'Child Rescue Ireland. As I was saying, if you are concerned, I'd advise alerting the Gardai. In any case in which a child or children have been abducted and there is a reasonable belief that there is an immediate and serious risk to the health and welfare of the child or children, the Gardai are allowed to seek the assistance of the public to help find them.'

'No ... Colin loves his children. I have no worries about their safety, he's a brilliant father,' I repeat.

Why is my head so itchy?

'Honestly, I'd suggest you both trying to figure this out without sitting in front of a judge. In relation to family matters, it is always best for parties to be amicable and to come to an agreement themselves. It is also much easier for parties to stick to an agreement they have made together than one that a judge may impose upon them. I'm sure Mr Devlin can find a place nearby and you can come to an access agreement.' Very deliberately and obviously, she checks the slim gold watch on her orange arm.

'It's only fair that I move out,' I blurt out.

'Ali!' Corina swivels on her chair to look at me.

'I wouldn't make any hasty decisions, dear,' Anita says.

'But surely this is my entire fault? Why should Colin have to lose out on living with his children every day ... I mean, where's the justice in that? It was all my fault!'

'But you are their mother and Colin didn't exactly behave like a gentleman!' Corina says.

'And he is their father. I made the mistake. I will get a flat in Ranelagh, and we can do something like they live with me half the week and at home with Colin the other half.'

Anita pipes up. 'In Ireland, dear, generally speaking, children will not live half the week with one parent and half with the other, or do weekly on-off or monthly on-off living arrangements. Judges generally don't like it and it's usually not practical and also not in the best interest of the children. Most usual is the children live in the family home with one parent and enjoy access with the other, be that every weekend, every second weekend and maybe a day during the week as well. Regarding what you said there about this all being your fault, in Ireland we have a no-fault-based system of divorce.'

Her tone of voice and the way she emphasised the word 'divorce' tells me our time with her is up. Clipped. Final. I wish she would stop saying that word. Divorce. This is all becoming too real.

She goes on, though. 'This means the courts won't apportion blame or penalise one person because of the breakdown of the marriage. The courts may take behaviours into consideration in cases where the behaviour is so gross and so unreasonable that it would not be in the interest of justice to disregard it, and then it is only taken into consideration in granting ancillary orders like maintenance and so on.' Anita rises now and we rise also.

I've heard enough anyway. I don't even want a divorce.

'Thanks so much, Anita … Sorry, tomorrow is Sunday, but I will have the home kits sent over to you by courier first thing Monday morning.'

She nods her head.

'Can you have them delivered to the office and not here, dear?' asks Anita and Corina nods.

'Thanks so much again.' I offer my hand and she shakes it limply.

'My pleasure, Corina is an old friend.'

Then Corina and Anita hug tightly and we leave through her massive electronic gates.

'Old friend, me arse,' Corina whispers. 'She wants the home Botox sets is all.' Corina opens her car. 'I only know her through that gym I once joined.'

As soon as I have clicked my seat belt, I press redial for Colin's mobile and this time it rings.

'It's ringing!' I shriek.

Colin answers after the fourth ring. I can hear wind and shouting.

'Colin, I want to see the children!' I yelp. I'm already sweating.

'Are you back? Where are you? Who are you with?' he asks in a very high-pitched voice.

'Yes, I came back last night too, late, I stayed at Corina's,' I shout.

He pauses, before saying, 'I'm at Mark's match. Maia is taking them to see the matinee panto at the Gaiety after. I can come over to Corina's then, if you want to talk?'

'Yes, yes … OK … yes, thanks.' I'm taken aback at his tone.

'See ya then.'

And the line goes dead.

17

Early afternoon. Corina's kitchen.
South Circular Road. Dublin 8.

I'm sitting barefoot at Corina's kitchen table. I'm not sure what to expect from this meeting with my husband on this otherwise seemingly innocent Saturday afternoon. This Saturday that could mark the end of my life as I know it. I push myself up and walk to the fridge, open it and take out a can of Coke. I never drink Coke, never allow the kids to drink it but I'm so nervous it's a distraction. The ring pull comes away with a hiss. I take a long fizzy drink and I belch loudly.

He's on his way to see me. What is he going to say to me? What am I going to do?

Corina walks in.

'Before he arrives, I want to talk to you.'

She pulls out a chair and sits and I take my Coke can off the countertop and join her.

'Like I said in the car on the way home: that advice Anita gave was all really beneficial. I know you are saying that you feel this is all your fault, but the marriage was in trouble, Ali, wasn't it? Worse than I think I wanted to believe before all this.'

Was it really that bad? I question myself now.

Didn't I only question myself last Sunday in front of my mirrors and come to the conclusion that I wasn't really that unhappy?

'Honestly, I don't know what to think any more,' I say, running my finger in the groove of the metal opening on the can.

'I have to ask, and it's not me being nosy, but have you spoken to or texted Owen since you got back?'

'Oh God, no!' I'm horrified she has even asked me that.

'This isn't about Owen.' I stare at her.

'Oh, but it is, I think he was the catalyst.'

'He was my excuse, my fantasy card, my escape: I used him to compare Colin to and that was really unfair.'

'So you aren't in love with Owen?' She shakes her head as she speaks.

'No. I fancied him, that's all,' I say.

'Well, it seemed a hell of a lot more than that to me,' she says.

'I was intoxicated by the fact he got me.' I drink the fizz and swallow the belch this time.

'And Colin doesn't get you any more, right?' Corina extends her hand and I pass her the can.

'Oh, Colin knows me all right, but he doesn't get who I've become. More, he doesn't want me to know this version of me. He doesn't want me to change, *ever*. I suppose I forced myself to admit, that night I wore the sexy underwear we were in an awful gridlock. If we could just stop picking at one another. You see, Corina, I can't actually physically fancy Colin when he's being a dick to me and without a sex life our marriage is in trouble. It's a no-win situation. Owen was a welcome distraction.' I speak the truth.

'So what are you going to say when he comes over?' she asks after she swallows her drink.

'Doesn't it depend on what he says?' I answer her question and take my can back.

'Oh, come on, Ali, of course not! Listen to yourself: speak up, love, say what's on your mind, get it all out in the open. *This* is the point where it matters what *you* want! All this cannot be in vain! You weren't happy. Your marriage has been damaged, badly damaged, and if you really want to fix it you need to work out the best way to go about it for *you*!' Corina is angry.

I don't know if I do want a separation. But I say this in my head.

'Why are you getting so cross?' I say.

'Because I need you to take responsibility for yourself, for your own happiness, if you aren't happy. Ali, he can't make you happy unless he's willing to change. Owen was just a diversion, agreed. I never thought you were in love with him, you just loved the fact he was so like you. You used the comparison to back you up on how different you and Colin have become. This point in time has arisen for a reason.' She turns to the window. 'Now it's the time to make up your mind but I want you to know, whatever you decide to do, you have my complete and utter support. I will always have your back.'

She winks at me as we both look out the window; the day is so dark his automatic headlights light up her warm little kitchen.

The sight of his car pulling into the small driveway is familiar and unexpectedly comforting. I take a long slow breath. The car stops. He gets out. Black jeans, black runners and a high-necked green hoody. He beeps the alarm on and his wing mirrors turn in. I rise and go to open the front door.

'Come in,' I say and he follows me through. Corina doesn't look up from her upside down magazine on the couch where she is now sitting, and he doesn't acknowledge her. We go through into the kitchen. I close the door as I hear Corina turning on the TV, volume louder than it needs to be.

'Tea?' I ask. He shakes his head.

He leans his hands against the back of the high kitchen chair. Supporting himself.

'OK.' I nod.

His nose is black and blue with specks of dried blood still visible. I have to ask.

'Is your nose not broken?'

He doesn't answer my question.

'What were you thinking?' he whispers loudly.

'About which part?' I say.

'When you sent him that picture of you in your knickers?' he snarls.

'I wasn't thinking, clearly—' I stop myself and start again: 'OK, I was thinking about how unhappy I was and how … and how I desired him.' I swallow.

Silently I thank God for Corina's presence next door.

The truth, the whole truth and nothing but the truth.

'How long was this going on for?' His voice is steady.

'Honestly, Colin, nothing ever went on. This last week I've been so miserable with how we were – the constant fighting, the effect it was having on the kids – and he was there. He's … he was only ever a good friend but then I started developing feelings for him.'

'Did you tell him this?'

'I did in Amsterdam after I'd eaten a hash cake,' I say.

He looks like I just told him I drowned a litter of newly born kittens.

'I'm not proud of myself, Colin.'

I feel strong suddenly and I have no idea why.

'I bet you're not,' he pants out the words. He is struggling to hold it together, the white of his knuckles tells me.

'Not ideal, Ali, for a married mother of two to be sending half-naked pictures to the object of her fantasy, is it really?' His face contorts with sarcasm.

'It's not. It's definitely not,' I agree.

'And now?'

I realise that he now knows I'm not afraid any more. Without the children in the same house I'm not afraid of a row. In fact, I'm going to say every damn thing I have ever wanted. I part my fingers and slide them through my side fringe.

'And now I don't know,' I say.

'Do you want to be with him?'

'No.' I am definite about that.

And I don't.

God, I know that sounds insane. I knew it the instant I got into the car with Corina at Dublin airport. I can't explain it – it just wasn't there any more. That feeling. Those emotions. They were gone. Owen had been my waking thought for months. He had made my blood rush and my feelings seemed so true, so real. What I thought I felt for him was an illusion, a fantasy, an escape from my suffocating marriage. None of it was real. It was all make-believe, my invention. And also Owen was never going to settle down and be part of the life of a woman with two children. I get that. It was always only going to be an affair. A dirty affair.

'So what is it you do want here?' he asks now, straight to the point.

'I want a separation ... for a while ... some space, Colin.'

Didn't realise I wanted that till this moment.

He rests his hand on his chin covering his dimple.

'Is that what you really want?' I can actually hear him swallow.

'Yes, it is.'

'You want me to move out of my own house?' His tongue sits between his teeth.

'Probably for the best, just until we see where we go from here.'

'You're an unfit mother, Ali.' His eyes are dark.

'That's not true,' I tell him.

He scoffs, 'I think the facts speak for themselves; oh, and the picture evidence.' He snorts.

'I made a mistake.'

'Why was he in your hotel room then?' he hisses at me.

I sigh. How can I say this to my husband?

'Why was he in your room, Ali?' he probes again, teeth slightly clenched.

'Because I thought I was going to have sex with him and I very nearly did.'

He throws the chair he has been clutching across the room and it bashes into a shelf and topples plant pots shattering to the floor.

'All OK?' Corina stands at the door, her face flushed, mobile phone in her hand.

'What's it to do with you?' Colin turns on poor Corina.

'Well, actually, now that you ask, this is my home you're wrecking, Colin Devlin, and I'd be very happy to press charges against you: you smashed my phone and intimated me.' She stands tall and waves the phone in the air.

'What are you?' He looks her up and down with disgust. She is wearing her funny pink onesie with smiley emoticons, her lounge wear.

'What am I?' She moves in. 'I'm a woman, Colin, a woman whose home you are standing in. I'm a friend of Ali's, now you show me some respect.' Corina's face is thunderous.

'Just because you can't get a bloke you don't want anyone else's relationships to work out. I know your sort, I have had you pegged from the very beginning!'

'As a matter of fact, Colin, I have stood up for you. I understand how hard and hurtful this all must be for you, so I'm to ignore your insults and accusations for now.'

He turns to me. 'I can't talk with her here. I'll text you later.' He turns and leaves.

'Colin! I want to see my kids!' I scream after him.

'They are in town. We'll arrange that later.' He strides away through the front room, opens the front door, beeps his car, gets in and skids out of Corina's driveway.

I sit slowly. 'If he shows Jade that picture of me, I … I just know she'll never speak to me again.' Tears roll down my face again now.

'He won't,' Corina says. 'He's really angry, Ali, really angry. Even though I know he knows nothing happened, he's angry you don't seem to love him any more. Did you see the way he looked at me when I said I'd stood up for him, a flicker of hope? As much as it pains me to say this after the way he's treated you, after the way he just spoke to me, I think you need to kill that anger with kindness.'

I can't believe I just said all that to him. But more than that I can't believe how OK I feel about it. It feels like a lead weight has been lifted off my shoulders. I never once thought I wanted to end my marriage, I'm still not sure, but those words just flooded out of me. My phone beeps.

I'm not moving out of my house. I will move into the spare boxroom tomorrow. Please don't come back until Monday evening. I need to think. I will drop the kids to school and see you back here at teatime.

'He wants to move into the box room and for me to come home Monday after work,' I tell Corina.

'Baby steps.' Corina sounds more confident than she looks but she has said her piece.

'Baby steps ...' I say and I tap back the words:

OK, see you then.

'I think it is wine o'clock, my friend?' Corina says stretching.

'Wine o'clock,' I agree.

I wholeheartedly agree.

251

18

Saturday early evening. Corina's house.
South Circular Road. Dublin 8.

Corina and I are sitting on the couch, feet tucked under us, drinking wine and watching *Bridesmaids*. Corina's phone rings.

'Oh my good God … it's Owen O'Neill!' she informs me, her face suddenly flushed.

'Answer it!' I say, as she mutes the TV, her mouth bobbing like a fish.

'Hi, Owen,' she says and I see her nod and nod.

'OK, sure … Yeah, sure … She is … She's here, actually … Do you … No? OK … Yeah … OK … Oh, right … OK … I will … Oh, you are? … I'll tell her that … That's great news … I will … OK … Talk to you then, bye-bye-bye-bye. Bye.'

She looks at me clutching the phone in her fist now.

'He was just asking about me helping him with his art exhibition.' But she looks embarrassed.

'He didn't want to speak to me?' I say.

'No. He's just in out-patients, said he thinks it's for the best if you guys don't have any communication for a while … and he said to tell you his hand will mend.'

He is right, of course he is. The funny thing is, if he

came to me on bended knee declaring his undying love, I'd have no interest.

What was I thinking?

Why didn't I seduce Colin that night and ask him could we do counselling about my job? Nicely tell him about Nancy Farrell and Kitty Tead and James Rafter of the Steffi Street gang? I wonder what will happen with my job. I'm going in on Monday to find out, that's for sure.

'Are you meeting him?' I ask her.

'No … I won't …' Her red hair flops around her head, she's shaking so wildly.

'Why? Hey, he's single, he'd be a great catch! He really likes you.' I laugh. I actually laugh.

'You're not serious?' Corina holds her wine glass by the stem and stares at me.

'What?'

'You think I could be with the type of guy who thinks it's OK to seduce and drug an unhappily married woman?'

'Ah, come on, that's not fair … he's not like that.'

'That's what it looks like to me.'

'It takes two to tango,' I repeat his words.

And a bigger person to walk away.

'Please, Corina, work with him, for me? He has some amazing pieces all ready to go while his hand heals. Help him put on a small kickass exhibition of his work? He didn't ask for any of this, I promise you that, and when I pushed him away after leading him on, he was so, so understanding … He's one of the good guys.'

'Hmmm, I might take a bit more convincing … but OK. We were texting about it before all this shit went down …

253

I'll work with him on his expo, but just for you.' She winks at me.

Maybe she's right. As wrong as I was, he was in the wrong too but I think he deserves to be forgiven.

'Can we go out, Corina? Can we go for a Chinese and a bottle of wine?' I ask suddenly.

'OMG! I'm starving out of my tiny brain! Yes, of course! Trevorweight will have to remain, I'm gonna pig the hell out!' She is delighted but pauses for a second before saying quietly, 'Will you hop into the shower before we go?'

'Do I smell again?' I gasp lifting my arms.

She draws a gap between her index finger and thumb.

'A smidgen,' she smiles.

'Shit … sorry, I was sweating profusely again with Colin here. I'm like a stinking sweat machine. Yes, OK, I will.'

I stand under the boiling hot jets and rub fresh-smelling apricot body wash all over me.

I can't change anything. I have to accept things and I will not lose my children.

I step out and dry off. I open Corina's wardrobes.

'Go ahead.' She hears me rattle the hangers. 'Take whatever you want, not that anything will fit you!'

I see a nice wrap-around red dress that I can wear with my black knee-high boots, so I put that on. It is too big but I pull the belt tighter. I dry my hair into a tiny sleek ponytail and clip back my fringe. I put on my make-up. I stare in the mirror. It's a new chapter. I'm a new person. I'm going to toast the week I ruined my life.

19

**Saturday night. Wott's Chinese Restaurant.
South William Street. Dublin 2.**

'To the week I ruined my life!' I hold my glass of red wine
by the stem out towards Corina and we toast with a clink.

'Oh, don't say that, it will be OK, things happen for a
reason and all that.' She looks less than convinced.

The small tea light candles in the silver, heated serving
dish flicker at us. The restaurant is warm and actually
I am a bit hungry. The truth really does set you free. I
miss the kids like crazy but I will be home Monday. My
new chapter waits to be written. I have no idea what will
happen or what it will bring. I haven't had an appetite
since those hot dogs on Friday. It seems like a lifetime ago.

'What do you fancy?' Corina's freckles catch my eye as she
holds the large, soft-backed, silver-embossed Wott's menu
out to me. Her red hair is tied back as always with the front
bits tumbling down around her, eyes heavy with mascara.

'Something simple, I might try a sweet-and-sour chicken
and fried rice.' I open it and read down my options.

'Mmmm.' She studies the menu carefully as gratefully
I sip my wine.

'I'm having starter, main course, sides and a dessert
– the whole shebang,' she tells me, then she laughs and

pours more wine into our glasses as she goes back to her menu. 'This is the first time we have been out that you don't have a curfew. Every cloud and all that.' She winks at me now.

I look around at the Christmas decorations and I wonder what the kids are doing. If Mark got to play for the Ranelagh Rovers Under 6s today. I wonder about the state of the kitchen. I wonder whether Colin read Roddy Doyle's book to Mark. If the uniforms are washed. If the lunches are made.

Colin tends to give Mark his iPhone to play games on till he falls asleep when I'm not there. It hits me. I should try now. With a shaking hand I put my glass of wine down beside the flickering flame. I grab my bag from the back of my chair and I pull my phone out and dial.

It answers on the first ring.

'Mummy?' My son's little voice whispers down the line. My picture comes up when I call Colin. It's a picture of me with my face full of spots when I got adult chicken pox. Colin thinks it's hilarious. It kinda is, I suppose.

'Baby boy!' I literally crush the phone to my ear. 'Hello, baby, how are you?'

'Where are you, Mummy? You said be home sooner.' He sounds so baby-like. His squeaky voice comes clearer over the line now.

I pant in relief because I can tell by his voice that he doesn't know what's been going on.

'I had to work a few days longer, I'm sorry, baby. I will be back to cuddle you after school, how are you? How was football? Did you get to play? I can't wait to see you, sweetheart.'

'Mummy, I'm in the middle of a 'portant game here …'
He's distracted.

'OK, well, is Jade in her room, sweetie, just for a second?' I shut my eyes tight.

'Uh-huh – I'm on level fours of surfer and Daniel is still on levels 3 … and—'

I interrupt.

'Baby, could you pop into Jade's room and let me talk to her for just one tiny minute?'

'Uh-huh, but I can't find my slippies, Mummy, so I have to go in my toes feet,' he says.

'That's OK, sweetie, toes feet are OK on the carpet, remember?' I urge him on.

I look up and Corina is staring at me. I give her the thumbs-up with my free hand. Heart bumping out of my body.

I hear Jade's muffled voice. Then I wait. Then I hear, 'Hello … Mom?' She drawls her American all over me.

'Hi, love.' I breathe out a huge sigh of relief as I hear her voice. Her beautiful voice. I don't care if she barks like an Alsatian or *uh-uh-uhs* like a monkey to communicate. Why was I letting her accent bother me so much? Who cares?

'Where are you, Mom, like … aren't you totally supposed to be home this evening and stuff? Like, er, Dad told us your show got cancelled and stuff, right, but I thought that you'd be here tonight?'

I close my eyes and I can see her. Soft pink headphones down around her neck now. Blonde hair piled on top in a messy bun. Probably in her cream love-heart pyjamas, as I washed and ironed them before I left.

They don't know. They don't know. They don't know.

'You heard that Dad bust his nose, though, right?' she tells me all very conversationally.

'I-I-I did,' I stutter.

'I mean, what kinda idiot falls off a treadmill at the gym, right? Like, Mom, he's sooo embarrassing looking…'

'I know, love.' My eyes are watering again. Corina passes me a linen napkin.

'Mom … why was Dad so mean to Corina at my gymnastics?'

'It's a grown-up problem, love, but it's all sorted now, nothing for you to worry about, OK?'

'I kinda felt sorry for her. She is a nice lady, she bought me a big bag of peanut M&Ms.'

'I told you she was a nice lady and she thinks the world of you … Daddy and her have made up now so it's all fine,' I try to convince her.

'I remembered what you said, Mom, about taking people as you find them and I'm going to do that from now on. If you were, like, trying to call Dad, will I call down to him?' I notice the more she talks, the less American she keeps up.

'No, that's fine, love, I spoke to him earlier,' I say as I dab the corner of my eyes with the napkin.

'I want my subway surfers game back, I nearly had a mystery box.' I can hear Mark.

'The annoying ant is pulling the phone out of my hand. See you tomorrow, Mom … Mom … ?'

'I'm still here, Jade,' I say.

'I miss you and … I love you, Mummy,' she tells me.

I'm taken aback that she's told me she loves me and called me mummy.

258

'I-I-I love you too, darling, so much …'

'So, so, so, so, so much … Remember when I used to always say that when I was a kid?' she asks quietly.

'I sure do,' I say. 'Maybe now that you are older and I definitely don't call you boo boo any more, maybe we could make up a new saying?'

'Yeah, maybe, Mom. That maybe sounds kinda cool, or maybe a quirky handshake? Gotta go.'

They hang up. I let out a long, 'Ahhhhhhhhhhhh.'

It comes from deep within my very core. A yogic breath. That conversation was medicinal. Healing.

'You talked to them? How?' Corina is clutching the soft black menu to her chest.

'Mark had Colin's phone in bed.' I smile brightly and put the napkin down on my lap.

'They're OK?' she asks.

'Yeah, seem perfectly fine.' I light up with a beaming smile.

'I mean, things are going to change for them obviously. They will ask why Dad is in the box room, but I'm going to be honest with them, insofar as I will tell them we are working through a few issues. Do you think Colin would ever tell them what happened in Amsterdam?' I ask her.

She is quick to shake her head. 'No. Never. He'd never hurt them like that. He loves those kids too much … Oh, would you ever look who it is?' Corina's eyes dart to the door.

'Who?' I dare not look around. My nerves are hanging by a thread.

'It's Trevor. Responsible for my Trevorweight, Trevor.' She sits up straight and licks her lips.

'He's coming this way.' She stares at me as a couple walk by.

'Hey, Trevor!' Corina pushes back her chair and stands up; she is only up to his neck. He looks quizzically down at her. The tall woman with him stands, with her festive, glittery silver bag clutched between her two hands in front of her. Her long pink polished thumbnails scraping at the glitter. They make a handsome couple. He's attractive, tall and dark with a goatee beard; she's sexy, voluptuous, blonde with a swinging high, sleeked-back, salon-prepared ponytail.

'Oh, 'ow ya doin'?' His Mancunian accent rings out around us.

'Couldn't be better, and how are you, pet?' Corina is bright and breezy as she pokes him hard in the chest. He is unbalanced slightly.

'Not bad, ya know … Keepin' busy, hun,' he adds. 'You know my girlfriend, Amanda, right?' For all his easy manner, I can see he still hasn't placed Corina. In fact I'd go as far as to say he hasn't a clue who Corina is.

'No, don't think I've had the pleasure.'

Amanda grimaces as she slowly looks Corina up and down and limply holds out her henna-tattooed hand.

'How was the wedding? It was last week, wasn't it?' Corina keeps eye contact, straining her neck in the process.

'Hmmm?' He looks uncomfortable.

'Your brother's wedding, the Pimple, wasn't it last week? You get through that heartfelt speech you were telling me all about, Trev?' Tilting her head to the side now, sporting a pretty convincing sympathetic face.

'Your brother didn't get married?' The sexy blonde

girlfriend says running one hand down her sleek ponytail. 'Who is yer one?' Her head does a dart in the direction of Corina.

'Did you call me a one?' Corina looks up at her.

'Listen, I don't know you nor do I want to. Me and Trev, we have only just got back together, it's a fresh start so whatever he did or didn't do to you is in the past, sweetheart, OK?'

'Of course, delighted for you both,' Corina says, nodding at the blonde before pressing Trevor some more. 'But I'm speechless the Pimple isn't married? And after all the effort you put into that speech, Trevor? You spent an entire evening telling me about how you guys swung on that same old battered tyre-tree as kids in Salford; latch-key kids, I think you called yourselves? About how your abusive dad drank himself to death and was found face down in Salford precinct in a pool of his own vomit by your schoolmates? About how you and the Pimple worked paper rounds at three in the morning to buy tins of tuna to live on?'

'Why did you tell her your dad was dead? Billy's not dead,' the girlfriend says now, frowning through a suspiciously line-free forehead.

'And how you lads saved up and sent your mum to Lourdes to try and cure her unidentified disease of the legs.' Corina turns to Amanda, all sympathy. 'She can't walk, as I suppose you know ... tragic ...'

The girlfriend looks around and I know it's for a hidden camera.

'But we just dropped your mum to Zumba class? What kinds of shit are you spilling to birds out there?' Her voice is hushed now. 'What the hell is going on, Trevor?'

'No, no, no, you have me mixed up with some other guy, love.' Trevor laughs unconvincingly and shakes his head, his feet shuffling. Desperately trying to think on his feet.

'But she knows the Pimple?' The girlfriend makes a good point.

All three of us stare at Trevor.

'Babe, there's a lot I don't want you to know about the Pimple, and trust me it's for your own good. I'm protecting you. You know he has a major problem with the booze. I don't know this chick … Ahhh, ya know what, our table is ready … Have a lovely evening … er … eh … um …' He puts his hand on the small of the other woman's back and they walk on, her ponytail swinging left to right.

'*Corina!*' she calls after him. 'C.O.R.I.N.A. Remember? It's your favourite name in the whole world. It's what you always wanted to call your firstborn if it's a girl, isn't it?'

The girlfriend does a double take.

Corina sits.

'Knob end!'

'Jesus, is this what you meant by "among other things"? I ask. 'You all right?'

'Just don't get it, Ali, I just don't. He's a mean liar. What sort of bullshit was he feeding me? Like, what the heck? Is he clinically insane? He's a mean liar. Why would someone make up such elaborate bullshit? And I feel bad for her, witch though she seems to be!'

'Some people are very odd, Corina. He's not worth it and she will find out what he's like soon enough … seems like they deserve each other, to be honest.'

'Are you ready to place your order?' We are interrupted by a very pretty Chinese waitress, in a tight red-and-black cheongsam. We tell her we are and I order my sweet-and-sour chicken Hong Kong-style with egg-fried rice. Corina has chicken satay skewers for starters, sizzling beef in black bean sauce, noodles and an extra portion of boiled rice, and we order another bottle of red, a rich Merlot.

'How could I have liked him? I think that's the most frustrating thing. I must be a very bad judge of character.'

'He told you what you wanted to hear. He wanted you to trust him,' I say.

'Just to get me into bed?'

'Well, it appears that way, doesn't it?'

'Do you think he actually didn't recognise me, because if that's the case I am literally going to go over there and dump my black bean sauce over his head!'

'He didn't seem to remember you, Corina, no.' No point in lying. 'However, I think that says a lot more about him than you.'

'I'm giving up the dating game. I can't be arsed any more, truthfully. I hate it.' She fixes her cutlery. 'Hurry up! I need food! Food is the one thing that never lets me down. Food is my Eros.' She sighs, twisting her head around to see if she can spot our waitress returning.

'I've never been in the dating game … but hey, who knows where my life is headed, maybe we can go at it together!' I try to cheer her up.

I hate seeing her so down on herself. That prick Trevor.

'Fun though that sounds, things will work out with Colin. You guys just need to have some serious counselling and time apart to see what you are missing and then get your little family back on track. Give it time. Regardless of all he's done, I know he isn't a bad man deep down.' She reaches in for the plate of prawn crackers our waitress has just delivered and folds one into her mouth.

'I hope so.'

'Really?' I decipher the word through her full mouth.

'Well, not like it is now, but I would like it if we could fall in love all over again, find a new respect for each other. Mind you, that would be little short of magic.'

'Wouldn't be a miracle though, I've seen it happen before. Liz and Richard?' she says distractedly, looking over at the blonde who is now sashaying into the ladies' room.

'What's wrong, apart from that absolute plonker back there?'

'I don't want this to sound all poor me, 'cause you know I'm not like that – I am the glass-is-half-full lady – but seriously, I think the way I look, guys just don't like it for the long term. I'm not arm candy, that's for sure. They just use me. I mean, come on … Look at the girlfriend compared to me!'

'Oh, come on, that's ridiculous, and you are gorgeous!'

'I'm not *gorgeous*, Ali, I know that and you know that …' Her face is serious.

'I think you are!' I hold my hand over my heart.

'Well, thank you.' She winks at me.

'And you go on loads of dates, Corina, loads,' I point out.

'Yeah, dates. Except that's usually in the singular: I go on loads of *date*. This *date* is never normally repeated. There is no omnibus. It's killing my self-esteem. I'm serious:

I'm out of the game as far as I'm concerned. This race is over.' She raises her glass to her lips and takes a long drink before reaching in for the prawn crackers. Holding the savoury, white, puffy crisp aloft, she says, 'I'm just gonna get really, really, really fat and then at least I have a reason why ... Sure, look, I'm halfway there already!' She pats her tummy. 'In fact, I should go for one of those feeder guys, what d'you say? Perfect! Ha! Why didn't I think of that before? I'm gonna get myself a feeder. Now I want him to be a good match. I don't want a feeder who wants me to eat tripe or rare lamb chops, I'd prefer a banoffee pie, Rice-Krispies-bar kinda feeder ya know?' She laughs again now.

'Do you want children?' I say in a low voice as I lean across the table. I have never asked her this before.

'Desperately,' Corina says without missing a beat, wiping the grease from the prawn crackers from her hand with her white linen napkin. I wait. She looks down and then she looks up.

'Ever since I was a little girl, all I've ever wanted was a big family. Kids running around everywhere. My clock is ticking, I'm thirty-nine next year, Ali, and single as a lone sniper. Without wanting to sound like a whining wagon, I am starting to panic about my fertility.'

I'm not having this.

'So what are you waiting for?' I say.

'What do ya mean?' She looks questioningly at me as she reaches in for another prawn cracker.

'You want a baby, there are plenty of ways of falling pregnant, you know. You don't physically need a boyfriend or a husband any more, Corina, this is the twenty-first century.'

'But I'd have to do it all on my own; that's not the way I saw it, Ali.' She shrugs her shoulders.

'Eh? Hello? What am I, Scotch mist? You wouldn't be on your own.'

'Wouldn't be easy.' She nibbles around the edge of the prawn cracker but I can see she's thinking. Deliberating, if you will.

'Nothing about having children is easy, Corina, but to be honest, given my experience of late, sometimes it is less stressful coping on your own with them. Look, it's your life, but if you're relying on a Mr Right that doesn't come along, you'll be cutting off the thing you say you are most desperate for.'

'But isn't it all about having someone to share the joys with?' Nibble. Nibble. Nibble.

'No, not always, it's very conventional to think like that. It's romantic but it's not realistic, marriages fail every second of every day … look at me …' I remember something. I snap my fingers at her.

'A-ha, I never told you this! So I know this girl, she's an actress, that one with the pierced downstairs area I was telling you about?'

Corina remembers and crosses her legs. I go on.

'Well, she did a play in the City Arts last year. She was forty, had been engaged for ten years, *ten*, imagine! She wanted to wait until they were married to have a baby – it was really important to her for her parents' sake – so of course they broke up. She told me she looked into all her options to get pregnant. She found a website that offered to match women with potential sperm donors. Put up her profile and photo, found a matching donor that offered

AI – that's artificial insemination – he came to her flat and did his business in her bathroom and handed her the jar of sperm, he left and she did her thing with her AI kit. Long story short, she got pregnant and he wanted to be involved, now they raise their little boy, Luke, together as friends. Isn't that mad?'

'Sounds like a film with Sandra Bullock and some relatively unknown up-and-coming hot young actor.' Her eyes open wide and she snorts. 'Up-and-*coming* … ha ha ha, get it?'

'I am serious here.'

Her laugh fades and she surveys my expression.

Corina would be a fantastic mother, I think.

'You really think these are realistic options for me?' Hope literally floods across her face. Like Charlie Bucket, when he peels back that silver foil to reveal just the tiniest peek of that wondrous Golden Ticket.

'One hundred per cent I do!' I feel all emotional.

'Holy crap,' is all she says as our food arrives, all loudly sizzling and smelling divine. After speaking to my babies I am now ravenous. When our waitress has placed all our dishes down I spoon some sweet-and-sour chicken pieces onto my warm plate and add some egg-fried rice.

'I tell you what … if we are still sitting here this time next year and you are still in the same position, let's seriously consider getting you pregnant. See how Trevor's fixed for a deposit? He owes you one.' I wave my knife behind me.

We howl with laughter.

'God, I wouldn't want to inflict a poor baby with his pathologically lying genes!' She pours her sizzling beef all over her thick noodles and twists her fork to gather. My chicken is sweet and tender and the flavours erupt in my mouth.

'I don't need a man, do I?' she says laying her fork to rest on the side of her plate.

'You don't.' I pierce a piece of pineapple with my fork.

'You're so right, why do I care if that idiot wants me or not? I deserve so much better.'

The penny has dropped.

'That's the Corina I know and love.' I smile.

'I deserve so much better.' She repeats the mantra under her breath and it seems to resonate and she smiles brightly. Raising her wine glass to me, she says, her eyes slightly damp, 'I'll always have you, right?'

'Damn right.' I look her in the eye and it's my turn to wink at her.

part
2

20

Six months later. Late Thursday evening.
My new apartment. Ranelagh.

I never knew loneliness could literally hurt. Or that regret could physically make you vomit. But they do. Not daily any more, but in the early days when I first left No. 13 to live on my own.

For the entire month of April I practically vomited every night before I crawled into my cold, lonely bed, curled into a ball of flowing tears. I know that all sounds very dramatic and it is getting easier, but I want to be honest.

Those first few months, I can't overstate how horrific they were. I'm coming to terms with where I am now but I still miss it all dreadfully. The family. The home. The unit. I just never thought it would be so harrowing and so traumatic. It comes in waves, the hurt, the guilt, the fear. From not being with my children as they drift off to sleep and missing out again when they wake early morning. No little worker bee team, running around our hive, seven days a week. Ironically, I miss Colin Devlin. Who knew? Not in a marital way at all, but I miss the person, the friend I married. It's like he left and just never came back. We talk, we communicate, but only about the children. Colin Devlin has completely shut me out of all other aspects of his life. He is more or less a stranger to me now. And that's just the way it is.

The hardest part is looking back with a clear head. Everything, events, situations, happenings, they are all muddled up. Almost like I was drunk for a long time before the break-up. Who really started that fight? Who really was to blame? At the end of the day, does it really matter? All I know is that we couldn't seem to live in harmony together any more, under the same roof.

Yes, a lot was wrong in our marriage but a lot was right too. Possibly it wasn't as bad as I made it out in my head, so why had I wanted a way out so badly? I honestly still don't know. Sometimes I'm still not sure that I did want a way out. It's mind-bogglingly confusing. But I wasn't happy. That is the one fact I believe to be true and I need to accept that.

That was a real issue.

I sometimes wonder whether I didn't purposely sabotage it all, just to get Colin to see how unhappy I was. I don't know. I do know one thing, though: I dearly wish I could rewind the clock to when the small cracks first appeared and sit and talk to Colin. Hold my temper and listen to him. I don't mean agree unquestioningly, or change my principles by any means, or allow him to overpower me; I just wish I had looked for and found a compromise. I wish I'd communicated better. Although I thought I was trying to make him listen, I never really knew how to speak to him. Not so he'd hear me. I have trouble with that even now. And when he became childish and vindictive, I allowed myself to as well. It had all gone too far. We just let it unravel to the point that it wasn't possible to roll it all back up. Now that we're not fighting all the time, when he drops the kids off or I see him at the house, I look at him and I think, *Mother of God, he's gorgeous*. So long as we don't speak to each other, part of me fancies him again.

It won't be long before he has a new partner.

Who knew I'd yearn for the constant running from A to B, the messy kitchen, the messy bedrooms, the messy bathrooms, the constant picking up of books, clothes, toys, underwear, Lego, DVDs. Ha! Sing it, Ms Morissette. Sing it loud.

There is an emptiness not being a part of it all any more that I can't explain. A black hole deep inside me, but it's filling up slowly, tiny grain by tiny grain. We split the children as much as we can. But a home is a home and Colin, Jade and Mark all live there together.

I am a new person. A different person. I'm still figuring out exactly who I am on my own. Time will tell. This was never in my plan. But you know what they say about the best laid plans.

★ ★ ★

So you want to know what happened.

On that Sunday night of the week I ruined my life, before I went back home, Corina and I went to see an Amy Conroy play in the Project Arts Centre. Afterwards we decided to have another Chinese on the way home and Corina and I ended up again drinking our body weight in red wine. The mass of prawn crackers and Chinese food did nothing to soak it up. All the staff had been sitting at a far table, arms folded, just waiting to get rid of us. And then who should pass us again but Trevor, this time without his girlfriend.

Corina had stood up, a bit unsteady now, using the table as support and slurred, 'Trevor, Trevor, Trevor, you think you're so clever ...' She had wagged a floppy finger at him here as she searched for words. I'd had to hold the linen napkin over my mouth to stop a burst of laughter. I was so giddy, excited because tomorrow I was going home!

'Ahh ... I don't give a shit, so hey ... whatever.' She'd thrown her floppy hand in his direction before her eyes lit up at me.

'Hey! That *was* a rhyme! Trevor! Clever! Whatever! Do your thang, girl!' she'd ordered and sat down.

And I did. I did my Marcel Marceau all the way round our table as Trevor and his very confused male pal looked on in horror. Corina'd had to dash to the loo, her legs literally crossed to avoid an accident.

'He's a bit of a spoofer, isn't he?' I focused on the pal, who nodded.

'Why do you have sex with girls and not call them back?' I slurred slightly at Trevor.

'Uh ... dunno, do I?' he managed.

The man's clearly a genius.

I went to work into the City Arts Centre, very hung-over I must add, the next day. Similar to the walk of shame, at nine o'clock I had gone straight to Colette's office and sat in front of her. Colette is a fair person and she didn't judge me per se, but after talking for almost a full hour about morals and discipline and fair play being the heart of the

City Arts Centre, I knew that my position in the City Arts Centre was no more. Colette had lost her respect for me. I could see it in her eyes, and I understood it. Colette didn't want to fire me or even reprimand me, she just wanted to reiterate her values, and I didn't feel comfortable knowing I had crossed that line.

Back in my office, I knew what I had to do. I sat down at my laptop to write my letter of resignation and two weeks' notice. I could have easily clicked send and walked but being a creature of habit and a professional, I also printed out a hard copy, put it in a white envelope, licked it, sealed it and walked back down to Colette's office. Michael had been sitting opposite her as I handed it over.

'My notice,' I'd said standing tall. Head pounding.

'You could have done great things here, you know,' was all Michael offered.

'Oh, I will do great things, Michael, don't worry about me and thank you so much for the opportunity.' My head was held high.

Colette, feeling the atmosphere, had sat back, twirling the torn envelope between her finger and thumb, and then had said, 'You can leave now, Ali, no need to work out your notice … with full pay obviously. Thanks a million for all your hard work and commitment to the centre, I will miss having you around. Whenever you need a reference just let me know, I'd be very happy to write you a glowing report.' She had stood up and hugged me tightly, the pen falling out of her ponytail. I picked it up and handed it to her.

'Keep in touch,' she had said as she slid it back into her hair and held my chin in her hand, then turning my face, kissed me on both cheeks. I returned to my office, packed all my personal belongings into a SuperValu cardboard box and said goodbye to no one.

Unemployed.

I just wanted to go home. I wasn't due back until teatime but I had nowhere else to go. Once inside No. 13, my home, I showered and happily started my clean up on the huge mess. I even changed all the beds and cleared out Mark's overflowing drawers. By the time Colin arrived back with the kids I had a lasagne made, a big salad bowl and baked potatoes in the oven. The kids had been over the moon to see me, as had Colin, I'd felt on that evening. Mark and Jade had fought over who got to watch what on the TV and the ultra-sonic hum of their raised voices hadn't bothered me at all. I welcomed it. Dinner was spent together as a family at the table and after, as he helped me wash up, I'd told Colin I'd been fired but I was going to look for another job first thing and I knew the exact job I wanted. He'd been really quiet but supportive. We had all gone to bed early and, as he promised, Colin had slept in the spare room and I had tossed and turned all night in our broken nest.

Tuesday morning, after the school run, I went straight to St Andrew's Resource Centre and asked about the newly advertised Senior Citizens' Entertainments Manager position. I got it on the spot. I was to start work the following Monday. Just one thing left to do and that was to fix my marriage.

* * *

It didn't work out with me and Colin. I could go through the ins and outs of what happened over the next few months but it won't change events. Colin couldn't get over the fact I sent that picture and almost slept with Owen, not that I blame him.

We'd made it through the Christmas but it was horribly forced and fake. The festive-looking house was an un-festive place to be. No fights, no raised voices, just a whole lot of nothingness. Simply put, there was nothing left between us. He tried. I tried. We tried together. I remember as I'd dried up with my Rudolf tea towel after Christmas dinner, staring out at the frost covering my back lawn, the broken scooters and half bikes. I knew deep down, it would be our last Christmas as a family in the house.

In January we'd decided to look into marriage counselling and so followed three months of talking with Dr Jane Higgins on Monday evenings. Laura babysat for us. Colin had organised it all with her help. Turns out Colin's opinion of shaky, old, past-her-sell-by-date Laura had changed dramatically. Neither or us complained or missed a meeting, we were model attendants and participants. In the end even Dr Jane told us that there wasn't much room left in our relationship for growth. Like a dying plant, we could keep ripping off the brown dead leaves but they would always keep coming back. This time no one was to blame that the second chance didn't work out.

'But I'm willing to do whatever it takes!' I had cried in sheer frustration and desperation one Monday evening, late into our run of counselling sessions.

And then I had seen the way Colin had looked up at me and that made me suddenly stiffen and stop. Dead in my tracks. I knew the look. It was the look he had for opposing managers or players after their team had beaten his beloved Manchester United. We were done. Cooked. Spent. I knew it.

But when our marriage ended for real, for ever, it was a Friday night. Valentine's night, would you believe, and we had booked Laura to babysit the kids and reserved a table at L'Ecrivain, a really exclusive restaurant on Baggot Street. I'd bought a new tight, red knee-length dress from River Island, had my make-up and hair done professionally in a local salon and wore a pair of strappy heels. He wore a suit. The kids were excited. Colin was still in the spare room and that was supposed to be the night: the set date when we were to try and go back to sharing a bed together, to make love and make it all, all right again.

Happily ever after.

* * *

'What do you fancy?' he'd enquired as we put down our menus at the same time.

'Steak, I think. You?' I answered.

'Steak too, I think,' he sort of answered.

No further questions.

We sat in silence. Not comfortable Corina silence, awkward silence.

Clearing of throats. Settling of cutlery. Twisting of glasses. Looking around. Various unnecessary toilet trips. Lame observations.

'Lovely place,' I said for the sake of speaking.

'It is,' he said.

'Popular, isn't it?' I asked.

'It is,' he answered.

Silence.

Silence.

Silence.

'Starving, are you?' I poured more water into my already half-full glass.

'Starving … yup … yup.' He seemed to be struggling to fasten the second button on his cuff. Concentrating hard on it. His dimple strained under his contorted face. His brown floppy hair hanging over one bright blue eye.

He never fastened that button.

'How was work?' he asked again.

He had asked 'How was work?' every single day since we started counselling. He no longer believed that me giving up work was the fix-all solution. Our therapy sessions had taught him that much. Dr Jane had made him understand that part of me and he respected my decision to work both outside and inside the home. It was all very PC.

'Good, yeah … you?' I replied.

'Good, yeah.'

I nodded.

'Be your biggest month of the year, yeah?' I'd already asked this on the drive in. We'd discussed it to death.

'Yeah,' he repeated.

And a split second before he spoke again, I noticed a tiny bead of sweat gathering on his forehead.

'This is over, isn't it?' he said quietly and calmly.

'It is,' I answered. A lone tear out of nowhere squeezed itself out and trickled down my face.

Salty and expected, in my sexy red dress.

'I'm sorry, Ali.' A lone tear escaped down his face also.

'I just can't fix it.' He wiped his sweating forehead with the back of his hand as tears gushed down his face.

I'd never seen him cry.

'Neither can I.'

We reached out at the same time and held hands across the beautiful expensive white linen. Two people who'd met as kids and produced two amazing kids were now strangers again. All the familiarity and knowing and understanding were defunct. Just like that very first day Colin had walked into my classroom, messy shirt and tie, khaki bag slung over his shoulder, I had no idea who he was. We had come full circle.

'I can't stop thinking about you and him in that hotel room, all those messages between you … the picture … I can forgive you, I truly can because I fully take responsibility for my part in it all … but I just can't forget it. God I wish I could, but I can't.' He pinched his nose to stop it dripping.

'It's OK, Colin. I don't know if I could ever forget either.' And it was true I didn't.

'I think it's the picture that bothers me most, Ali. It's like I just never knew you. You aren't the person I thought you were. You were the last person in the entire world I thought would send a picture of yourself in your underwear to another man.' His voice cracked on every word.

It was never going to go away.

'You know, when things were really shit, when we were rowing all the time and there was no sex … I wanted to say … I wanted to say … I-I-I …'

He had to take a second to compose himself, napkin covering both his nostrils.

'I wanted to say … "Let's go away, Ali, for a weekend

on our own … I love you and I appreciate all you do … I'm just scared of losing you." I saw what happened when my ma worked in Londis, she was never there any more, she was now a working mother … I know she had to … It just scarred me … That's what this is all about … but I couldn't … I couldn't let it go … my pride … Couldn't let you feel like you had won … beaten me … I knew how pathetic I sounded telling you I wanted you chained to the kitchen sink … and Jane is right, a lot was my making … my mantra now is: let go.' He is inconsolable and sobs come hard and he struggles to catch his breath.

Let go.

Let go.

Let go.

Let go.

The words dance around both our heads.

And we did.

We physically let go of one another's hands across the table, as he tried to compose himself, then he said, and I was waiting for it, 'I'm never leaving my home though, Ali. I'm never leaving my kids. Please don't make me.' His uncontrolled breath still catching on each word.

'I know you're not, Colin,' I said. 'And you shouldn't have to.'

We were both crying freely now.

'I'll go,' I said.

★ ★ ★

It wasn't an on-the-spot decision. I had been thinking about it for a while, to be honest. All through Dr Jane's counselling I felt us slip away. In the beginning I thought maybe we could reinvent ourselves but as time passed and we began to speak openly to each other, I began to see Colin wouldn't be able to. We were just a life-support machine waiting to be unplugged. Jane had mentioned a couple in similar circumstances to us, where the mother had moved close by and left the father in the family home. It had stuck in my mind and so, four months later, I left my family behind and moved out.

I cried for days and days. Colin cried for days and days. Our kids had cried for days and days. So why did I make that call? Why did I walk out?

Because shit or get off the pot, that's why.

I made a tough, selfless decision. A heart-wrenching one, I will not belittle it, but one that I felt was the right one for all of us. For my kids. It was the only decision that would cause the least interruption to the kids' lives. I knew I would cope way better on my own than Colin ever would. Colin would have crumpled. I could have battled to get him out of the family home, of course I could, and I would probably have won, but I didn't think it was fair. Also, he is the main breadwinner, so it made more sense financially that he continue paying the mortgage, the household bills, and looking after all the things the kids needed. The norm remained in the home. I felt I could make my own way, rent a small place and my salary was better in St Andrew's Recourse Centre than the City Arts Centre so I could get by independently. Just. Colin had offered me a few bob every week but I turned him down. The only thing I asked was that he still pay my tax and insurance on my car.

When we sat them down and told them, Jade had taken it way worse than Mark, obviously.

'Why don't you love Daddy any more?' Anger, her first emotion. Her cross expression and folded arms, bright blue eyes blazing. Body language so closed off.

'Oh, love, I do love Daddy, very much and I always will, but it's just better that we have separate places to sleep because we don't love each other that way any more.' Dr Jane's advice.

'Is it because I told him that man was here that night and that Corina used his good wine glass?' Her eyes were on the grey slate kitchen floor. Occasionally they darted up at me and then straight back down.

'Not at all, love!' Colin said.

'No, darling.' I gathered her into a huge bear hug. I pulled out the red kitchen chair and sat her on my knee.

Mark didn't really bat an eyelid. He had so many friends in his class and on the Ranelagh Rovers Under 6s whose parents were separated, divorced or just never lived together to begin with. Nor does he bat an eyelid to mixed-race parents, same-sex parents, transgender parents – thank God for the changing, modern, accepting world we now live in.

'Can I go out to Daniel's now?' was all he wanted to know.

'Do you understand what we are tellin' ya, pal?' Colin looked across the kitchen table at him.

'Yeah, Mum's gonna be living in a different house and we'll stay there too at weekends?' The way he said it, it was so clear in his head we didn't have much to add.

'But we still love you and I will be around whenever you need me,' I told him.

'Can I get the *In Space We Brawl: Full Arsenal Edition* for your new place?' he asked, all excited.

'We'll see.' I uttered my magic words and that was enough to make him happy. Dirty football tucked under his arm, he set off with Colin to walk him up to Daniel's.

My daughter and me remained at the kitchen table.

'Mom ... I do like it when you call me boo boo,' and suddenly Jade burst into sobs, still sitting on my knee, her head now deep into my shoulder. Hot tears from a broken eleven-year-old heart. I'd closed my eyes tight and made soothing sounds as I'd choked back rock-hard lumps of tears. I did the whole 'it's not your fault', but kids are kids and they will always think they are to blame. I have to live with that every day. We had sat at that table for over an hour just holding one another.

So when we all felt ready, Colin and the kids helped me find my new home. It had to be within walking distance to the house, that was a deal breaker. I'd seen this block of apartments, Ros Mor Heights, which were a five-minute walk down the road. Colin negotiated the rental lease for me and a car park space and I began my move slowly at first, a night here and a night there, making the transition as smooth as possible. Heart-wrenchingly harder than I had ever imagined.

Jade, bouncing back to my delight, complained at the beginning once I had fully moved myself in, and I brought them to show them their room.

'Uh, do I have to, like, share a room with the ant?' Blowing her newly cut blunt fringe up in the air. But when she'd seen the bunk beds and her white princess pull-around privacy curtain her face involuntarily lit up.

'OK … that seems cool, Mom,' was all I got as her Uggs climbed up the small wooden ladder and pulled the curtain.

Mark had loved them.

'Oh, Daniel is gonna be so jealous! Green face! Can he come for a sleepover, can he, Mummy, can he, can he?' he'd begged.

My apartment isn't a new building, but it's well maintained, with quiet occupants. Myself, I'm based in the small bedroom, which fits a double bed, a bedside table and my bedside lamp from home. I'm on the first floor, 1B. The sliding doors from my living area open onto a little patio area, where I have treated myself to a wicker table and two chairs and some potted plants. The wicker reminded me of home. It's a compact living area and kitchen combined; with Corina's expert eye we have decked it out in creams and yellows. Cream carpet and sharp glossy yellow tiles in the tiny kitchen area. The walls are papered in a cream diamond pattern. The sofa is black leather and on the facing wall is a plasma TV. One bathroom, with no bath just a toilet, sink and shower. That's it. My new home.

21

A gloriously hot summer's day.
Malan's Restaurant. Dawson Street. Dublin 2.
I gaze around my little apartment now as I stand on the
small red button on my Dyson vacuum and the cord zips
away. I have always wanted a Dyson. My power toy. It's
not eco-friendly but by God does it give the carpets a
great clean! My compact apartment is neat as a pin. The
air is heavy with the scent of the lavender Shake n' Vac
I've just liberally sprayed all over the carpets. I walk to the
small cloakroom and store my little Dyson away. Moving
into the double room, I run my hand down the soft maple
wood on the bunk beds and tuck Jade's privacy curtain
up under her pink pillow. Tomorrow night my two babies
will be snuggled up in here and I can't wait.

It hasn't been easy on them, any of it, but I can't change
the past I can only move forward and be the best mother I
can be. Jade has grown up a lot over the past few months
but Mark still seems to have come through it all fairly OK.
I think ever since he got to play on the Ranelagh Rovers
Under 6s he's been in a world of his own. In the end, I had
to have a quiet word in Erik Clancy's shell-like. Sometime
you've gotta do what you've gotta do.

Four months pass and, like the old saying goes, time is a

great healer. I gave up my right to stay in the family home and now I have come to terms with that. I wholeheartedly stand by my decision. My mistake. My punishment. Don't get me wrong, I am acutely aware of the part Colin played in our eventual demise. But I'm still devastated I was the straw that broke this family.

If Colin and I had kept going. If I had left my job as I had intended to, to be a stay-at-home mummy and none of the rest of it ever happened, I still would eventually have come to resent being at home full-time again. I love my kids so, so much, but to be the best mother I can be, I need to work outside the home too.

Colin is a good guy, but even if what happened with Owen hadn't happened I think it would have ended eventually. Probably not for many more years. We would have got on with it, like so many other couples do, and made it function, but that's not right either, is it? How is that fair on either of us? I hope one day that Colin meets a fantastic woman. I truly do. In the meantime, we've arranged it so that I have the kids from Friday after school to Monday morning, when I drop them to school, and he is happy for me to help put them to bed every Wednesday night at No. 13. Believe it or not, afterwards I usually have a quiet cup of tea with him. One day, he may want me as a friend. Not yet, but I am going to keep trying. After our cuppa, I wash the cups and then I say goodnight.

I stroll back to my little apartment with my new cutlery and my fridge full of food from wherever I like to shop. I put my mini dishwasher on. I stay up as late as I want with my heating blasting all around me. I light my gazillion candles. I drink me some wine. For the first time in my life I am not answerable to anyone and when I manage to block out the guilt it is OK. Actually, if I'm perfectly honest? If I could take away the gut-wrenching guilt over what it did to the kids, the independence and peace is slowly becoming a welcome thing.

That's terrible, isn't it?

So that's the deal. Twelve years over just like that, after one crazy week.

★ ★ ★

You will have noticed by now that I haven't mentioned Owen O'Neill. I still don't know why I felt the way I did about Owen because I feel absolutely nothing physically for him any more. Oh, I still love him and we are still great friends and he's OK by the way. Working away on his paintings. He is still having physical therapy on his hand – all of which Colin is happily paying for – but he can still paint with it. Owen never took a legal case against Colin, and when he returned back to work after two weeks, he also handed in his notice. Again, Colette accepted. He then dutifully called me up to tell me and asked me out on a date. To see. I said no. His relief was audible.

Owen admitted what happened between us had given him a fresh creative muse and it had, his new works are incredible. It's now his full-time job. The work is filled with passionate desire, and pain, and illicit sex.

We discussed what happened and we both agreed we had chemistry and we should both have nipped it in the bud straight away. We should not have spent so much time together and I should never have told him my marriage was in trouble.

You live and learn. Harshly.

I adore my new job. Seriously, I laugh so hard day in and day out. With Colette's kind help, I was able to secure the funding for the St Andrew's Resource Centre old folks bus and I take them every Friday afternoon for activities to the City Arts Centre. We do wonderful things with them, from painting, to writing little plays and putting them on for family and friends. The Steffi Street gang are even trying to teach them some of the sign language they've been learning. Honestly, now hand on heart, I'm glad I didn't give up my need to work. I love it. I love how it makes me feel.

I, Ali Devlin, have moved on.

My phone beeps on my outside patio wicker table as I shield my eyes from the sun. I pick it up. It's Corina.

Will be running ½ an hour late soooooo sorry!

I'm meeting Corina in Malan's. Our Sunday get-togethers are now on Thursday evenings as my weekends with the kids are too precious to give up.

I move inside to my living room, my bare feet drown in the warm sun-heated cream carpet. Ruby Bomb, my newest toenail colour, hidden in the thick threads. Corina is still with Owen, I'm guessing. Owen had a phenomenal response to his art exhibition last night. Corina, as ever, had been amazing as event coordinator and PR guru. The Paschal Art Gallery on South Eccles Street had been very dimly lit with tiny, blindingly bright spotlights over each of his works. Owen had been on hand to answer any questions and hand sign any sales. Patricia, from the Beans in the City Arts Centre, had done the food just as Owen had hoped one day she would. Tiny nibbles of freshly grown foods that were mouth-wateringly delicious. Owen had looked really smart. In a white granddad-style shirt, black suede suit jacket, with ripped jeans. I was super proud of him.

I stand very still and look at one of his paintings now on my living room wall. I bought it. At least, I part bought it. I'm paying him off week by week. I know it's us, but no one else would. Well, I'm sure he told his girlfriend. Those two are inseparable and I know they have no secrets. I step in closer and study the work. There are two straight thick black lines down each side of the painting, only curving at the end, going where who knows. A couple of shimmying lines, obviously dancing figures, stark black against the yellow of the walls, and in the background a cigarette on a table, where a candle might be, releasing dark greys of curling smoke. The centre is a huge piece of chocolate cake and all over the painting are mini Pac-Men and Pac-Women. It's beautiful. The yellow and black so opposite. So extreme. Abstract yet vividly telling our colourful story.

I check my watch. It's four o'clock and we were due to meet at five. I grab my phone and dial Malan's to push our reservation back. I set about getting ready. Not having a bath is strangely liberating. I'm not a big fan of the shower so it's in and out. I don't waste time. I used to linger in the bath for hours. Jumping under the hot jets I quickly wash my hair. Pulling open my wardrobe door I choose some cut-off denims (imagine approaching thirty-six next week and in cut-offs, just who do I think I am?) and an aquamarine-coloured tank top. Slipping into my outfit, I dig out my flip-flops and go do my make-up.

A rare hot, bright, sunny evening it is and people are seated outside every bar and restaurant as I walk down a lively Dawson Street. Summer whistles a happy tune at me and Christmas seems like a lifetime ago. I've gone a bit mad for the jewellery. Long silver necklaces hang around my neck. Jade borrows them all the time.

Colin hated me in shorts and he hated dangly jewellery (as he called it). I've noticed that all the things he didn't like me doing, I do all the time.

My lengthening blonde hair is freshly washed and has dried naturally in the sun on my walk into town. I get a few glances as I pass people on the street, I know I do, but I have zero interest in dating. A full body glance from a sunburnt guy swaying to light a cigarette with a half-full pint of Guinness in his hand makes me think, *Why*? It's not that I don't see myself ever in a relationship again, it's just I like this stage of my life. It's taken a hell of a lot to get me here so I need to understand why I'm here. I like the freedom from being in a bonded relationship. Part of a couple. Right now that is; that might all change. Hey, Tom Hardy might come knocking yet.

I'm over the moon that Owen and Corina got together. I texted her last night to bring him today, that I'd love to see him for a chat, celebrate the exhibition last night, but she'd said no, this was our time.

Oh, sorry did I not tell you that they are dating?

She's the girlfriend I mentioned earlier. They have no secrets. They have been dating since she organised his first exhibition in the Powerscourt Townhouse in February. He even refused the successful place he was offered on the course in France to be with her. He moved into South Circular Road with her after three weeks. He gets just how lucky he is.

He gets her. He's a lucky man.

The door to Malan's is propped open with a triangular wooden wedge to let fresh air in and I tell the waitress I have a reservation. She points me to the desk.

Owen still feels horrendous about what we nearly did, he tells Corina all the time. At first she was unsure about his morals until she saw his regret and his continued work with the Steffi Street gang outside of the City Arts Centre. Owen rents a room in his local community centre, at his own expense, on a Sunday morning and those that want to see him go. They paint and read and just talk. James Rafter was even an usher at the gallery expo last night. Wearing a little suit and red dickey bow he looked amazing. By all accounts he's a clever little storyteller. There is talk of a childrens book of James' tales, for which Owen is supplying the illustrations. It's about a boy who once painted a picture of a ballerina. Owen told Corina, who of course told me, that being privy to these kids and their broken homes caused him to realise he had almost spilt up a family; it made him do a lot of soul searching to work out what he wanted in life.

So she forgave him. They set about working together on his exhibition. He had pursued her, wooed her, wined her and dined her, taken her to Paris, taken her to Rome. Romanced her. Flowers, chocolates, jewellery, he'd done it all. Corina fell head over heels in glorious, vivacious, buoyant love.

I like to think I brought them together! Ha!

Our reservation is under my maiden name, Ali O'Dwyer, I tell the impeccable-looking maître d'. He ticks off my name and I make my way with him to our usual booth, exchanging pleasantries and making small talk about the insufferable heat. I slide myself in. Lean back against the familiar soft, red leather-backed frame of the booth. I pick up the thin, hard cardboard menu and fan myself with it for a moment. For some reason, I am taken back to that Sunday afternoon before Christmas, sitting here, when I texted Colin and asked if I could stay for another glass of wine. I stare out the window, at the Mansion House. Back to the future.

Imagine he had said, 'Yes.' Imagine he had said, 'Go on, love, enjoy yourself.' Imagine he had said, 'Of course, you deserve a break, say hi to Corina and I will see you in the morning.'

Life turns on a moment. In my heart I know if he'd said that and I arrived home happy and tipsy to a warm reception, we'd have made love. We might have stumbled back onto our path. We might have rolled that unravelled ball of string right back up. Good as new.

Or imagine I had come home, without a bottle of wine in hand and told him I understood he had been up early. I should never have asked. Thanked him for how hard he worked for us.

Imagine.

Out the window I see Corina strolling down Dawson Street. Smiling to herself. I continue to watch her as she moves nearer to me. She has her red hair pinned up as usual with the tumbling strands around the sides of her face. Corina hates the sun and is porcelain white against the tanned people sauntering up and down past her. What a friend she has been. She genuinely wouldn't date Owen if I wasn't in full, total agreement. If I hadn't actively encouraged it. When she came to my work and told me there was an attraction she was actually horrified. She sees me through the glass now and waves madly.

'Beautiful day! Yeah, yeah I know it is ... but I am sweating like Miss Piggy in a fleece onesie!' She is beside me and kisses me on both cheeks and then slides in opposite me.

'Will ya stop, it's gorgeous. Oh, by the way, my landlord, greedy Greg, has been forced by the residents to open that communal area up the top, so we can use it for barbecues. I was thinking maybe for your fortieth we could have a little steak and vino get together?' I say as our waitress puts down a large jug of water and bobbing lemons in the centre of our booth.

Corina smiles at the waitress before leaning in and asking me intently, 'How's all, Ali, everything OK? You doing OK?'

I answer my usual.

'I'm fine, Corina! You honestly don't have to ask me every time you see me any more. I'm getting better ... The new routine, we are all getting used to it. It's getting easier. However, I have agreed to take the St Andrew's regulars on our brand spanking new 161D bus to the Gleneagle Hotel in Killarney next month for the week. God help me, Kitty Tead will have me up singing "Paddlin' Madeline" all night ... They are hyper-excited. I—'

'I'm expecting a baby, Ali.' Her mouth is wide open as

though she is about the scream at the top of her lungs. I can see her tonsils.

It takes me a second to sink in.

'Wwwwhhhaaattt?' I jump out and run around and hug her. 'Oh, I'm thrilled for you … thrilled for you both … What amazing parents you will make!' I hug her, not too tightly, before bombarding her with questions: 'When are you due? How are you feeling? When did you find out? Oh my God, this is amazing news!'

'Our baby is due in January.' She is literally beaming. Shining. Luminous. Hands gently placed over her treasure.

I stand over her and look down at her. My heart is bursting with joy for her.

'Owen is outside Cafe en Seine, will he come in? I don't usually want him at our time but this is a special occasion, I think. We literally just came from our first hospital appointment.' She beams up at me.

'Yes! Of course! Get him in here now!' I say.

'OK, great, maybe just for a few minutes, he's so excited … but I want us to have our own chats too,' she says as she tap-tap-taps furiously on her Blackberry.

I pour us each a glass of cold water. It all makes sense now. It's all all right. All as it should be. Things really do happen for a reason. Corina and Owen are going to have a baby.

I mentally check my facts. I might not have done it all perfectly. I might not have created the ideal television Cornflake ad family, with the perfect marriage, the perfect high-paying career or the perfect home.

But my children are doing OK.

I am doing OK.

I think it's really important for me to be OK.

And then it hits me.

My Oprah 'A-ha!' moment. What's the only thing that matters and the one thing I have always wanted? To be a great mother. That's my complete goal. That's my life. Me and my children. I will always be there for them. That is the one thing I am sure of.

And out of nowhere, an old poem springs to mind, one that Bernie O'Dwyer read to me over and over again. I recite it in my head:

One hundred years from now
It will not matter
What kind of car I drove
What kind of house I lived in
How much I had in my bank
Nor what my clothes looked like.
One hundred years from now
It will not matter
What kind of school I attended
What kind of typewriter I used
How large or small my church.
But the world may be …
A little better because …
I was important in the life of a child.
- Forest Witcraft

I, Ali O'Dwyer, am important.

Acknowledgments

To my husband Kevin and daughters Grace & Maggie. Thanks for all the support and understanding when mammy locks herself away in Maggie's bedroom to make up stories! And to Dad, Mam, Samantha and Keith. Love is too small a word to express how I feel about you all but you all know that, right?

Caroline Cassidy and all my extended family.

To the usual suspects, all my amazing friends, I am so lucky to have you all.

Black & White Publishing, thank you so much to you all. Campbell, Alison, Laura, Simon, Chris, Thomas and Daiden, it's been an absolute pleasure working with you all on this novel.

Thanks to Park Pictures, Gill Ness, MacFarlane Chard and a special nod to all the fantastic women I work with on TV3's Midday.

Susan Webster, thank you for so graciously giving me your time and legal knowledge on family law.

For my granny, Margaret Kilroy.

I can't believe this is my fifth novel so the biggest thanks to you reader for buying my storybook. I really hope you enjoy this one.

Love Caroline.x
@CGraceCassidy